JINX BOUND

JINX BOUND

Sam Stone

The Jinx Chronicles
Book 3

First published in 2018 by Telos Publishing Ltd, United Kingdom

Telos Publishing welcomes feedback
feedback@telos.co.uk

Jinx Bound: The Jinx Chronicles Book 3 © 2018 Sam Stone
Cover art © 2018 Jim Burns

ISBN: 978-1-84583-971-0

Cover Art: 2018 © Jim Burns
Cover Design: David J Howe

The moral right of the author has been asserted.

British Library Cataloguing in Publication Data. A catalogue record for this book is available from the British Library.

With Thanks To …

Katherine Easton-Campbell, Kerry Hawkins-Edwards, John Guilor, Alan Kenney and Andrew Petch for their support of the *Doctor Who* Merchandise Museum. I hope you enjoy being a part of *The Jinx Chronicles*.

The Story So Far ...

JINX TOWN

High School Teacher Jasmine Regis is on a school theatre trip when the Jinx arrive in Manchester via a mysterious vortex. Within minutes the aliens have devastated the theatre, killing men and taking the women back into the swirling maelstrom. Jas is only able to save one pupil, Andrew Carpenter, and they hide out in the theatre.

Two years later, Jas and Andrew are managing to survive in a brutal post-apocalyptic world. As one of the few remaining women on the planet, Jas disguises herself as a boy for her own safety. She is able to do this with a form of magic, but doesn't know how she has this ability.

When Andrew gets a serious infection Jas finds her way to the Trafford Centre in search of antibiotics. There she meets Taylor Arch and his band of soldiers. She and Andrew join Taylor's team. But during a training session, Taylor Arch discovers Jas's secret: they begin an affair.

Learning the truth about Jas's gender, Gerald Avery, a doctor with a dark past, threatens to expose Jas and Taylor unless she sleeps with him.

Not wishing to compromise Taylor, Jas and Andrew return to their previous hiding place at the theatre – here Jas is taken by the Jinx and she discovers firsthand what has happened to the women they took.

On the Jinx planet, Emin, Jas learns that the Jinx – the Arrak Nah Tiamen (Warriors in Space) – had suffered a devastating blow when a virulent plague attacked and killed the females of their race. Left bereft, the Emperor, Arven, led the Jinx attacks on Earth with the aim to repopulate their race.

In a bizarre marriage ceremony, Jas bonds with Arven, but even with powerful Jinx magic holding them together, Jas's own inner strength leads her to the seduction of Arven's Al Kuzemen mage, Kale, whom she persuades to help her return to Earth.

JINX MAGIC

Once back on Earth, Jas and Kale realise their error: not only does Jas have real feelings for Arven, but they have returned to Earth three years later than they should have. There Jas finds Andrew, now a young man; and Taylor – her former lover – married with a family. They are all living in the Trafford Centre, which they have turned into a fortress and city.

But there is something seriously wrong with the planet and its atmosphere.

Taylor discovers that his former Major, Handley, is behind the toxic air. Handley and Colonel James are just two of the powerful military men who have gone to ground in secret bunkers – MD59 and MD1 – which are basically underground cities. At these bases terrible experiments are taking place. Women are used as breeders or whores and Handley and James are building an army of drones that are almost invincible.

Jas and Kale have discovered that Earth women are adept at magic – and begin to train those who show ability.

Through a series of live surveillance cameras the military are watching the Trafford Centre survivors. They intend to use this new, growing population for their own future ends. But Jas finds one of the cameras and alerts Taylor. As the truth becomes apparent, the Trafford Centre survivors learn that there are sleepers among them – ex-soldiers, on enhanced hypnotic drugs, living as ordinary citizens until activated.

Meanwhile, back on Emin, Arven is fighting his own battle. Not only is he suffering from the loss of his *chio mien* (soul mate), Jas, but some of his formerly loyal councillors are plotting against him. Observing the changes in his people since their exposure to the Earth women, Arven realises that he needs to delve into Arrak history to discover why his loyal mages are saying the Arrak Nah Tiamen are cursed. He sets off with Malachi and two trusted warriors to the Eleventh Moon. Unbeknownst to him and Malachi, one mage, Ballin, and Councillor Marlin, are plotting his downfall. As he arrives on the planet, the mage traps them there, making it impossible for the Emperor to return.

Back on Earth, Handley and James decide to attack the Trafford Centre – they need new female stock as breeders, and the former soldiers will make useful drones. But as they attack, Jas and Kale raise another vortex, and take the survivors to the only place they can think of to save them – Emin.

Part 1

New Beginnings

1

The Eleventh Moon was a wasteland. As Emperor Arven and his mage Malachi, with warriors, Prins and Elee, stepped out from the vortex, the swirling wind picked up. It battered the Arrak Nah Tiamen until Malachi was forced to close the vortex for fear that it would rip this already unstable world apart.

'It's difficult to imagine how this world remains: there's nothing living here,' Malachi said. 'As we would expect.'

He held aloft an ancient scroll that showed a map of the area.

'There should be ruins from the city,' the mage said. 'East of here.'

Malachi tapped his staff down on the black sand. A feeble light came from the diamond embedded in a gold setting that was moulded onto the top of the wood. The light showed them the direction and Malachi turned and began to walk. The small group followed.

The wind continued to build and brought the sand with it. They carried on walking, armoured face shields protecting the Emperor and his warriors. Malachi wrapped his head scarf around most of his face and squinted out into the blowing sand until he could no longer see through the maelstrom.

The wind grew ever stronger and the sand swirled around them until the group were forced to halt.

'We must take shelter until this calms,' said Malachi.

Then he raised his staff, tapped it down twice and conjured a tent before them.

The Emperor entered first. Inside, the magic of the mage bolstered the fabric as the wind whipped at it, and there was barely a sound from the outside world. But the tent was empty. A surprise to Arven, but even more so to Malachi.

'Highness!' Malachi said. 'I apologise. There should be furnishings for your comfort. I don't know what happened.'

'Save your magic,' said Arven. 'This place may drain you. I can feel … death and waste in the air.'

Malachi nodded. He was always impressed with how sensitive the

Emperor was to magic, even though it was not his calling. Arven knew enough though to feel when the energy wasn't right, and Malachi realised he had been foolish not to explain the risks of this planet more to Arven. He should have realised that the Emperor would understand.

They were here to find answers, and answers they would find when this sandstorm abated enough for them to move on.

Prins and Elee took up point at the tent entrance as though they expected an assault on the Emperor at any moment, but Malachi was sure that his senses were accurate: there had been no life on the Eleventh Moon when their tribe had departed centuries ago, and nothing lived here now.

Malachi studied the scroll he had brought with him. He had found this among the historical scrolls kept by the senior Al Kuzemen, a mage called Kale, who had once held this role before he had decided to run away with Arven's Empress, Jasmine. Malachi knew there was an important reason why this had happened. It was all linked to the history of the Arrak Nah Tiamen; and this scroll, as well as the few others he had found, told him that there was something important left behind on the Eleventh Moon. Something that would explain the troubles the tribe had suffered over the last few years. Those troubles had started with the death of all the Arrak females to a mysterious virus. An occurrence that had not only devastated their population to the point of extinction, but had also led the tribe to Earth in a desperate attempt to find compatible mates, and repopulate their land.

This plan had been executed by Al Kuzemen Kale, and had seemed to be the solution to all of their problems. But then, the people had begun to change following their contact with the Earth women, and not always for the better. A problem that was growing worse by the day.

'We cannot have our people turning on each other,' Arven had said.

The Emperor was right. Some of the Arrak men who had not bonded with a human female had become jealous: a trait never experienced in their culture before. There had been fights breaking out among the warriors, culminating in deaths. And, following the murder of Garuk, Kale's replacement as Imperial Al Kuzemen in the capital of Sharik, Arven had called to Malachi for help. It was as though they were cursed, and this became a stronger suspicion every day.

'Kale had hinted at it,' Arven had explained before their journey. 'He knew there was some link with our past. But not why it was affecting our future as it was. I suspect he left with Jas because this curse made him. We are all victims of destiny, are we not?'

Garuk had investigated further, helping the Emperor come to these conclusions, and Malachi had found nothing in the scrolls that negated their opinion, and so he had taken up the Imperial Al Kuzemen mantle and aided the Emperor on what some might have considered a fool's mission.

A few hours passed before the storm began to calm and the explorers could move on. Malachi took back the magic and the tent disappeared. He led the way with Arven by his side and Prins and Elee following closely behind, hands on their swords, ready always to defend the Emperor. Each of them had their helmets pulled down to protect their eyes from the still-flying grit but the storm had abated enough for this not to be such a problem.

They walked for an hour or more until Malachi came to a halt in the middle of a wild, desolate desert. Blackened sand was all around them, and the wind whipped it up in thick gusts, making it difficult to see beyond a few feet at a time. The air was cold, a concept that the Arrak Nah Tiamen had been unused to until their many excursions onto Earth had introduced them to varying temperatures. It wasn't as hard on Prins and Elee for this reason; Arven and Malachi felt it more, for they had not journeyed to Earth as often. Aching with the cold, legs hurting from the exertion, they soldiered on regardless.

The landscape was austere, gloomy and intimidating in its never-ending barrenness. Malachi's power was diminished with every step and the map that was forged in his mind faltered. He could not *see*: his third eye showed him nothing, his extra senses were impaired. It made him feel weak and vulnerable.

'It should be *here*,' said Malachi. His fingers, clutching at his staff, were rapidly turning blue with the cold.

'There's nothing. Only sand,' said Arven. 'Miles and miles of dunes. Are you sure this is the place?'

Malachi didn't know what had gone wrong. There were no ruins to be seen as the map indicated. He didn't say it, but he had expected to find tall, ancient buildings rising into the sky. He turned in a circle, bemused by their absence – frightened by the planet's dark tainted soul.

Had the centuries destroyed everything, turning it all to dust?

'There should be *some* residue,' Malachi said.

Arven walked forward, surveying the area as he began to traverse a towering dune ahead. Feet sinking into soft black sand, his leg muscles strained almost to breaking point, but the Emperor pushed ahead to the top of the dune. At the top he peered through his fingers and the swirling sand and then his heart lurched in relief.

'Here!' he called.

Malachi and the warriors struggled to his side.

At the top they looked down. They were on the pinnacle of a large triangular structure that had, over time, become the buffer for the sand.

Ahead, in a gully, lay the ruins they sought. White, sand-bleached buildings – square and impersonal shapes – protruded from the ground. Even after many millennia they left their stain on the dead planet. And the centre of it all – the huge structure on which they all stood – towered like the personification of an ancient evil.

'What is this building?' Arven asked.

'We are on the top of a pyramid, Highness. It is the heart of the city we seek.'

'It's made of stone,' Arven observed, 'Or else the magic that created it would have failed long ago.'

'I feared as much,' said Malachi. 'The second tribe … our ancients … originally brought the technology from their birth world through the vortex to this place.'

Arven felt the weight of the structure as though it were above him not below him. His inherent revulsion for anything scientific gave him a sickening vertigo.

'We have to go inside,' said Malachi. 'And find the scroll room.'

'What do we hope to learn?' asked Prins.

'The secret to our curse and how to save ourselves from it,' Malachi said.

They began to make their way down into the gully. Prins and Elee led the way, and the hard gravelly sand slipped under-foot, making the descent slow.

At the bottom the ground was more stable but the four Arrak Nah Tiamen walked carefully, heads down against the driving wind as they circled the ruins.

Arven looked up at the large structure that they had traversed.

'This would have been the palace of their Emperor,' Malachi said. 'Unlike our domains. On Earth these became burial tombs for kings and queens of ancient lands. Probably our closest ancestors.'

The pyramid screamed power, aggression, avarice and abuse of science. All of the things that the Arrak Nah Tiamen were against: science was the evil presence that was forever lurking in their dark past.

'Explain this to me,' Arven said. 'We couldn't have come from this …'

Malachi looked up at the pyramid and frowned. 'We did. I'm sorry, my Emperor.'

'Why wasn't I told?'

'All mages suspected that science was somehow our darkest secret – we did not reveal it so that the burden was not passed to you or any other Emperors since the first who led us from *this* place. We were made to protect you and the Arrak Nah Tiamen from this. Now I realise how we have failed. We mages should have known what would happen but somehow the knowledge was lost. There's a story here that we were forbidden to remember … otherwise it would have been passed down, and we could have saved our world with this hidden knowledge.'

'I don't give in that easily,' Arven said. 'We aren't doomed yet. We can fix this. The new life that the Earth women brought us was proof of that. Otherwise our species wouldn't have been so compatible. We had no choice but to do what we did … Our race would have died. Now we must continue to fight on, or everything we are is for nothing. Everything we've done was pointless.'

Malachi looked at Arven, his eyes round with wonder. 'You believe that?'

'I believe we wouldn't have been able to bond if it weren't meant to be with the Earth women. And those bonds are strong. More powerful than any of us have ever experienced.'

Malachi looked thoughtfully at Arven. The Emperor, more than anyone, knew about bonding with an Earth woman. He had paid a higher price, but had won the biggest prize of them all. The Empress was strong, and Malachi knew that she would return to Emin in triumph, just not when.

'Now how do we get inside?' asked Arven.

Malachi's mind returned to the present and he walked the edge of the structure. Using magic to clear away swathes of sand he found a section that was arched and appeared to be a doorway. Arven, Prins and Elee were by his side when the sand blocking the entrance was drawn out. The use of magic, unlimited on Emin, tired the mage quickly, as though he had physically removed the sand with his own hands.

'Rest awhile,' Arven said.

Malachi sank down beside the door, utterly exhausted, and Arven considered how this small expedition onto the planet was proving far harder than it should have been for them all. Perhaps they should just raise a vortex now and return to Emin, coming back with more men and mages?

The hard wind dropped and the pyramid afforded them some shelter; that at least was a blessing.

'Perhaps we should enter one of the smaller structures and rest?' Arven suggested, but at that moment Malachi struggled to his feet.

'The sooner we find what we came for the sooner we may return,' he said.

The others followed him and they found shelter in the huge entrance of the pyramid. It was a spacious cavern, unnaturally clean under the circumstances, and Malachi expressed a thought that this must have been a reception area.

Inside they met yet another blockade. This time in the form of a solid rock door below an ornate arch that was carved with a million faces, all turned toward the entrance as though guarding it from invasion.

'This structure drains me,' Malachi said. 'It is the opposite of magic and therefore pulls against me.'

'Science …' Prins gasped, realising what Malachi and Arven already knew. 'Arrak magic didn't make this.'

'No,' Malachi said. 'It couldn't have.'

Prins made a sign to ward off evil as his eyes followed the line of the rock door.

'I can't use magic in here,' Malachi told them. 'It is as though I have been disconnected just by being inside.'

'How do we open it?' Arven said.

'By using the means they used. There will be a mechanism somewhere.' Malachi surveyed the door.

'There. That wheel carved out of rock. We must turn it.'

Prins and Elee hurried to do as instructed. It took all of their strength to turn the wheel a fraction. It wouldn't move further and the stone door remained unopened.

'There must be some technique to it,' Arven said. He looked closely at the wheel but couldn't make out how to move the mechanism. He placed his hand on the wheel. The rock felt hot to his touch and he quickly pulled back. Then, the wheel began to spin on its own and the big stone door began to open with an audible crack. The rock scraped along the sandy floor, shovelling away the remnants of the sand.

Arven stepped back and Malachi gripped his arm. '*You* were the key. There must be *some* magic here, and it recognised you!'

The door opened fully and the space beyond lay like a black hole before them. As Arven and Malachi approached, light burst open before them. They looked inside to see a long straight corridor lined with torches that were miraculously lighting themselves.

'Wait,' said Malachi as Arven made to enter.

Arven pulled himself free of the mage's restraining hand: Malachi's fear was irrational. They had already established that there were no life forms here, so what did they have to fear other than knowledge?

A strange buzzing noise came from the other end of the corridor, and as Arven considered moving beyond the doorway, a black swarm poured toward them.

Arven threw himself aside, just as the wave of flying creatures poured out into the reception area. Prins and Elee had drawn their swords at the first sign of trouble, and now they swung them through the air as the large, bird-like creatures flew around them.

Elee ducked as one of the things snapped at him with a beak that hosted serrated teeth.

'What are they?' cried Arven, covering his face again with his helmet. He squatted down behind the open doorway.

Malachi raised his staff and, despite his earlier claim that he couldn't use magic here, he forced a burst from it. The reception area lit up and light flooded over the creatures. They squealed and fell, or cannoned into the walls, but invariably they were cowed or dying.

'They must have lived inside here for all of the centuries,' Malachi said. 'They are not equipped to cope with light. It must have been the torches that scared them out in the first place.'

'How could they have survived in there?' asked Prins. 'What would they live on?'

'That we will learn,' said Arven.

The remaining creatures died or flew out of the reception area and onto the planet surface, possibly for the first time in the course of their development.

Arven stood and walked cautiously into the corridor, followed by the mage and his two warriors. They passed through the tunnel until they came to yet another door. Another mechanism similar to the first awaited there, and Arven did not hesitate to touch it, even though it burned him. The door ahead slowly opened and the four Arrak Nah Tiamen passed through.

More torches lit their way. Fortunately, there were no more of the flying creatures, and so the small group walked safely through the corridor until they came out into a furnished chamber.

Malachi looked around. Because the building had been sealed there was very little dust, and the red plush throne at the end of the chamber appeared to be undamaged. Not even the creatures that had inhabited this place had sullied it. Perhaps they had hibernated all this time, until disturbed by the return of the Arrak Emperor? Or maybe they had been left to guard its secrets from any but the rightful explorer.

Malachi scanned the room for signs of magic. But it appeared that this was a natural phenomenon, an accidental mummification of the room and its contents, because the air had been trapped and unmoving inside.

'So this is how my ancestors lived. They did not worship the magic that makes us, they worshipped their leader.'

'Yes,' Malachi said. 'Not in the way that we revere you, my Emperor. I suspect that this man was a warlord: he controlled his people with fear. But let us not forget that your ancestors turned their back on these evil ways. They left here, found Emin. They evolved in spirituality.'

Arven heard the voices of a thousand Earth men screaming inside his head. Already he was beginning to see the message that had been left for him. No one but he could have entered this place. No one but he could fully understand.

'Search this room,' he said now. 'We are looking for an ancient scroll that will explain our present circumstances.'

Prins and Elee began the search. None of them noticed as the stone door quietly closed behind them – sealing them inside the chamber.

2

The two moons of Emin shone down to make a pathway for Jasmine Regis and the mage Kale as they made their way through the camp. Magic was in the air and the night desert was the perfect temperature. Jas was calm – she should have been afraid – with Kale by her side she knew she was not in any immediate danger.

They had travelled a long way, back from Earth to Emin with a group of human survivors. The frazzled and frightened group of around 500 survivors was now safe in the hidden camp that Kale had raised using Jinx magic. For the first time they were able to eat, drink and sleep in safety. The irony was that they were now closer to the enemy than they had ever been, because they were on the Jinx planet, right under the noses of the Arrak Nah Tiamen.

'You're safe here,' Jas reassured them. 'You'll see.'

'But what if they find us?' asked Sylvia Bennett. She was a member of the council and always first to question everything. Mack, her husband, sat by the camp fire, unusually quiet: he had not said a word since they had exited the vortex.

Jas noted how Sylvia's once grey hair had now turned pure white. It shone as though she had silver glitter sprinkled in the strands. The old woman's skin was no longer sallow, but glowed pink with health: as did the skin of everyone else in the camp. The change in the humans was occurring rapidly – it was all for the good that they had left Earth's poisonous atmosphere.

'Kale has the camp covered with a protection spell. You are completely invisible to anyone on this planet. Even if they are standing just beyond the barrier,' Jas said, bringing her mind back to the discussion.

The barrier itself was only faintly visible to the occupants inside. It looked like a blurring in the air. The type of effect you get on a hazy summer day as heat rises. The blockade surrounded the town like a huge dome. It flowed over and above their heads, and from outside no-one could see or hear the bustle and movement of the survivors inside. But up close, there was a vague hum. It reminded the occupants that the shield was there and was a warning not to cross it.

'What happens if we do cross?' Sylvia asked.

'You'll find yourself out in the desert. You may not be able to return without the help of Kale. Your presence may be exposed to the Jinx mages. It will endanger the entire camp. I urge you to stay clear of the barrier, and keep the children safely within its walls at all times.'

Sylvia nodded. The crowd of council members around them murmured their agreement. Sylvia and all of the other survivors would do as they were told. They were used to following orders for their own safely, and so were the children. The thought of this saddened Jas briefly, before she shook the negative feeling away: she and Kale would soon be able to change things for the human survivors. At least, she hoped they would.

Jas considered their current dilemma. They had hoped to be on their way to see the Jinx Emperor, Arven – Jas's husband – by now. Less than a year ago, when Jas was brought to Emin, she and Arven had bonded. But Jas had resisted the magic that held them together, foolishly persuading Arven's chief mage, Kale, to help her return to Earth. Kale had fallen under Jas's considerable spell, not realising that the Empress carried inside her a tremendous proclivity for magic. Only when they reached Earth did the spell fade, and Kale understood the enormity of his error. However, Kale's ardent loyalty to his Empress had not faded but grown, and he took her orders and helped her and the survivors at every turn. When their final fortress at Manchester's Trafford Centre had fallen, Kale and Jas had used Jinx magic to bring the survivors to safety at the only place they could – Emin.

That safety, however, now depended on Arven's ability to forgive his wife for fleeing, which meant that the time had come for Jas and Kale to face Arven and atone for their misdemeanour. Jas was both excited and afraid at the prospect of seeing her husband again. Now they were back, both she and Kale would have to face the consequences of their somewhat foolish departure from Emin. Jas would have to explain her impulsive behaviour, and gain a pardon for Kale for his part in it all. She believed that forgiveness would not be difficult to obtain from Arven, but perhaps his subjects would question it, especially some of the more radical Arrak Nah Tiamen council members.

The only problem was, Arven was not on Emin.

Jas's mind raced over the last few days she had spent on Earth. Her heart beat with apprehension as she recalled their sudden, terrifying flight from the army and their poisonous drones. *Horror movies of old would have portrayed them as zombies,* she thought. They were the stuff of nightmares. Violent, cannibalistic, and no matter how much they were wounded, the creatures appeared to feel no pain.

Jas shuddered as she recalled leading the terrified Trafford Centre survivors through the vortex, knowing that she was taking them to enemy territory – but if they had remained they would all certainly have died at the hands of the drones, or worse. Even so, she did not regret what she had done. Part of her believed it had been imperative to return to Earth. There was a reason behind it all; she just wasn't sure what. But saving the lives of her friends was important to Jas, if nothing else. And for now at least she had been able to do that. She couldn't have left them to the fate that they would have certainly faced.

Julia, one of the escapees of the military base in North Wales – a place called MD59 – had revealed to them how the fertile women among them had been used as breeding stock for the military, or prostitutes for the single men. In her days as Major Handley's secretary, before the attack of the Jinx, Julia had been privy to sensitive material, and because of this, also suspected that the drones were subjects of unethical experimentation with drugs and hypnosis. She had later been used as a breeder at the base: a process that had almost killed her.

Of course, Jas understood that ethics meant nothing now on Earth. The planet was dying, Handley and his army may not realise it, but their experiments, and the poison they were pumping into the air, had, in just five years, completely destroyed what remained of Earth's ecosystem. Jas had tried to explain this to the survivors. Although some were open to the information, others found it difficult to accept that Kale had used his magic to predict Earth's lack of future.

One thing the survivors had realised was that the moment they stepped into the vortex, Earth was lost to them forever. There was no going back. And with the state of things there, that would only be a good thing.

Of course, deep down, the way the shit had hit the fan wasn't a surprise to anyone, given the state of Earth politics, starting in that fateful year 2016, when the United Kingdom had voted out of the European Union – and Brexit had brought to the fore all that was unsavoury about humanity – and then the United States had voted a perverse businessman, Donald Trump, into the White House as their President. Even then it had been as though the world as they knew it had been coming to an end. What had followed – and many men and woman in the supposedly enlightened world of the time had been shocked to realise it – had been that life for women, gay, lesbian and transgender people, as well as anyone from any ethnic minority, had in fact changed. Black lives didn't matter. Neither did anyone else's. The rich were getting richer and the poor were being trodden back down. Gone were the days when entrepreneurialism paid off. There was no longer a middle class and therefore the divide grew bigger. It was impossible to better yourself – if you happened to make or come into any money, then it was all taken away from you in tax. People were giving up hope of a better future long before it was over.

It had been subtle at first. Life had limped on for a few years in a semblance of normality. Then, quiet expulsions of immigrants. Women and those of the LGBTQ communities began to lose high-profile, well-paid jobs, on ridiculous technicalities. Their straight, less competent, male counterparts were promoted above them. They were slowly being forced back into domesticity or the closet – where, the likes of Handley would say, 'they belonged'.

Away from Earth, Jas began to see all of this clearly. She knew things had been wrong for years before the Jinx arrived, and now she suspected that the military, with their bigoted leaders, had been moving their forces into place, ready to force humanity to take those backward steps. And the media had helped them by stirring the race pot over and over again.

The arrival of the Jinx had played perfectly into their hands.

'This can't be so,' Taylor Arch, a former Captain under Handley, said after Jas explained her realisation to them.

A discussion erupted between him and his men and anyone listening.

'It is,' said an attractive redhead. Jas knew her: Katherine Easton-Campbell – mostly referred to as Kat – because she had been attending Jas's magic classes, and had proved very adept. 'I felt it. I had this great job, and suddenly I was made redundant. My job was then given to a chap who had worked under me. After that I found it impossible to find work that wasn't menial. And those lower-end jobs were rapidly becoming available in abundance. Especially when they started sending immigrants back to the countries they came from.'

'Kat's right,' Jas said. 'I was a teacher, but as a female I was constantly being questioned, even though I had qualifications coming out of my ears. Just before the Jinx, the education secretary had brought in a new ruling about female teaching staff. I never saw it, but rumour had it that we were heading toward serious demotion.'

'What if this is all true?' Andrew Petch, a former pastor in the old world, said. 'It doesn't make any difference now. We can't return to Earth.'

'I'm glad you realise that,' Jas said. 'Because we have to make it work here on Emin. And I believe we can. It's going to take patience and trust on both sides.'

More discussion followed, and fear of the Jinx was at the heart of it. Jas couldn't disagree with any of these terror-filled arguments. The Jinx *had* attacked Earth, they had killed anyone who resisted, and they had taken the women away to become breeders. How were they any different from Handley and his men?

'What you say is right,' Jas had explained. 'But the Jinx aren't intentionally evil. They didn't do what they did for greed. They aren't Viking raiders raping and pillaging, though it does seem like that. They have no understanding of any of these concepts. You see, they don't treat their women badly – they put them on a pedestal if anything. Though I agree how they live is very different from us. And our understanding of *free choice*. I don't agree with their methods, any more than you do, but the fact is they did this to survive. If I can, I will change things here. Now that I see the full picture.'

'Noble idea, but how do you plan to do that?' asked Petch.

'Think back. The way our politics was going, I'm sure we wouldn't have liked Earth very much, even if the Jinx hadn't arrived. Even if the air wasn't polluted.' Jas said.

'Well we sure don't like how it is now …' Margery mumbled from the back. 'But you didn't answer Pastor Petch's question.'

'You've got to understand, I fought against the Jinx too. And I don't have a rose-tinted-glasses view of it, just because I bonded with the Emperor. I just know that Arven doesn't want any more bloodshed. He is full of regret for how they handled things. He too wants change. And that is where our negotiations will start. The fact is we need to survive, and we're going to do that, whatever it takes.'

'That doesn't mean we should all just forget what happened …' Petch had said. 'The opposite in fact. The problems on Earth started because we had forgotten the lessons that two World Wars had taught us. That racism and bigotry were not acceptable.'

'True,' Jas had continued. 'We need to use our knowledge and understanding of our human mistakes now to save all of our lives. To try and find a way to live in harmony with the Jinx. And to teach them how to compromise too.'

'I can't help feeling afraid,' Kat said. 'Why do you so strongly believe that the Jinx can live with us, without reverting to the behaviour they had when they attacked Earth? Technically we women are safe, but what about the men here? They are surplus to requirements for the Jinx – as clearly they have enough of their own.'

'I know what you're saying. But they are learning. Their contact with us has changed them all, and mostly for the good. All I can do is draw comparisons. Do you believe that Handley and his army could change? When they have the world totally under their control now? Those men are the pits of humanity. And why? Power? Corruption? Or was it always lurking there in the background? I believe the Jinx are more capable of growing and accepting than the soldiers back on Earth who were supposed to be the people we trusted. But look how we were betrayed by our own. The Jinx don't have bias and bigotry. They have accepted all Earth women here in all of their colours and races. True, they have a bit to learn about freedom, and our various sexual preferences, but that will come in time. Handley on the other hand will never learn. Will never change his views.'

'Jas speaks the truth,' Julia had said. 'Handley was the most evil man I've ever met. He was a bigot of the worst kind, and he and others like him bought into his *Handmaid's Tale* version of what our life should be like. I thought our world had truly grown up, but we regressed so quickly that it made me realise how, deep down, most of us pretended to be tolerant when we really weren't. Doesn't that terrify you? That we lived this lie and the first chance we got to come out we took it …?'

'It does scare me,' Taylor had said. 'I was afraid for my wife and daughter back there. But I'm still afraid here.'

'Your fear is rational.' Jas walked around the campfire as she spoke. 'You should be afraid. We all should. I don't know how this will go down. All I know is – I have to try. And if it doesn't work, maybe Kale can find another place for you all to go and be safe. But I'm asking you now to give me a chance to talk to Arven. He won't send his soldiers here. He won't hurt you. That I do know. And he is the only person who can protect you from his warriors. And believe me, the Jinx follow a code of honour. Treachery is unheard of here. They won't go against the Emperor's final word, no matter what.'

'You have a lot of confidence in him,' Kat said. 'But I hope love hasn't blinded you to his faults.'

'I do love him,' Jas had said, surprising herself and the others with the admission. 'I'm not given to sentiment. Never have been. But it took leaving here for me to realise it, with my stubborn Earthling ways. And I don't doubt my personality will continue to get in the way of our relationship. But, I think, like men and women of all eras, we will find a compromise.'

'So what now?' Taylor asked.

Jas glanced at Kale.

'We go and see the Emperor,' Kale said.

'Just the two of you?' Sylvia said.

'Yes,' Jas answered. 'It's the only way.'

'You're sure the camp is protected?' Jas asked Kale as they stepped over the barrier.

'Yes Empress. No other mage will be able to sense their presence.'

'But what if some of Arven's warriors stumble on the camp?'

'Empress, you *know* I have hidden them. No-one can see, hear or sense them. Be at peace, Empress. You have saved your people. You did the right thing. And now you must be reunited with the Emperor. Then all of these bad times may be forgotten,' Kale said.

'All right. I believe you, you know that. We've been through so much together, how can I even doubt you?'

Kale nodded, but as per his usual modest way he said nothing.

'I'm afraid. *For them*. Not me,' Jas continued as they drew closer to their destination. 'They are so fragile and the Jinx so strong.'

'The Emperor will protect them,' Kale said, repeating her own words of earlier.

It was Jas's time to be silent as she hoped that this was true, that Arven would protect and help her people. For a time she became lost in her own thoughts, wondering how Arven would greet her. What he would do? Surely there would be some punishment for her flight from Emin? Arven would have to show how in control he was to his people. You can't have your Empress running away with your mage ... But she hoped she could persuade him of her true nature and her motives: she understood that the subliminal call she had received to return to Earth had been destiny. She had been unable to fight the urge to go back, regardless of her bond with Arven. The truth was, she now believed that she had been brought back to help the others and it had been no coincidence that she had arrived three years later than she had left, when her friends needed her the most. The timing was somehow crucial.

'And I will attest to that,' said Kale.

For a moment Jas wondered if she had been speaking aloud, and then she recalled the mental link that she had with Kale. She closed her mind off to him, afraid that he would see her self-doubts and fears too.

'The only problem we have,' Jas said, 'is that I still can't feel Arven's presence.'

'That's why we have to go to Sharik. A mage could be hiding him. With a shield like we have.'

'But why?' Jas asked.

Kale didn't answer.

At the Jinx oasis Kale tapped his staff down on the sand. A swirl of air and a small vortex opened before them. 'We can move unnoticed with minute bursts of magic.'

They stepped inside the swirling portal and within seconds the vortex closed and reopened. Jas found herself staring at the Sharik skyline. It looked truly beautiful highlighted by the twin moons.

'Empress?' Kale said.

'We're cloaked, right?'

For all of her brave words to the survivors, her own doubts still emerged.

Kale nodded. 'Not even another mage could see though this magic.'

But of course, Kale was the best of the mages – that was why he had been Arven's Imperial Al Kuzemen. Now, back on his home planet, Kale was displaying incredible power again. It made Jas aware of how much the Earth's poisonous air had been affecting him. And herself. She too felt strong. Stronger than ever before. In fact she could almost see the magic dancing in the atmosphere. It had a colour too, lilac sometimes, deep purple at others; a colour, she now realised, that she had always seen here, in her peripheral vision.

She turned her head to survey the outline of the town. Magic danced over the tents, the oasis grass, the pens of the animals. All of this was possible because of the power the Arrak Nah Tiamen had. And Jas now had the ability to see it too.

'Come,' said Kale. 'There is nothing to fear. The Emperor will be happy to see your safe return.'

'If we find him …' Jas sighed, and then she and Kale began to walk through the broad, straight sandy pathways that were the streets in Sharik. *Jinx Town*, Jas thought suddenly. This was the name that the Earth women had given to the capital city of the Arrak Nah Tiamen, once called the Jinx because of the way their magic affected Earth technology. Jas couldn't recall the moment when she had stopped thinking like an Earthling and begun to think like one of the Jinx. It had been sometime soon after she had returned to Earth. She realised how much she had changed. How different she was from the survivors. How lucky – and that was an oxymoron in itself – she had been to have been captured by the Jinx. For she had not had to live the life her former friends had been forced to endure. She didn't know what she would have become, who she would have been, if she had remained as they had for those further three years. They had been shadows of their former selves. Even Andy – still a young man – was much changed. Poverty, starvation, the daily grind for survival had worn them all down. And during that three year gap between Arven capturing her, and her return, the Jinx had ceased all further visits to Earth. That was a mystery that Jas did not understand. Even now. After all, Arven's plans were to capture all remaining females on Earth – regardless of Jas's disapproval of their methods.

They reached the centre of Sharik. Arven's tent lay ahead, and next to it was Kale's former residence. Jas had a feeling of both *déjà vu* and unreality, but neither of them stopped. They walked straight ahead.

There was a guard on the entrance as always, but this was a warrior Jas did not recognise.

'Wait,' said Kale.

'He can't see us though? Or hear us?'

'No, but I have a bad feeling.'

Kale turned away from the Emperor's tent, and he and Jas passed down the side between the mage's tent and the Emperor's.

They moved silently around to the back, and there Kale halted.

'What is it?' Jas whispered.

'Can't you feel it?'

Jas shook her head.

'The Emperor is definitely *not* here.'

Jas had been holding her emotions in check, but at Kale's revelation she let out that part of herself that recognised Arven.

'I feel the same as I did on Earth. Arven is nowhere near me. And my heart hurts because of it. I had hoped this feeling was just nervousness at seeing him again ...'

'I know,' Kale said.

'Where is he?'

Kale put out a search that stretched away from Sharik and ran onto the next town and the next, until he had searched the whole planet.

'As we thought, he's not on Emin,' he said.

'But ...'

'I don't *know* where he is. I can't *feel* him anywhere.'

Jas was lost in anxiety. This was not good. Not good at all! Had Arven gone to Earth to find her? And if so, how would the toxic atmosphere affect him and his men? Were they even now fighting the drones?

'We have to find him,' Jas said. 'Or none of us will be safe.'

'There is another mage in my former tent,' said Kale. 'If I open up more, I have to drop our cover. They will surely sense my presence.'

'Don't take the chance this close,' Jas said.

She took Kale's hand and led him back toward the front of the tent.

They both came to a halt as they heard the warrior guarding Arven's door talking to someone.

'No-one is to come in,' said a voice that Jas didn't recognise. 'The Emperor is not to be disturbed.'

'Councillor Marlin,' Kale said. 'But why is he pretending that Arven is still here?'

Jas's heart skipped a beat: maybe Marlin knew where Arven was? Perhaps there was nothing to fear after all.

'We'll return to the camp,' Jas said, 'and wait it out while you do some discrete searching. Arven obviously doesn't want anyone to know he's absent for some reason.'

Kale nodded.

From their vantage point they watched Councillor Marlin walk away toward the mage's tent. Jas began to walk back but Kale stopped her.

'The tent is cloaked,' he said.

'Arven's tent? Maybe he is in there, just having complete privacy ...'

'No. I mean ... yes, there is a basic cloak on the Imperial tent – but not enough to block me. He's not there. It's my ... the mage's tent. Heavily cloaked. Marlin passed inside and it was as though he completely disappeared. Invisible, as we are to them.'

'So, the new mage is hiding something?'

Kale shook his head. 'It's not our nature to be deceitful. Our prime objective is to serve the Emperor.'

'Maybe he *is* serving Arven. He might be keeping his absence a secret on his orders.'

'Maybe ...' said Kale, but Jas could hear doubt in his voice.

She was so in tune with Kale that she always knew how he was feeling. This disclosure of his suspicion, despite his words, brought about new concern for Arven's safety.

Kale made several attempts to penetrate the cloaking on the mage's tent, but to no avail.

'When Garuk died ... he sent me images. I made no real sense of them at the time. But it was a warning. Of betrayal.'

'Why didn't you tell me this before?' Jas said.

'I thought, with Earth's poisonous air, that I had misread the images. I couldn't believe it to be true.'

'Who is the traitor, Kale?'

'I don't know,' he said. 'But I ... *felt* a warrior's blade cut him down.'

When Marlin left, both Kale and Jas followed at a safe distance. The councillor turned left toward the council tent but carried on past it. Then he entered the warriors' quarters. Marlin paused at one tent, glancing around to see if he was being observed, before he ducked inside.

This tent was not cloaked as heavily as the mage's had been, but it was still a void to Kale's basic scan.

'I could push through this one easily, but it would mean risking exposure,' Kale said.

'Let's do this the old fashioned way,' Jas said. 'They can't see or hear us, right? So we'll just walk inside and eavesdrop.'

Before they had time to do that, Marlin came out of the tent with one of the warriors.

'Elidon,' Kale said. 'One of the more outspoken warriors. He was spreading a great deal of discontent before we left.'

'What would Marlin have in common with him?' Jas asked.

'I don't know. I have never known Marlin to spend any time in the company of warriors, except when being escorted somewhere by them. '

Marlin walked away from the tent and Elidon went back inside, only to exit again a few moments later with several other warriors. They hurried to the el lien meck pens and saddled up the camel-like creatures while Kale and Jas watched at a safe distance. Elidon was the first to mount, and the others followed suit as he galloped out of the pen and down the wide pathway toward the open desert.

'Wonder what that's all about?' said Jas.

'Marlin must have given them some orders. Perhaps direct from Arven,' Kale said.

Jas didn't answer. She had an odd feeling in the pit of her stomach that just wouldn't leave. It was a vague sickness that had nothing to do with her pregnancy, and more to do with a feeling that something was very wrong in Sharik. She just didn't know what it was yet. The one thing she did know for certain, however, was that it was not a good time for Arven to be absent. Their reunion would have to wait, and the fate of the survivors would have to hang in the balance a while longer.

3

'This place is magical,' said Julia as Kale and Jas returned to the camp.

Many Bedouin-style tents had been erected and the camp resembled a smaller version of Sharik with its wide, sandy streets. Each family unit had their own tent with sleeping quarters, a living space and a room with a small pool for washing and bathing.

Plant life grew in and around the new homes of the Trafford Centre survivors. There was a large central campfire, and several smaller ones dotted around where families cooked their own food. Jas saw Corporal Kline and Sergeant Harvey and their wives among those serving food to a group of orphaned children from the central fire – the former soldiers had taken up their previous role of ensuring everyone had food – especially those with no family to care for them.

A river ran alongside the camp now with fish leaping in and out of the water. Someone had been smart enough to cast a line and as a result several large, salmon-like fish were grilling on a spit above the fire.

It was indeed magical.

Jas noticed the healthy glow in Julia's cheeks. She hadn't looked this well back on Earth; in fact all of the survivors had looked decidedly sick at the Trafford Centre. Jas noted now that they were rallying far better than she would have imagined they could after years of poisonous air and a difficult life.

'How are you feeling?' Julia asked.

'Me? Fine,' Jas said. 'Better than on Earth.'

'Me too,' Julia said. 'And Kale seems … strong.'

Jas nodded.

'These people haven't eaten this well for months. But I'm sure there will be a moment when I'll have to explain how Kale has created it all from Jinx magic,' Jas said.

'It's amazing,' said Julia. 'And when the time comes, I doubt any of them will object to it.'

'Can you image how Jinx magic could have cured world hunger?'

Raised voices some distance away drew their attention from the camp's centre and fire. Jas and Julia hurried to see what was wrong.

A few tents away they found the doctor, Gerald Avery, in the middle of the altercation. The other person involved was Dawn, Taylor Arch's wife.

'What's going on?' said Taylor, running across the camp.

'Keep him away from me. And from Lucy,' Dawn said. Then she turned and walked back into the small tent that she occupied with Taylor and their daughter.

'What was that all about?' Taylor asked Gerald.

'I don't know. She's acting weird. I wanted to check she was all right after she tried to …'

Gerald glanced at Jas but didn't finish the sentence. They all knew of Dawn's breakdown, and how she had almost shot Jas before they escaped from Earth.

'If she doesn't want your help stay away from her,' said Jas. 'I suspect she has good reason.'

Gerald turned and walked away. His face was red with anger.

'What reason would Dawn have to dislike the doctor so much?' Taylor asked.

Jas shrugged. 'I don't trust him and never have,' she said. 'Anyway … I need to speak with you.'

She took Taylor aside and out of earshot of the other survivors.

'Arven isn't here,' she said. 'He's not even on the planet.'

'What does that mean to us?' Taylor asked.

'It means we need to remain hidden until he returns. He is the only person who could guarantee the safety of everyone here.'

'You say that like you think he *will* guarantee it. But we're alone right now, so you can give it to me straight. *Are* we safe here?' Taylor asked.

'I believe we will be. I have to.'

'Where is he?'

Jas shook her head. 'Kale is trying to find out, but his presence here mustn't be detected by the other mages. Not without Arven being around to protect us. He'll have to be discreet.'

She explained again how the mages could sense each other, and how Kale's magic was the only thing protecting the camp from being discovered.

'Call it some kind of cloaking device. Only it's magic, not science.'

'I'll go and talk to the others about setting up a perimeter too,' Taylor said.

'It wouldn't hurt,' Jas said. 'But remember your weapons are useless here. Kale is our only real weapon and defence. He needs to be respected and protected at all cost.'

'Agreed,' Taylor said.

Jas went to look for Kale. She had been up all night and really should need to sleep but the planet energised her and she didn't feel tired at all. She walked instead through the camp. Saw the homes and camp fires, the children running around playing, for the first time in a while, as though they had nothing to fear. The smiling faces that greeted her made the effort of their flight all the more worthwhile. Jas knew they were all safe. They could rest, regroup and regain their strength and vigour. The Emin atmosphere was pollution-free, and every breath cleared away the residue of the poison from Earth. She had no doubt that they had done the right thing bringing them all here, even if, at some point, they had to leave again. But for now she hoped that wouldn't happen.

'There you are,' she said.

Kale was standing by the river. The gem at the top of his ornate wooden Al Kuzemen staff glowed, and light fell onto the water as the mage held it aloft.

'There are many fish here now,' he said. 'Soon, we'll have other beasts too. They will be attracted to the camp and then ...' He cast his staff in the air, and wooden-looking posts began to emerge from the sand, forming into an animal pen. 'We will capture them and keep them here. Your people will survive until the Emperor returns.'

'Thank you,' Jas said. 'This is amazing and they do appreciate it.'

'Now I have to go,' said Kale.

'Go? *Where?*'

'I cannot see the Emperor and I fear for him. I need to travel to another town and find a mage I trust.'

'Why can't you trust the one in Sharik?'

Kale was silent for a moment.

'There's something you aren't telling me,' Jas said.

'Prestin is there. It has to be him, and he is too involved with Marlin. I'm *suspicious* of them both.'

'But you told me that mages can't be disloyal,' Jas said.

'I believe things have changed. We have been ... tainted by our deeds. And my suspicion is something I have to thank you for.'

'What do you mean?'

'You have opened my eyes in many ways, Empress. I fear that my people are not the same as they were before their contact with Earth's women. We now have jealousy, greed, and murder among us. Remember what was happening *before* we left? These things are not natural to the life of the Arrak Nah Tiamen.'

'Yes. I remember the man who murdered his relative because he was jealous that he had bonded with an Earth woman. Your people are evolving. It had to happen.'

Kale nodded. 'For this reason we may not be able to trust all mages either. Just because they carry the magic for our people, it does not mean that they are all wise.'

Then Kale took his leave, promising to return within a few days. Jas walked to the edge of the camp with him and saw an el mien meck saddled and waiting.

'Hurry back, dear friend,' she said. 'Bring news of Arven, but be safe.'

Kale mounted the animal and set off across the desert away from the camp. Jas turned back to the camp.

'Can you help me?' said a tear-filled voice behind her. Jas turned to see Caroline and her two children, Jamie and Selene, looking out of one of the tents. 'He isn't here. I've looked everywhere.'

'Perhaps you should go to the camp fire and get some food?' Jas suggested to the children.

Jamie and Selene looked confused and frightened, but Jas's suggestion immediately lifted their mood and they ran from the tent toward the campfire.

'Can I come in?' Jas asked.

Caroline stepped back to allow her entrance to the tent.

Inside Jas saw all of the familiar Jinx furnishings and knew that each tent would have beds and tables and chairs, sofas for the occupants to recline on, and behind a curtained partition a small bathing pool. This was just as she had lived in Sharik, though these tents were on a much smaller scale as the magic Kale had drawn on was deliberately low-key.

Now she wondered about everything she had ever seen at Sharik. Her impression of the town, the tents and the pens had led her to the conclusion that someone, somewhere, had created them by actual work. But after watching Kale build their small outpost from nothing but sand, she now understood that this was how the Arrak Nah Tiamen lived. Magic was everything. No wonder science and machines seemed like sacrilege to them.

She sat down on a low stool opposite Caroline, who sank down onto a chaise as though her energy had finally failed her.

'Where is Donovan?' she said.

'I don't know. I think he must have been left behind,' Jas said. 'I'm sorry.'

'We can go back, though?' Caroline said. 'You could take some of the soldiers back to find him.'

'For the moment we have to conserve our strength and keep everyone else safe.'

Jas didn't reveal that Kale had left the camp, or that Arven was also not on the planet. Some information was best left out of a conversation with a possible widow grieving over what may have happened to her husband back on Earth. Jas suspected that Donovan was dead. What else would have prevented him from finding his way back inside when the drones had penetrated their defences? Jas knew enough about Donovan to realise that he would have tried to reach his wife and children – if he'd been able to.

'Try not to worry,' she said now. 'And think of Jamie and Selene. They need you to be strong.'

'I don't need a pep talk,' Caroline said. 'I need Donovan back.'

For once Jas was at a loss for words.

'Come out to the campfire and eat something,' she said finally. 'Perhaps one of the others saw him. If we can pinpoint his last location ...'

Hope blossomed in Caroline's eyes. 'You could go back for him?'

'In the coming days we'll see what we can do,' Jas said, afraid to commit more or make any promises that she may not be able to keep. She knew that Kale could not leave the planet and keep his magic in place to protect the outpost, and for the sake of one man, the lives of many had to come first. But she couldn't bear to see the distress in Caroline's face. Part of Caroline doubtless knew that it was more than likely that her husband was dead, but she didn't want to face that fact, and Jas did not want to be the person who told her the truth. Not yet anyway.

Let's at least have a few days of peace, she thought now as she took Caroline's hand.

'You must keep up your strength, for your children's sake,' Jas said.

Caroline went with her to the fire, where they found Selene and Jamie, fed and watered, playing happily with the other children, despite their mother's anxiety.

Sergeant Harvey held out a bowl to Caroline and then filled another for Jas.

'I don't need ...' she began.

'Sure you do. Everyone does. You need your strength like everyone else, Empress,' Harvey said. Then he winked at her. 'No more rations.'

Jas took the bowl. It contained a thick vegetable stew and a portion of the cooked fish. She began to eat and was surprised at how hungry she was. The fish was delicious. Though she knew no Earth fish lived on Emin, it tasted like salmon. She ate quickly, because it was the nicest, cleanest-tasting food she'd had in a long time.

'This is good,' she told Harvey.

'I know. Amazing, right?' He looked around as he spoke, and Jas saw the wonder in his expression. 'Feels like I'm dreaming.'

'You're wide awake, I promise,' Jas said. 'And safe.'

She didn't add, *for now*, but for the first time in her life Jas wished she had seer ability. What she wouldn't give to be able to see just a few days into their future. The return of Arven would be a good thing right now. But she was as powerless as everyone else in the camp and would have to wait for time to reveal their destiny.

She left the campfire and found her way to the tent she shared with Julia and Kale. Inside were three separate curtained cubicles with beds, as well as the usual furnishings. On one side she discovered a wardrobe with imperial robes, just her size, and on the other side Jinx female clothing for Julia. Another wardrobe held mage's robes for Kale. It seemed he had thought of everything, and all in the blink of an eye.

Jas looked down at her Earth clothing now with some dismay. The camouflage trousers and black T-shirt were dirty and she was decidedly dishevelled. Taking one of the robes and a set of undergarments, which consisted of a pair of harem-style bloomers, she opened the curtain that led into the pool room. The pool wasn't as grand as the one she had in Arven's tent back in Sharik but it was filled with steaming, perfectly warm water. It was sunken into the ground, with four stone steps that ran across the side and down. Stripping off her worn and tired clothing she stepped in.

She sank down into the water, relishing the flow of it on her skin. It was an age since she had been able to clean herself this well. The facilities at the Trafford Centre hadn't been exactly luxurious. Now she washed away the grime and remaining taint of Earth from her skin. It felt good, as though she were ridding herself of any final connection to the planet.

She paused. Earth was doomed, hadn't Kale told her so? But she did feel a moment of regret that there really was no going back there now, no matter what. She scooped up water in her hands and splashed her face. The water muddied, then immediately cleared, taking away the last of the dirt. Leaning her head back, she dipped her hair into the water and rubbed at her scalp. The dirt washed away, and her head was immediately cleaner. No need for scrubbing or soap, the water purified without that, but it felt good to massage her skin anyway.

Once clean, Jas walked back up the shallow steps and picked up a towel from a conveniently-placed stack at the side of the pool. She wrapped it around herself. Then left the room and went back into the main tent.

In her own cubicle with the curtain closed, Jas dressed in the clean clothing and put aside the military trousers and T-shirt. She would have to wash these at some point in the pool, but she was weary now. It had been a long and arduous 24 hours and she felt a wave of fatigue.

She lay down on the bed fully clothed and closed her eyes.

4

Alan Kenney met Michael Harrington as planned, and they made their way unobserved to the P Sector. John Guilor was in the booth as expected.

'If anyone comes along, you're just asking the status of booking one of the girls …' John said.

Alan nodded.

'Here …' John continued. He held out a swipe card. 'Triple A – you can open any door with this.'

'Where d'you get it?' asked Harrington.

'I cloned it from Handley's personal pass. Even with this area in quarantine, he is the only one who would still go in and use them. Dirty fat bastard. He's in here most days and he doesn't care who knows it.'

'He makes me want to puke,' Alan said.

'After this we get my sister out of here, okay?' John said.

'And Tremaine and I can be together too,' said Harrington.

'Yeah,' said John. 'We should live the way we want to.'

'Tremaine said the P Class girls will need help after this. They've been through a lot, and the withdrawal from the drugs might be difficult for them,' Harrington said. 'He gave me some meds for them.'

Alan listened as Harrington gave instructions.

'It's gotta look like they got themselves out …' John said.

They went over the plan again.

'You know the rendezvous point?' John said when they were all clear on what they were doing.

'Yes,' said Harrington.

'We'll all meet you there in a few days.'

Alan was familiar with the layout of the sector, and although he had never been with any of the girls, he had often booked one for an hour – then just sat and talked with them. In his own way he had been giving them respite, but also it had to appear as though he was one of the men in the same way. Alan wasn't gay; he just couldn't bring himself to do what the others did. He couldn't treat women that way, and he didn't understand how some of the others, whom he had known and worked with for years, could. But he no longer had to bear this burden alone. Since Alan had learnt that Dr Tremaine was sympathetic, gay and in love with Mike Harrington, Alan had done all he could to help them both. The doctor and soldier had in their turn helped him, and his friend John Guilor – whose recently widowed sister, Kerry Hawkin-Edwards, had been scheduled to be sent to the breeder programme. Hearing of their dilemma, Tremaine had volunteered to marry Kerry, sparing her from this awful fate while helping his own cover as a straight male.

Now Alan led Harrington through the maze of client rooms until they found the main holding area.

Neither of the men had been back here. This area was off limits to all but the medical staff. So Tremaine had explained in detail where the women would be.

'It's an airlock,' Harrington said when they found the door. 'We go in, and the other door won't open until the one behind us is closed. Crazy thing about this is, this area is the most secure in the entire base, and these girls are so drugged up and conditioned they couldn't even attempt to leave.

Harrington swiped the card in the security pad. Nothing happened.

'It's not working,' he said.

'These things can be temperamental,' Alan said. He took Harrington's card, wiped it on his uniform, then swiped down slowly.

The door made a quiet beep and began to open.

'You're sweating,' Alan said. 'Calm down. It's all going to be okay. Handley is busy dealing with James today.'

'How do you know?'

'I was on the door when James arrived. Handley will be getting his arse kicked about the Trafford disaster. He really screwed up and James had to send his men in to rescue our guys from the drones.'

'I didn't know that. What happened?'

'The drones turned on our guys. Not surprising really: they are bred to kill, and Handley's regime proved too efficient. The drones are insane, feral, and therefore not easy to control. We need to be aware of that when we get out of here too. They are dangerous, and so is anyone else living out there, breathing in that zombie poison. Promise me you'll be careful, Mike?'

'I will. I just want out of here with no hiccups,' Harrington said. 'I'll get the girls to safety and wait for you all to join us as planned.'

They stepped into the airlock and Harrington pressed the *Close* button on the door. As it sealed shut behind them, the door ahead began to open.

They hurried through as soon as they could.

'Should we close it?' Alan asked.

'No. The medical team is off duty today. Tremaine made sure. And the women are fed automatically by default. So no chance of bumping into catering staff either. They make sure they have as little human contact as possible. Except when ...'

'Yeah. I get it,' said Alan. '*Sick*. Really sick.'

They found themselves in a sterile-looking corridor. The whitewashed walls were lined with large windows. As the men passed them they realised that each was a two-way mirror looking into a small private room.

'This is where they keep them for conditioning,' Harrington said.

It was so cold and calculated that Alan had to look away.

He checked his watch for the time. 'The P Sector main room camera is supposed to be offline in two minutes. Are there cameras on this corridor?

'No.'

'Good. Where is the main room?'

'This way,' said Harrington. He led Alan down the corridor to the door at the end. 'They keep them together in here when they aren't working.'

Alan waited a few minutes to make sure their timing was good, then he swiped his card down the security panel. The door opened immediately and he and Harrington moved in.

There were thirty women in the room, and they lay on couches, eyes closed. They were wearing identical grey boiler suits. Above their heads was a dull swirling light, and mood music played at a low volume.

'Wake up,' said Harrington. 'We are getting you out of here.'

None of them moved. Alan and Harrington exchanged a look, then they moved to the nearest couch.

'The meds that Tremaine gave you ...' Alan said.

'Yes of course. The blue vial is to help wake them. They'll be very compliant and take orders. So it shouldn't be difficult for us to encourage them out of here.'

'Jesus. Those bastards really do a number on them, don't they? Drugging them like this?' Alan said. His stomach was rolling with sickness. The thought of what some of his colleagues did horrified him more than the Jinx ever had.

Harrington injected the first girl, then moved to the next. Alan waited beside the first until she began to rouse.

'What's your name?' he asked her.

She was a petite little thing, barely in her twenties and so thin that Alan wondered if they deliberately starved her to keep her this lean. It gave her a child-like appearance. Alan knew this fetish was something that the old world would have abhorred. The thought increased the feeling of sickness in his stomach.

The confused girl sat up and rubbed her eyes. 'My name ... Gina. I'm Gina. What is your pleasure?'

'Come on, Gina,' he said. 'Get up and stand by the door.'

Gina did as she was told, and Alan followed Harrington around the room, encouraging the waking girls to wait by the door.

They formed an orderly line, like robots.

Alan took up the rear as Harrington led them all from the room toward the airlock exit.

'We can't all fit in there,' Alan said. 'You take the first ten through, and I'll send the others to you.'

They began to move the women out. As Harrington passed through with the first batch, Alan waited with the others. They were eerily quiet. No chatter or gossip among them. And, they showed no fear.

'We're gonna get you out of here,' he babbled to break the silence. 'Just do as Harrington says beyond the door and you're all gonna be free.'

The women stared at him with blank uncomprehending eyes.

'Don't you understand? No-one is going to treat you like this ever again.'

'Yes master,' said Gina. 'Whatever you want.'

The airlock closed on the other side and Alan swiped it again and filled the space with more of the women.

'When the door opens, pass through. Okay?' he said.

They all nodded in response to his words. Then Alan backed out and closed his door. He heard the click and saw through the panel that Harrington was opening the other side. They continued this process until the last batch was inside the airlock.

Alan was about to leave with them when he became aware that someone was standing in front of one of the two-way mirrors halfway down the corridor. He sent the girls on alone and turned back. They had glanced briefly into the rooms beyond but had thought them all empty. Now he saw one woman alone.

'Thank god I saw you!' he said. 'But how do I get you out?'

He glanced down the corridor and then turned in the direction of a door he had seen at the other end – the opposite end from the containment room where they had found the women. He used his card again and the door opened for him. Here he found another corridor. This one led behind the small rooms, and he counted along until he found the one he thought contained the woman.

He swiped his card. There was a long pause, but then the door began to open.

'Hey?' he said. 'I've come to get you out of here.'

The woman remained facing the mirror. Looking at her reflection.

'Come on,' Alan said. 'You're gonna be free.'

He entered the room and went to her. She was wearing a hospital gown and nothing else. Alan looked around but found neither clothing nor a robe.

He took her arm and led her back to the door. She came without resistance, and they soon reached the main corridor.

He glanced through the panel and noticed that the airlock was now empty. He used the card again and, as the panel opened, he took the woman's hand.

'You're gonna be fine,' he said to her, his voice calm and kind.

The airlock closed behind them. Only then did Alan look at the woman properly.

Her eyes were black, as though the drugs they had given her had dilated her pupils to the extreme. Her mouth was slack, and drool slipped from her lips and fell onto her chest, soaking the front of her hospital gown.

'Jesus!' he gasped.

The woman turned to him then, and her mouth flapped as though she were trying to talk.

The airlock in front started to open.

'Come on Al,' said Harrington. 'We gotta get outta …'

Harrington stopped talking when he saw the woman with Alan.

'She's a vegetable,' he said. 'We can't take her. Tremaine told me you can't help some of them.'

'But she was in a room. *Alone*. I couldn't leave her there,' Alan said.

'Come on. We'll sort this out later.'

'What about that *other* injection. Maybe it'll help her too,' Alan said.

'Yeah. I'll try it,' Harrington said. He retrieved one from his rucksack, which now stood on the floor next to a case of gas masks.

Then he rolled up the sleeve of the woman's hospital gown and injected the solution into her.

'What's that one?' Alan asked.

'Supposed to be an antidote to the drugs they pump into them to condition them.'

'Right. So that will help with withdrawal?'

'Yeah. Might bring her out of this. You never know.'

'Help me get some outdoor clothing on her,' Alan said.

They pulled a coat and trousers up over the woman's hospital gown. She remained quiet and dazed despite the injection.

Harrington gave the others orders to put on the outdoor clothing over their boiler suits and place on the gas masks. The women all complied.

Alan pulled on his own gas mask and placed one over the head of the woman. He took her hand and, with Harrington now taking up the rear, led the way to the damaged area of P Sector. This was the reason they had been able to enact their rescue plan: especially when Handley's superiors had feared that the P Class women had been contaminated by the small amount of poisonous air that had leaked in from outside.

'There's a hatch up out of here,' Alan said. 'It was breached and can't lock, so they've disabled the alarm on it until the repair crew get to it.'

They opened the airlock to the hatch and a rush of outside air made Harrington check his mask and those of the others. Then Harrington led the way to the top as Alan ferried the woman up the steps after him. He gave each of them a bag to carry, containing provisions that should be enough to get them all to the pre-arranged rendezvous point. But he knew there was also a truck parked conveniently near the hatch, left there by one of the fifth columnists.

The hatch above pushed open easily, and Alan could see Harrington helping the woman out one by one. As he came to the final woman, Alan was beginning to regret bringing her. She was rocking from side to side, twisting her head at weird angles that would have hurt anyone normal.

'Go on,' he said to her. 'Up the ladder.'

She stopped moving and stared at him as though she had just noticed him for the first time. An odd expression came onto her face and she began to stroke his arms. He began to feel intense anxiety. Maybe it was because she was so odd and he feared being able to get her out before their presence was discovered. Or maybe it was because she appeared to be more animated than earlier – but not in a good way.

'I'm sorry,' he said. 'I think I'm going to have to put you back.'

He pulled her away from the hatch, then looked up and waved to Harrington. As planned, he closed and locked the inner airlock. Some of the polluted air had crept inside the sector, but not enough to set off the alarm or to cause real damage.

He pulled the woman further away, then removed her mask. She was watching him intently. It was predatory and it creeped Alan out. He led her back to the main sector airlock and then rooted in his pocket to find the security card. He found the card but it slipped through his fingers and fell to the ground. As he bent to pick it up, the woman grabbed him.

For a minute Alan didn't know what was happening. Then she bit his arm. Alan screamed in pain into his gasmask as he felt her teeth ripping his flesh. She forced him down to the ground. Alan's training kicked in. He used her own weight and momentum and rolled her body until he was on top of her, then he scrambled to his feet. In the roll his mask came away from his face and clattered on the concrete floor.

She rose slowly. Deliberately. Her teeth gnashed against her bloodied lips. Alan backed away. His arm hurt and he gripped it. She was insane. And maybe the injection Harrington had given her had caused it. He had to warn Harrington not to give it to the others, but how could he do that right now?

The security card crunched under his foot.

He could still get that door open, push her in and close it. Couldn't he?

She was moving forward now, faster than Alan could back away. And he couldn't risk disadvantaging himself again by trying to retrieve the card. Perhaps it was best to lead her to the security checkpoint, get help from John Guilor.

He turned and began to run, but she brought him down as she threw herself onto his legs in a perfect rugby tackle like a trained athlete.

She crawled up his body, fingers digging into him through his uniform. Alan struggled, but she had the strength of the insane. He tried to roll again in order to shake her off, but she felt impossibly heavy.

Fingers and teeth bit into his skin through his clothes. Then she bit down into the back of his neck, teeth gnashing and sawing as though he were a tasty steak that she had to have.

Before he died, Alan thought her heard shouting. His blurred vision imagined he saw the rush of feet running toward them. Help was coming! It was ironic that he could end this way, killed by someone he was trying to save …

And then welcome blackness took away the pain …

5

Kale had been travelling solidly for 14 hours when he saw Renik in the distance. The el lien meck he was riding was tired. He set up camp and looked out over the desert, raising a patch of grass and a shallow pool of water for the animal. He didn't summon any more magic this close to the town for fear that the Al Kuzemen within would feel his presence.

Kale was finding it difficult to accept this concept, even as he thought of it. It was unnatural to be suspicious of members of his own order: they were sworn to protect the Arrak Nah Tiamen and their Emperor, and how could any of them break this oath? Yet someone had. Therefore he had to test any mages he met at a safe distance, when their guard would be down. It was the only way he could be sure whom to trust. That at least he had gleaned from the knowledge Garuk had attempted to send to him in his final moments.

Kale tried to decipher those images even now. But they always ended in Garuk's pain and death – a pain that he had shared with Kale in order to make that passing easier. If the mage's corpse were near, Kale knew he would be able to look into his eyes, and possibly see the killer there, but the body would have been burnt by now, as was their custom, and so this was another avenue closed to investigation.

The moons rose above his head. Kale felt the cool glow touching his skin and enjoyed the energy it gave him.

The animal could be revived with a little more magic, and he would be able to continue his journey if he wished, but he revelled in his solitude. How long had it been since he had been able to enjoy his own company? Something that Al Kuzemen normally took for granted. They did not live as hermits, but would have done so given the choice. Their calling was about individuality, magic, wisdom and servitude to the Emperor and the people. Al Kuzemen never married: it just never occurred to them to seek to bond with another when they were already tied so completely to their magic.

Being alone with his thoughts brought about new revelations for Kale.

He was confused by his own emotions. Once he had believed himself to be in love with Jas, but he had been the victim of a spell she had subconsciously cast over him because she had needed his help to escape back to Earth. He did not, even now, know how she had done it. Love could not be created by magic. It was one of their unspoken, but true, impossibilities. That was why Kale had thought his emotions real. Now he had feelings for Julia. Partly of the reason why he helped the survivors was that he could not imagine leaving this beautiful woman to that terrible fate. She had been through too much already.

But, where did these new feelings leave him? He was an Al Kuzemen – and none had ever bonded. Was it even permissible?

Kale did not know the answer to this question, because the situation had never presented itself before. This dilemma, however, made the idea of it seem more possible than it should be. If none had done it, did that mean that they couldn't, or that they could but had chosen not to? It was all so complex.

Kale let his thoughts drift and he pulled into his mind's eye the many scrolls he had read, bringing their images before his eyes with barely a flick of his wrist. It took such little magic to give him total recollection, and he scanned the documents telling of the Al Kuzemen history, looking for answers.

The scrolls did not discuss the personal lives of former mages though. All they described was how a mage could use his magic; how he must have a lifetime of learning and dedication in order to perfect his art.

His mind fell on one scroll. It was history from centuries ago. A 'mythological' tale, Jas would probably call it, because there was no proof that these events had ever really occurred. He and Jas had enjoyed philosophical discussions about faith and religion, and he knew her views on the Bible and other religious texts that claimed to be the retelling of actual events.

'The biggest fairytale of all,' she had called it. 'Yet so many believed it was true.'

'In your world, magic was fantasy too,' Kale had pointed out at the time. 'And yet, you now know it is real.'

Jas had grown as thoughtful then as Kale was now. He knew that in those moments she had been questioning everything she had formerly believed in. He found himself doing the same thing now, months later, with so much adventure behind them. The events that had taken place had changed Kale too. He hadn't craved his solitude as one of his calling should; somehow he had thrived on helping Jas, on being among the humans, even as their dying planet had drained his strength.

'And look at me now,' he said to the animal as it chewed at the magically-created grass. 'I'm out on yet another adventure. This time alone.'

It was unheard of! And it gave Kale pause.

I'm no warrior, yet I am behaving like a hero. Rescuing Earthlings, rushing out into the desert to find allies. Kale began to laugh. The sound pouring from his lips echoed into the desert. He stopped, shocked at this very emotional response. It was so unlike him, and laughter was not something an Arrak Nah Tiamen mage indulged in. They were always so restrained.

It felt good to let go of his serious side for once.

The al lien meck stopped eating the grass and began to drink from the oasis pool. The animal was content and so was Kale.

Kale lay back on the sand and looked up at the red moons, and the clear Emin sky. He closed his eyes, letting his mind drift in and out of the ancient scrolls as the magic continued to play out. It was a good way to stop himself thinking about Julia. And the very male urges he had when around her. Feelings and emotions he had never felt before, not even in his brief infatuation with Jas.

The Eleventh Moon scroll fell before his eyes, and Kale began to absorb the information again. Ah yes, the two tribes. Now wasn't that the stuff of fairytales? He drifted into meditation as he read. Following the path of the tribes and their disagreements many thousands of years ago.

On a planet that it was said was Earth – or Earth-like.

He had forgotten that aspect of the story, and yet wasn't it what he had been thinking of when he had led the Arrak Nah Tiamen there in their search for new mates? They had already tried other planets and galaxies to no avail, because other inhabitants had been too different from them to even conceive of making them their mates.

Kale squeezed his eyes shut in a reflex to the memory of the story. He had grown up on it. Part of the mage teachings. A given, that it was all some impossible story but they had to defend its authenticity fanatically in their own spiritual journey. Just like Jas's Bible. Which, after their discussions, was one of the books he had read while being in the Trafford Centre. His arrogance had even identified with the character of Moses, doing great evil for the sake of saving his own people. But religious stories were all something future generations could identify with. Kale understood this in his own way even more.

His thoughts stumbled. Why was he thinking about Earth religion and philosophies? He suspected it was because they were somehow intertwined.

'What do we have here?'

Kale opened his eyes. He was surprised to realise he had drifted off to sleep and now he found himself surrounded by a band of warriors.

He sat up, but the Arrak warrior who had spoken, perhaps the leader among them, pushed him back down with his foot. He was wearing a wrap across his lower face, and Kale could see only his eyes. They looked at him with curiosity and then recognition.

'What is the meaning of this?' said Kale.

'We got ourselves a traitor,' said the warrior, removing his scarf.

Kale realised that Elidon and his warriors, out on their mission for Marlin, had stumbled across him. It couldn't have been a worse coincidence. Kale now regretted sparing his magic, for being caught by these warriors was far worse than being noticed by another mage at a distance.

'I'm on a mission for the Emperor,' said Kale.

'Hmm. The Emperor is not on the planet,' Elidon said.

'How do *you* know that?'

Elidon gave a harsh laugh. 'Get him.'

His warriors jumped to obey, and Kale was grabbed by callous, strong hands and lifted to his feet. His staff, never far from his hand, was knocked aside as he reached for it.

'Let me go,' Kale ordered. 'There will be severe punishment for anyone who mistreats an Al Kuzemen …'

'The way we see it,' said Elidon, 'you left your order when you ran away with the Empress. That Earth harridan killed a friend of mine the day she bonded with the Emperor. I never understood why they just didn't slit her throat there and then.'

'You're vile,' said Kale. 'No-one but the Emperor can touch the Empress.'

A fist hit Kale hard in the face. If the other warriors had not been holding him he would have fallen back with the force. More fists flew, and Kale's ribs erupted in pain, the wind was knocked from his lungs. He was dropped to the sand, and a rain of blows and kicks soon followed. Kale felt himself losing consciousness, and then his hand fell on his staff.

His magic sparked in defence, and the warriors fell back as a flare of light shot up into the sky and an invisible force field surrounded the mage.

'Kill him!' cried Elidon. But even as their swords whipped through the air, Kale's power kept them at bay. They couldn't penetrate the shield.

Kale climbed painfully to his knees. He was badly bruised, suspected that one or more of his ribs was broken, injuries that could easily be mended once he was clear of these rogues. But he felt the call of his order around him and realised that the magic spark had revealed his presence to all of the mages on the planet.

The need to hide himself forced another blast of magic from the staff as Kale pulled himself up to his feet, and his considerable height towered over the warriors. They all stepped back, covering their eyes, as the full force of his magic shone as bright as Emin's suns.

Kale wasted no time: he slammed the staff down onto the sand. The only way he could escape was to open a vortex.

The ground was torn up by the energy; Kale was doing this alone, so the force field was unstable. But he knew he could travel this way for short distances at least without the aid of another mage to stabilise the power. The Arrak warriors fell away as the ground beneath them churned up, showering sand over the area for at least half a mile.

As soon as he could, Kale threw himself into the vortex, and slammed it shut behind him, leaving the perplexed warriors behind.

The vortex reopened and Kale tumbled to the ground. He was exhausted. Too injured even to help himself up.

A loud cry brought him staggering to him feet with the last remaining strength in his body. Where had he arrived? What more was he about to face?

'Look! Out there!'

He raised his staff. And then …

People, humans, were running toward him. Kale fell into their welcoming arms. Somehow, he had brought himself back to the camp, and the Earthlings assisted him now – unbelievably they had crossed the barrier to *help* him!

Relief swept over him. They felt like his friends and he trusted them. How had such an anomaly occurred?

'What happened?' asked Taylor Arch, and Kale realised that he was leaning on the captain as he limped back to the fire.

'Attacked …' he managed to mumble.

'Get him to our tent,' Jas said as she appeared before Kale's blurred vision.

They led him into the tent and Kale was placed down on his bed.

'Let's clean him up,' said Jas, and then Kale saw Julia looking down into his battered face.

'My God, Kale! What happened?'

She gripped his hand, and Kale held onto her. 'My staff,' he said.

Someone behind her handed the large thick wooden staff to Julia, and she placed it down beside the mage.

'Had to raise a vortex. Felt *his* presence … knows …'

'Who?' asked Julia.

Kale drifted into sleep holding her hand.

'He needs to rest,' Jas said. She sent away the survivors who were milling at the entrance of the tent. 'I'll tell you when he wakes.'

Then she brought a chair to the side of the bed for Julia, who sat down without letting go of Kale's hand.

'He's been beaten,' Julia said. 'Who would do that? I thought mages were gods here?'

'They are. Usually,' Jas said.

She pulled up another chair and collapsed down into it beside the bed. She was shocked to see Kale in this state. 'This is not good.'

Julia looked at her sharply. 'What does this mean?'

'Kale was right. There are traitors among the warriors and the mages. We're all in great danger. I only hope they didn't manage to follow his magic back here.'

Prestin jerked awake and stared up at the ceiling of his tent. The vision went on for a few more moments. He saw clearly that Kale was back, and Marlin's warriors had found him. He experienced a moment of pleasure as he saw the men beat Kale, then the mage pulled out some more of his impressive power, escaping through a vortex. Something Prestin himself would never have attempted alone, because it was foolish and dangerous.

The vision ended, and Prestin was left with the distinct sensation that Kale was still on the planet. He could taste it, bitter in his mouth. But somehow the mage had managed to cloak himself once more, and so Prestin couldn't locate him.

Prestin got out of bed and walked toward the entrance of his tent. He looked out. It was still night, and he sniffed the air, trying to sense that trace of magic, that residue that would give away Kale's location, but there was nothing.

He had always admired, and envied, Kale's power. It had been what had brought Kale to the attention of Arven, after all, and why he, above all others, had been made the royal mage. Prestin had wanted the role himself, and had tried out for it when the Emperor's former mage had crossed over to the other plane. It had been soon after the Arrak Nah Tiamen females had contracted their fatal virus and died. All hope for the future had been lost, but one among them, Kale, had had a vision that had led him to the Emperor's door. He had been hailed as a saviour, yet he was weak. Only a weak soul could have been corrupted by a woman.

But now he was back, and Prestin knew his own current elevated position was in jeopardy. At least it might be, if Arven ever made it back to the planet; and if he didn't, the Arraks would be in the position to vote in a new leader for the first time in centuries.

Prestin winced as his fingernails bit into his palms. He relaxed his hands. He had an ally – Marlin wanted the throne. Prestin had agreed to help him obtain it. A logical alliance had been struck: the mage did not even see this as a betrayal of his order or his leader, because in his eyes Arven had sullied himself with the Earth woman anyway. He had let her betray him, corrupt his mage and escape the planet. She had made a mockery of his leadership. This vulnerability made the Emperor a failure in Prestin's eyes: not fit to rule.

Of course leadership was a birthright under normal circumstances, but as there was no heir, Marlin could put in his bid for the position, and it was unlikely to meet opposition. No-one else wanted the throne. They saw it as a burden that an Emperor was born to carry. But Prestin and Marlin saw it as a new opportunity to change the order of things.

He sent an astral image of himself to wake Marlin.

A few minutes later the councillor arrived at his tent.

'What is it?' he asked.

Prestin explained his vision.

'He's back? Then so must the Empress be.'

'Possibly. I cannot find a trace of either of them. And if she is with him, why was he in the desert alone?'

Marlin sat down as Prestin poured him a calming brew. 'This could upset our plans.'

'There is no need to worry. Arven is blocked and cannot return to the planet – he and his mage are trapped on the Eleventh Moon. Nothing can survive there. They will perish before long. And when he does, all of the mages will feel his death and know it to be true. You'll be able to act on your ambition, and I will support you. Just as we agreed.'

'You really feel no guilt over this?' Marlin asked, amazed that Prestin's training and faith could be so easily put aside.

'I have thought long and hard about this. Arven is the source of our misfortunes. It is time for us to change, or else our people will all perish.'

Marlin took the brew from Prestin and sipped the hot liquid. His shock began to fade, and his resolve returned.

'We must find Kale,' Marlin said. 'Send word to Elidon that I want his men to start searching.'

'Of course,' said Prestin. 'But I suspect that he will be more careful of discovery now.'

'Where was he, anyway?'

'Near Renik.'

'I wonder where he was going?'

Prestin said nothing, but he suspected that the mage had wanted to reconnect with one of his own kind. After so much time away from the order, it was logical to assume this was exactly what he would need to do to regain his full strength. And, as long as he remained hidden, that wouldn't happen.

'We have to warn the other mages. Tell them of his treachery. He must not find an ally among them.'

Prestin nodded, though this request would be far more difficult to fulfil than Marlin realised. It would take all sorts of magic and guile to prevent the mages from seeing inside himself – to stop them learning what he planned. And to make contact with them meant dropping his shields.

'Let me think on a way we can do this ...' he said, though he did not explain his dilemma to Marlin. He did not want the future Emperor to realise that he had his weaknesses. He wanted him to have total faith in him, otherwise he may ask another to be the Imperial Mage. And Prestin was determined not to be overlooked again.

6

'Where did they go?' asked Major Handley.

Lieutenant Steve Donovan's face and head were wet with sweat and blood. He was tied to a chair in one of Handley's interrogation rooms, and his arms ached as they strained against the handcuffs and the tight rope that was wrapped around his body. The thought drifted through his head that Handley was even more obese than the last time he had seen him. It was five years ago when he had been under Handley's command, and the major had sent Taylor Arch's platoon out to fight the Jinx. They had been lambs to the slaughter – it was a miracle that any of them had survived.

'Tell me, damn you!'

'I don't know,' Donovan slurred.

'You're wasting your time. He knows nothing,' said James.

James had travelled specially to MD59 from his own stronghold MD1 when he had heard of the sudden disappearance of the survivors from the Trafford Centre.

'We should have taken them sooner,' James said. 'What about the security cameras?'

'Unfortunately the survivors found them before we attacked. We went in blind, and there's no footage of where they could have disappeared to. The place is deserted, and they left with nothing more than what they could carry. My men reported that the Jinx mage opened a vortex. They took the people through it to God knows where.'

'A pity,' James said. 'We needed some new female stock. The breeders we have are tiring. Some have become infertile.'

'What should we do with him?' Handley asked.

'Lock him up for now. He might prove useful in the future. Maybe as a subject for our experiments.'

James left and Donovan was dragged away. He was battered and bruised, but hearing that the survivors had escaped had given him the strength to withstand the torture – and Handley knew it. Handley hadn't finished with him, but for now had bigger fish to fry.

Handley was left alone in the interrogation room now. Furious at the attacks that Arch and his men had made on his base. The damage meant they had a leak in one of the sectors. Some of the gas that they had been pouring out into the atmosphere had got inside. That entire area had been quarantined while the people inside were given a vaccine. Handley had overseen the whole operation, and it infuriated him that the pleasure drones had been in the centre of the leak. There would be no respite with any of the women until they knew they weren't going to go feral.

Handley's sex drive meant that it was difficult for him to go without relief for more than a day, so he had already paid a visit to his favourite whore that morning. Only the sentry on the post saw him, and he wouldn't be telling anyone if he knew what was good for him. The recent turn of events though made Handley feel even more frustrated. As a result, he contemplated heading back to the P Sector for another session with Gina. But once a day was all he could risk and remain under the radar. The knowledge that he was using one of the girls, while his men weren't allowed to, wouldn't go down well, and so he had to be discreet.

'Damn those doctors. Damn those bloody Trafford Centre scum too!'

Handley left the interrogation room and headed back to his own office.

'I want a casualty report from the Trafford fiasco,' he said to his secretary, Peter.

The man looked up and nodded. Handley was struck by how weasel-like he was. His pinched eyes peered through dense glasses, and his mouth was tight and prudish as he studied the Major. Handley almost felt the man's discontent. Surely he wouldn't dare to question the way they lived, after all that James and Handley had given him?

'It's on your desk, Major.'

Handley shrugged. Maybe the man was just humourless by nature.

Handley turned away and entered his own office. He pulled up a chair and sank his considerable bulk down into it, then stared down at the thick file on his desk.

He reached reluctantly for the document, flipping open the file to scan the top page.

Inside was a blow-by-blow account of their attack on the Trafford Centre, and Handley did not enjoy reading about the total failure of an operation that should have been easy for his men.

'The drones caused many problems ...' he read. The drones didn't take orders well, and insubordination had led to them turning on the base soldiers when the survivors had made their escape. This meant that the technology, including medication and hypnosis, had failed to control the feral masses.

Several of Handley's men reported being bitten during the battle that had ensued between them and the drones. Others had been accidentally exposed to the gas and had died because it was so potent.

Total disaster had been avoided when James's surplus men had swooped in and saved the day. These, Handley knew, were the individual soldiers whose intense conditioning had made them impervious to pain. These soldiers would fight to the death, unlike some of Handley's cowardly regulars. But the fight that had followed meant that a lot of drones had died, along with Handley's regular soldiers. Leaving his own base badly depleted.

'What a fucking mess,' Handley muttered.

At that moment the red alert began to chime all over the base.

'What the fuck now?'

Handley pulled himself out of his chair with some effort and hurried to the door. Outside, his secretary was no longer at his station.

Returning to his desk, Handley retrieved his service revolver – a Beretta M9 – from his top drawer. He placed it in a holster on his belt, and threw a handful of spare clips into his jacket pocket. Then he walked out of the office and locked the door behind him.

He headed to the emergency assembly point, wondering if this was merely a drill sprung on them by James. It would be just like him to do that today. As if Handley didn't have enough to contend with.

A group of soldiers scurried through the bland corridor ahead of him.

'Hey!' he called. 'Anyone know what's happened?'

Only one of the soldiers stopped and saluted him.

'We were told we were needed over in the P Sector,' the soldier said.

'Why?'

The soldier shook his head.

'I'm coming with you,' Handley said.

There was a truck waiting outside the office sector, and Handley climbed up into the front seat with the driver as the soldiers scurried into the back.

'There's been another breach, Major,' the driver said. 'We were told to wear masks. There's a spare one under the seat.

The driver pulled his mask on, and checked that all inside were ready before he turned the truck away from the offices and drove north toward the P Class quarters.

Handley reached under the seat and retrieved the mask, placing it over his face.

When they arrived, the zone, and the border control, was in chaos.

The border guard was hiding inside his booth and refused to come out until he saw Handley.

'Put a mask on!' Handley barked at the man. 'Then get your ass out here.'

The man did as he was told.

'Name and rank?' Handley asked.

'Private John Guilor,' said the man.

He saluted Handley with a trembling hand.

'What the fuck's going on here?'

'Drones,' said John, looking around. 'They got out, Major.'

'Who got out? This is the pleasure sector …'

'Some of the girls …'

'You're scared of a few whores …?' Handley shoved John back against his booth. 'You were hiding in there from a few crazy fucking whores?'

'They … grabbed one of the soldiers. They dragged him away. I set off the alarm but they came back around the booth and … one of 'em had his head. They'd ripped it clean off.'

'Is this a joke?' Handley said.

'N … no, Major.'

Handley gave orders for the soldiers to search the area. 'Shoot to kill. We aren't screwing around here.'

Then Handley returned to the booth and picked up the phone.

John stood awkwardly as Handley closed the booth door on him. He didn't know whom the Major was calling or what he said.

John was terrified. Alan Kenney was dead and there was one crazy running around down there. He glanced at the booth. The door handle was smeared with blood, and John hadn't been lying about Alan's head. The bitch had been carrying it: gnawing on his face like he was a tasty treat.

'Jesus. Jesus,' John said.

He dropped his mask-covered face into his hands. He only hoped that the others hadn't been like this one. What would they find when they went into the P Class area? Would Harrington be dead too? And how was John going to explain all of that?

Handley came out of the booth.

'Whose blood is this?'

'Sergeant Kenney. He came down to see when the bookings were gonna start again. Said a few of his men had been complaining …'

'Yeah. It's been a difficult few days,' Handley said. 'So what happened?'

'I … d … don't know … We were talking and then …'

There was a round of gunfire. John was pleased Handley's informal interrogation was interrupted. It gave him time to think. They had a story ready. He just had to use it.

'Yeah … well … then the girls all came running out. They went crazy. I don't know where they went but it was back that way.'

John's confidence grew as Handley, distracted by the noise and yells of his other soldiers, appeared to be only half listening.

'I think …' he continued, 'they might have …'

'Major!' called a voice.

Another soldier ran toward the both. John felt his cheeks redden with guilt as he saw the man holding a blood-soaked security card.

'We found this and one woman. We took her down, but it took a shitload of bullets. There's a body too – missing a head.'

'What about the others?' Handley asked.

'P Sector door lock shows several entries. I went inside and there's no-one in there.'

Handley left the booth, and John sighed with relief. He went inside and picked up the phone, but then thought better of contacting Tremaine in such an obvious way. The doctor would probably find out what had happened soon enough when they brought in Alan's body anyway.

'Shit! What a fuck-up.'

Handley returned to the booth.

'Looks like they left through the damaged hatch,' Handley said. 'Did anyone else come by here today?'

John shook his head. 'Just the Sergeant. Like I said. At least, on my shift. I can check the log ...'

John made a show of looking in the log.

'There's no visitors listed ... except ...' John glanced at Handley, '*you*, Major. At 6.00 am.'

'Right. Yes. I came down to ... check that everything was okay.'

John said nothing. He was confident now that Handley wouldn't pursue any suspicions he might have about his part in this. After all, the girls were supposed to be off limits to *everyone* right now.

'Phone the medical team to get down here and remove these bodies. I want an autopsy done on this freaky bitch,' said Handley.

John picked up his phone and, with a steadier hand, rang Tremaine's number.

'Doctor. Something terrible happened ... I've got Major Handley here with me, and he asks if you can send down some people to collect two bodies.'

Tremaine was quick to take up on John's formal tone.

'Sounds serious. Tell the Major that I'll come right away.'

A short time later a military ambulance arrived at the P Class checkpoint. Tremaine was in the front with the driver. In the back were two more medical crewmen.

John came out of the booth and glanced inside the back. He noted the body bags, but said nothing. Then he passed the doctor and the medical truck through.

'Hey, John,' said Private Mark Trainer.

'What are you doing here?' asked John.

'Come to relieve you.'

Trainer looked beyond the booth and saw the soldiers and medical truck in the distance.

'What's been happening?'

John related his practised story, aware of how much this 'fake' account had now become real.

'You telling me we have no P Class females in there now?' Trainer said.

John nodded. 'I just don't know what went down. But ...'

John glanced around, making sure that no-one else was in earshot.

'But what?' asked Trainer.

'Handley was here earlier. Think he might have *done* something to the girls.'

'Well, if he did, the cameras will show it.'

'Yeah. Good thinking. I hadn't remembered that,' John said.

'Listen, are you okay to stay here a little longer?' Trainer said. 'I just need to go and do something ...'

'Yeah, sure.'

John watched Trainer leave. A grim smile flickered over his lips. Tremaine had marked Trainer as one of James's informers. If this was so, then the second half of their plan would now be put in place. Trainer would report any suspicions he had about Handley to James, and hopefully this would throw distrust toward the Major.

'In order to bring down any regime, you need to spread dissent in the ranks ...' Tremaine had said.

John suspected that Tremaine's suspicions about Trainer were true, and that Handley and James would soon have another wedge between them. Handley and James had a very close relationship, and a history that none of them understood, but the fifth columnists hoped that a little mistrust would work under James's skin enough to make Handley's life the living hell he deserved. With the P Class women gone, there would be a lot of upset and frustrated soldiers. Who knew where that might lead? Maybe even another coup ...

7

'I can't open it, Emperor,' Prins said. 'It's sealed shut.'

Malachi tapped his staff down on the stone floor of the throne room, but there wasn't even a spark of magic released.

'It's a magic dead zone,' he explained. 'We can't escape by these means.'

Arven looked around the room. There was no obvious route out other than the way they had entered, but something inside him knew that this was all part of some kind of test.

Even so, Prins and Elee continued to try to prise the door open with their swords.

'Save your energy,' Arven said. 'There is only one way in and one way out.'

Malachi glanced at Arven, surprised by his words.

'I remember something,' Arven said. 'About this place.'

'Remember? Emperor, our ancestors left here millennia ago. How can you ...?'

'Before the mages, the Emperors held the Arrak Nah Tiamen magic,' Arven said.

'So it is said. But we have nothing but stories to support this.'

'It is true,' Arven said. 'And now I am here, I feel the magic return. I also know things. Things that I shouldn't know.'

'Such as?' asked Malachi.

'The way out of this chamber. Follow me.'

He led the mage and the two warriors toward the throne. Arven walked around it. Behind the throne was a panel that he knew would open, but couldn't summon the knowledge how.

'The throne,' Malachi said. 'Maybe you should ...?'

'Of course,' Arven nodded.

It was obvious really. The room had recognised him and had allowed him to enter. Was it possible that the throne held some power that he could awaken also?

Arven walked to the front of the throne, then turned around. He looked out at the empty chamber before slowly sinking down into the seat. He sat on the edge, tense, waiting for something to happen, be it the door reopening or the panel behind him sliding aside, but nothing changed.

'What do you feel?' asked Malachi.

'Nothing,' said Arven. 'Nothing at all. No more memory flashes and no more …'

Arven slumped back into the throne. Prins and Elee moved to help, but Malachi waved his staff before them.

'Wait! Don't touch him!'

The torches grew brighter as the chamber filled. The room was full of his courtiers. They came daily to hear his wisdom, listen to his commandments. The power grew inside him until he felt as though his physical being could no longer contain it. Their worship gave him supremacy: he was a god in their eyes. For that alone he would continue to rule them.

'Emperor,' said his advisor, Suleman. 'The people await your judgement. Shall we return to Earth?'

Arven coughed and found himself back in the chamber of the present.

'Emperor?' Malachi said. 'What did you see?'

'Another world. In this room. But years gone by. Maybe many millennia …'

Malachi waited as Arven gathered his thoughts.

'It was a fragment. But for a moment I was in the head of the Emperor of that era. I … he … was worshiped. He had magic. But no-one else did.'

Malachi's grew thoughtful as Arven relayed what he had seen.

'What did he decide?' Malachi asked.

'I don't know.'

Arven stood up from the throne. He found it difficult to relate to this all-powerful Emperor, a person so like himself … but with magic overshadowing his good judgment. In the Arrak Nah Tiamen world he knew, only mages had power, and they used that magic wisely, for the good of the people.

Magic should not be in the hands of just one man.

Where had he heard that before? Who had said it? There was a deep-rooted memory buried inside him, and the Eleventh Moon held the key to unlocking that mystery.

Arven turned. His hand moved of its own volition as he drew a symbol in the air. Behind him Malachi gasped. The wall behind the throne shifted and groaned. It began to open.

Elee and Prins held their swords at the ready, but this time there were no night creatures waiting to burst out.

Behind the wall lay a long corridor lit by torches either side.

'This way,' said Arven. 'In order to find the truth of the present we must continue to search for the mistakes of the past.'

The four Arrak Nah Tiamen passed the throne and entered the corridor. As Arven stepped across the threshold more of the torches lit up. Ahead the corridor split into two, but only the left side illuminated. Arven strode on toward the lit corridor, certain that he was being shown the way to the answers he sought. Behind them the wall closed, blocking off the throne room.

Malachi glanced back as the panel closed, before turning to follow Arven. He had never seen the Emperor so determined or driven. Magic glowed in Arven's aura, yet Malachi couldn't access his own power. It was as though all the mystical energy from the planet had been transferred to the Emperor and he alone controlled it. Though the mage didn't know how this was even possible. Arrak Nah Tiamen had roles in their society: mages were born with magic just as Emperors where born to rule – in all of history Malachi had never heard of an Emperor who had magic.

The corridor came to an abrupt end, but Arven was undeterred. Once again he drew a symbol in the air, and another wall opened for them.

Malachi was amazed. He didn't recognise the symbols that Arven somehow knew. He couldn't even retain their image in his head. It was a power for the Emperor alone to have, and he wielded it with confidence and expertise as though he had always held it.

Arven opened several more doorways along the corridor before they came to a large chamber.

In the centre of the room was a huge bed. Stone pillars at each corner were engraved with the royal symbol. Ancient writings covered the bare walls. There were luxurious furnishings: tapestries; large free-standing vases; a dressing table with a polished gold mirror; a low table with a jug and goblets.

'The Imperial bedroom,' Malachi said, though his speculation was unnecessary: Arven knew where he was.

'I ... *he* rested here.'

Like the throne room the chamber was immaculate. Though air was in abundance it was as though the place had been frozen in a vacuum. It was almost as if the Emperor and his people had only just left.

Malachi watched Arven as he walked around the room. In the corner, the dressing table was laden with jars and bottles, unguents and perfumes.

'No. This was *her* room ...' Arven said. Though he knew the Emperor had been at home in this suite also.

'An Empress?' Malachi asked.

Arven didn't answer. An image of Jas floated behind his eyes: she was the only Empress he wanted to see, not some distant ancestor, the bonded concubine of a long-lost dynasty. Even so, he knew he had to go there. If there was some truth to be revealed then he must find it. He had been led to this chamber for a reason.

He lay down on the bed as Prins, Elee and Malachi looked on. Arven was aware that his warriors and mage were feeling helpless for the first time in their lives. Malachi's magic was useless here, but Arven was strong, dominant, and for the first time truly powerful. He liked the feeling, almost as much as his ancestor had done. It was addictive.

Now he would use that power to learn the truth, wherever that led him. He closed his eyes.

She was leaning over him. The room was in shadow, and her dark hair fell over her shoulders and down to cover the silhouette of her naked breasts. It was too dark to see her face, but he knew she was beautiful. His angel, his soul-mate, his wife, and a seer too … They had bonded and now she was his, would always be his.

Magic danced on her porcelain skin; a lilac glow indicated her propensity – for the third eye was always purple. There was a slight bulge to her normally flat stomach. Maybe the movement of their child, growing inside her perfect body, had awakened her, for the power within her was new.

'Don't go back to Earth,' she said. Only then did he realise she was in one of her trances. He pulled himself into a sitting position.

'What will happen if I do?'

'A terrible curse on future generations.'

He didn't reply, but soon afterwards she sank back onto the bed beside him, her message delivered, soon forgotten, as she fell into a dreamless sleep.

The Emperor was left to mull over the dilemma. To return to Earth, or not.

He stroked her hair as she slept; it fell over her face, hiding her features.

What did the future matter? His people needed to reclaim their old world. This place, the Eleventh Moon, was not good for them.

A poison had been brought to them by the bite of those night creatures: a plague was claiming the lives of his subjects, and even with all of his power, he could not fight it.

He looked at Shamila sleeping beside him. Like all other times, she would not remember the trance or her warning. She at least was safe within this chamber, locked as it was to the outside world at night.

'Kil'n …' she murmured, as though she knew what he was planning.

'I have to take care of our present …'

Arven opened his eyes and looked around the chamber. His mind was swimming with the thoughts of the Emperor. Kil'n was his name, and somehow Arven knew he hadn't read it in any scrolls or heard it in his boyhood history lessons. No, this was an Emperor that the mages never talked about. Long forgotten, perhaps even buried in an unmarked tomb. There would be only one reason why the details of such a powerful Emperor were lost or – as Arven was beginning to realise – had been wiped from all record.

Kil'n must have committed some terrible crime.

Now Arven was zinging with this Emperor's power, and he was elated by it.

'I *own* the magic ...' he said. 'I never knew what it felt like, until now.'

'Such power is not for one man ...' Malachi said, quoting the warning that had floated through Arven's mind earlier.

Arven sat up on the bed in much the same way that Kil'n had in his vision.

'His name was Kil'n, and he was the Emperor.'

'There is no mention of Kil'n,' Malachi said. 'I know all of the Emperors' names throughout time.'

'We know all of the Emperors who have led us since we found Emin. But not before,' Arven said. 'Wasn't this why we came here? To find the information that we left behind? It has always been our belief that there was none before the parting of the two tribes. Yet, this was where our descendants ended up. We knew that. But there was no mention of Kil'n's immediate reign here.'

'Tell me what you saw, tell me about Kil'n ...' Malachi said.

Arven didn't comply immediately. He glanced down at his hands; his fingers glowed with a golden shimmer. Magic was all over him, and the more he connected with Kil'n, the stronger it became.

'Highness ... Magic is a potent elixir ...' Malachi warned. 'It takes mages most of their lifetime to learn to wield and control it safely, and we have only a fraction of the energy I'm sensing from you now.'

'Kil'n was a *mage*. He wielded this power by birthright, *not* by learning.'

'Magic is a seductress ...' Malachi said.

Arven did not reply. He swung his legs off the bed and stood. He felt supernatural. Every step he took in the room brought a rush of memories and flashes of images to him. It was as if they were his memories, now returning.

'You have a strong connection to Kil'n,' Malachi said. 'Please let me help you decipher what you see.'

Arven nodded. He revealed that Shamila was a seer and held some other mystical qualities.

'The Emperor and Empress were all-powerful,' Arven said. 'And the more that their subjects worshipped them, the stronger they became. You were right when you said it was seductive. Kil'n was enamoured with his power.'

'We need to find the scroll room. There would be a record of their reason for being here and why they needed to return to Earth,' Malachi said.

'The scrolls were destroyed,' Arven explained. 'Kil'n ordered it. I saw it in a flash of recall a few moments ago. Though I don't yet know why he did that. I'm not receiving the information in order. But some of his major decisions were made in this room, with the Empress. I'm connecting with him through the magic because of our bloodline.'

'Yes,' said Malachi. 'The only thing we can do is try to unlock more of his thoughts. Try to learn what was happening and why it is affecting us now. But such an endeavour may endanger you. And I have no magic to help you. We should return to Emin and seek help from the Guild of Mages.'

'I'm willing to take any risk. I can't leave until we discover what we came here for.'

Malachi nodded, but Arven could tell that the mage was apprehensive nonetheless. Perhaps, without his magic, he felt vulnerable for the first time in his life. Now that he had experienced this power for himself, Arven knew it would be difficult to let it go.

'Meditation may be the way to access Kil'n's memories,' Malachi suggested.

Arven returned to the bed, and with Prins and Elee standing guard, he lay back down and closed his eyes.

Light streamed into the room from a portal that opened up in the side of the pyramid. Shamila was sitting at the dressing table. A servant girl stood behind her, combing the long dark hair that almost reached the floor when she was sat, but touched the back of her knees when she stood.

Kil'n lay on the bed waiting for the girl to leave. He needed to love Shamila, even though the baby that had swollen her belly was almost due. It was morning and Shamila was being prepared for her final duties before confinement. She would appear in the grand hall with Kil'n when he announced his decision.

A decision he had yet to make.

'Leave us,' he ordered the servant girl. She placed the comb down on the dressing table and hurried away.

'Come to me,' Kil'n said.

'The assembly will be waiting …' Shamila said.

Kil'n stood and walked toward her. He wasn't given to being so decadent, but he had to touch her, had to be with her, once more before he faced what was to come.

He stroked her hair, pushing it aside as he bent to kiss the back of her neck. Smooth white flesh, as soft as silk. Her purity of skin was always a fascination for him.

'Kil'n …' she sighed.

He closed his eyes and pressed his lips against her throat, moving toward her cheek. Shamila turned her head and found his lips.

8

Kale woke to find Julia asleep in the chair beside his bed, and he knew without doubt that she had stayed there all night. Just as he had watched over her at the Trafford Centre as she recovered from her ordeal escaping from MD59. He quietly pulled himself up into a sitting position, and found himself watching the sleeping woman for a few moments.

Just looking at Julia made him feel happy and oddly vulnerable. All of the thoughts that had gone through his head before Elidon and his warriors had attacked him the night before, now returned. He had a strange compulsion: he wanted to walk into the bonding tent with her and see if they were a match. Could he remain a mage and bond with a female?

'You're awake!' Jas said, peering around the curtained bed.

Julia stirred and stretched, then, realising she had fallen asleep during her vigil, flushed with embarrassment.

'I'm sorry!' she said.

'What for? I'm fine. And you needed your rest,' Kale said.

'How are you feeling?' she asked, leaning closer. Kale could smell her human scent: musky, sensual.

'I'm mostly healed. The rest repaired my injuries.'

'Glad to hear it!' Jas said. 'Now … what happened?'

Kale told her of the attack and the momentary flare of magic that had revealed his presence to Prestin and every other mage on the planet.

'They'll be actively looking for you now. You mustn't leave here again. Not until we know where Arven is,' Jas said.

'They can't …' Kale began to cough and choke as his throat dried up.

Julia hurried to fetch a jug of fresh water and poured some into a chalice for him. 'Drink this. You need to rehydrate. You were unconscious for at least 12 hours.'

Kale took the drink, and the water soothed his throat. 'Where's my staff?' he asked once he could speak again.

Jas reached for it by the side of the bed, and as her fingers touched the wood a wave of purple energy sparked the staff into life. It glowed with a unique lilac flame. Surprised, she let go of the staff and it fell toward the bed, caught by Kale's swift reflexes.

'I have seen a staff react that way only once before. It happens when a mage touches another's power source. My staff recognised you as an influential power.'

'But ...' Jas said, 'we know already that I can do some magic. Just not of the calibre that you can.'

'Not like that,' he said. 'You are *malia* – an anomaly. Your magic has just shown its strength for the first time. Being here, on Emin, being pregnant with the Emperor's child, may have stirred something more in you.'

As though to reinforce his words, the child inside Jas kicked for the first time.

'Ooh!' She wrapped her arms round her stomach. 'I felt that! What does this mean?' she asked.

'I don't know,' Kale said. 'But for now it must remain a secret between us.'

Julia nodded her head in agreement.

Kale began to cough again. This time a smear of blood coloured his lips.

'You're still hurt!' said Julia.

'Internal bleeding ...' Jas said. 'I'll get the doctor.'

'No. It is a punctured lung,' said Kale. 'And why I needed my staff.'

He lay back down on the bed and raised the staff above his head. A blue light ran over his body, pausing over his chest. The light intensified to the point that both Julia and Jas had to look away. Then it faded and finally evaporated with a last spark of blue.

'There,' said Kale taking a deep breath. 'I'm fully healed.'

'Maybe so, but I think you still need some more rest,' Jas said. 'In the meantime, I'm going to find Taylor and talk to him about your attack. If that flare of power leads the warriors here, we may have a fight on our hands.'

Jas left the tent and hurried toward Taylor's and Dawn's tent. It was still early and the camp was quiet. As she weaved in and out of the tents, the silence gave her time to think about what she would say to Taylor and the council. She had hoped that bringing the survivors here would ensure their safety. Now, with Arven off planet, and Kale's presence revealed to the other mages, she could no longer guarantee this. For this reason, she paused at the smouldering embers of the campfire, close to Taylor's tent. She needed to gather her thoughts before she spoke to him.

Maybe they should leave Emin? Go back to Earth, but return to a different place, away from the Trafford Centre?

But no.

Earth was doomed. Kale had already explained that; and wherever they went, they would not have the clean and pure air, the fresh produce, and the relative safety that this camp afforded them. Nor would Kale's magic be so powerful. Kale's exile from Emin had taught them this much: he had magic elsewhere, but it was stronger when he was fully connected to his own planet.

They would have to wait it out until they learnt where Arven was, or until their presence was discovered and they were forced to flee once more. Then they could decide where to go. What impact that would have on Kale's power, Jas could only speculate.

'Morning …'

Jas looked up from the embers and saw Taylor standing in the doorway of his tent.

'You okay?' he asked.

Jas nodded. 'Kale is awake, but resting. Even with his magical ability to heal himself, he took quite a beating.'

She told him the details of the attack, omitting that Kale's magic may have revealed his presence. For now, she wouldn't worry him.

'As a result, he didn't make contact with the mage he was looking for. Someone he believed he could trust. Someone he thought could help us find Arven.'

'No sign of your … Emperor … then?' Taylor said.

'No.'

'Where do you think he went?'

Jas thought for a moment, then shook her head. 'I don't know. A wild goose chase, looking for me perhaps?'

'To Earth? But that could mean …'

'He's not dead. Nor is he in immediate danger,' Jas said. 'I'd know.'

Taylor didn't question her. He had experienced so much within the realms of the supernatural since Jas's return that his natural inclination to disbelieve no longer applied. He *did* believe. Everything. But, unlike Jas, he was not *entirely* certain that this far from Arven she would know whether he was in danger or not. But that slight doubt he kept to himself, because he was certain of one thing: Jas needed to keep having faith in Arven if Taylor was to keep the survivors happy. They had to see no fear or concern coming from their leaders. They had to stay strong. Hidden. Safe.

If Jas had known what was going through Taylor's mind she may well have revealed everything. In a peculiar parallel, she too wanted Taylor to remain positive for the good of the camp.

'We're safe,' she reassured him. 'But we need to remain vigilant and always within the camp boundaries. The magic on this planet is … I'm not sure how to describe it other than to say *real*. But it is intelligent too. And I suspect that Arven's absence is being hidden from the other mages by the mage in Sharik. More than likely on his orders. Which implies to me that he is doing something important right now. So, I have to trust that he will return. And when he does, I'll go to him. I'll make him protect you all.'

'I wish I had your faith in the Jinx, I really do …' Taylor said.

'Trust me,' she said. 'Trust Kale. He wants only the best for you all.'

'He's a Jinx. This could be a trap.'

'No,' Jas paused. 'And I'll tell you why. Kale has always been loyal to me, but now there is something else he cares about. He's in love with Julia. He doesn't know it yet; but even so, he would never endanger her, irrespective of his loyalty to me or Arven. He wants to keep her safe and he feels … a kinship for Earthlings now too.'

'Why would he?'

'Because one of us knew he was in danger and raised the alarm. He saved us by bringing us here, and then, *you saved him.*'

'How do you know that means anything to him?'

'I feel his emotions, and he has many confusing moments now. All of this, his contact with us, has changed him. Just as it has changed me by being his friend, and getting to know his people.'

'I still don't know what difference that can make to his loyalty overall. He's been a Jinx all of his life. A few months on Earth won't have changed that.'

'Under normal circumstances I'd be saying the same,' Jas said. 'But not in this case. Kale is fiercely loyal and … he feels responsible for you all. Just as I do. It may be a Jinx thing, but I'd also call it a human thing. That ability to *feel* for others who are different from yourself. To show compassion.'

'I hope you're right,' Taylor said.

Jas glanced over at Taylor's tent. There was no movement from within.

'How's Dawn?'

'She's getting better. Something went on in her past. She's hinted at it. Told me it was to do with the military … but she doesn't want to relive what they put her through.'

'They fucked with her mind?'

'That's one way of putting it …'

'Sorry. I wasn't very tactful … She almost lost it before we left though. Perhaps Kale can help her?'

Taylor glanced back at the tent himself then.

'No need. Our daughter, Lucy. She's *fixing* her. Day by day. I see them whispering together and I … My little girl has some of that magic you keep talking about …'

'Yes,' said Jas. 'She does.'

They both fell quiet, considering the implications of a small child holding such ability. For some reason it didn't scare Jas: it gave her hope for the future.

'Take care of them both. They'll be all right. We all will.'

Jas left the camp fire and walked away from Taylor's tent. Instead of heading back to her own she walked the perimeter. There she saw some of

Taylor's men on look-out duty.

'Jas,' called Sergeant Harvey when he saw her approach. 'How are you this fine morning?'

'Good,' she said.

They exchanged pleasantries for a few moments – a rarity. Jas couldn't help noticing how light-hearted Harvey was now. Despite the soldiers still being cautious, they were beginning to feel safe for the first time in years. Jas marvelled at the ability of humankind to survive and flourish in all circumstances. *Humans are incredible. That's why we've survived so long. That's why we will find a way to go on.*

'Is there anything we can do to improve our safety?' Harvey asked, even though he was relaxed and appeared to be unconcerned.

'We're invisible to anyone on the planet right now, but remain vigilant,' Jas said.

'I can't find Selene! Harvey, have you seen her?'

Jas and Harvey turned to see Caroline Donovan with her little boy Jamie.

'When did you last see her?' Jas asked.

'Last night. I put her to bed, then I fell asleep too. It had been a long day … I was exhausted … When I woke this morning she was gone. I thought she might have come to see your children …'

'No. I haven't seen her,' said Harvey.

'We'll help you search the camp,' Jas said.

Harvey yelled to the other perimeter guards and the search began. Jas noticed how the tension returned to the soldier immediately, despite his earlier calm. He was always going to be on full alert at short notice, because that was the way they had lived for so many years.

'She's probably playing with one of the other children,' Jas said, trying to reassure Caroline. 'Or exploring the camp. Children are naturally curious.'

Caroline gripped Jas's arm. Her eyes were filled with unshed tears, and the fear she felt seeped into Jas's skin.

'I can't lose my little girl as well as my husband.'

'We'll find her!' Jas promised.

9

'Dr Tremaine was in the medical centre the whole time. There were several witnesses who say he was there,' Peter said.

'We have no reason to doubt their word?' Handley asked.

'None. And security footage confirms it.'

'But the cameras in the P Sector were all offline for maintenance?'

Peter nodded. 'Looks like an unfortunate coincidence. The repairs had been scheduled for a while.'

'I'm not sure I believe in coincidences,' Handley said. 'Check through all of the records. Find out who was doing the maintenance and let's talk to him.'

'Yes, Major.'

Peter left Handley's office and found Dr Tremaine waiting outside.

Tremaine's hair had gone whiter in the last few months, and his grey-white shade was at odds with his relatively young face. He had a scar on his cheek – a present from the soldier who had tortured him after his previous disobedience, when he had helped a breeder by the name of Julia escape. Tremaine's skills were needed or he wouldn't have been left alive after the betrayal. Nevertheless, Handley hadn't forgiven or forgotten this transgression, and his first thought was that Tremaine was somehow involved with the escape of the P Class women too.

'Major Handley is expecting you,' Peter said. Then he knocked and reopened Handley's office door. 'Dr Tremaine …'

Tremaine went inside and closed the door behind him, shutting Peter out. Handley wasn't the only one who found the man repugnant to be around.

'You have a report for me?' Handley said.

'Cause of death: she was beaten and then shot to death – 131 bullets riddled her torso, face and head,' Tremaine said. 'A little "overkill" don't you think?'

'She attacked and killed one of my men and then fought the others off. So of course the soldiers killed her.' Handley said without emotion. 'What was wrong with her *before* that?'

'There are signs of toxin in her blood. She had certainly been affected by the leak. I believe she had been separated from the other P Class women?'

'Yeah. She was acting weird. Not responding to instructions,' Handley said. 'The hypnosis and drugs weren't working as they should have.'

'I can't tell you more without having access to her files.'

Handley thought for a moment. The P Class females, and the drug and hypnosis programme, weren't something Tremaine was normally given access to. However, a fresh pair of eyes on this might help. Maybe his other doctors had made some error that Tremaine might find. Plus, his evaluation and report on the incident would show significant loyalty to MD59. It might also get James off Handley's back about killing the doctor, when Handley believed he needed him.

'I think you might be on the way to redemption,' Handley said. 'Someone screwed up and I want you to check the research and tell me who. I'll be especially happy if it leads to any other base than ours.'

'I was stupid once,' Tremaine said. 'But I have tried to show my loyalty since. I'll be happy to prove this any way I can.'

'I appreciate that, doctor. Stupid isn't the word I'd use for what you did, but we can all have our head turned by a pretty woman.'

'Fortunately my wife has forgiven me,' Tremaine said. 'All I need is your trust again now Major. And my life can return to normal.'

'Peter!' Handley shouted.

Peter scurried back into the room.

'Give Dr Tremaine access to the P Class files.'

'But Major …'

'That's an order.'

Peter left, looking disgruntled as always.

'Don't let me down …' Handley said.

'I won't,' Tremaine said. 'Believe me, I intend to get to the bottom of this problem. We can't have maniacal women sleeping with our soldiers, now can we?'

'We can't have them murdering and eating them either …' Handley said as the door closed behind Tremaine.

Private John Guilor returned to his quarters. He hadn't heard from Dr Tremaine, so he opened up the e-mails on his personal desktop computer. They never emailed each other directly, but Tremaine had a process set up between a few of the other soldiers they trusted, by which they would all receive an e-mail containing a coded warning if something went wrong. If such a warning went out, it would be every man for himself, and they would all simultaneously exit the base by any means possible. Once they were out they would meet up at a previously-agreed rendezvous point.

John was still shaken about the morning's disaster and hoped that Harrington was safe, despite what had happened to Alan Kenney. It was a terrifying prospect that they might have released the women, only to learn that they were all psychotic. And why wouldn't the women be damaged after what Handley and James had put them through?

He left his computer open and got a beer from the fridge. He hadn't used his last month's alcohol ration, but now he needed a drink to steady his nerves. He still saw that crazy bitch grinning at him through the glass of the booth, while she bit into Kenney's face.

He swigged the beer, wondering what to do. He wasn't on duty again for another 24 hours, but he was twitchy.

His computer made a soft ding and John walked to the monitor, beer in hand. An e-mail had come in from head office.

He clicked and opened it. It was an encrypted message from MD1. Once he confirmed his identity, it opened fully.

FROM: COLONEL JAMES
SUBJECT: REASSIGNMENT

Private Guilor,
You have been selected for reassignment to MD1. Please pack your
belongings and report to Colonel James by 16:00.

John printed the transfer document that was attached, then closed the e-mail.

The time had come to flee the base. He would appear to be following orders, but would in fact slip away to the rendezvous point and meet up with Harrington – if Harrington and the women had made it there!

John began to pack his personal belongings. He was calm. Relieved that the time had come.

MD59 was fucked, but there was no way he would willingly put himself into the direct service of James. He knew where that led. He took his gas mask out of storage and placed it on top of his bag, then zipped it up. It was unlikely that he would be searched, but he stowed his sidearm in his boot, ready for easy access just in case he was challenged. He would leave this place and be free or he would go down trying to escape.

He collected the transfer document from the printer and lifted his bag, scooping it onto his back. Then he walked to the door.

He didn't glance around the room that had been his home for the last five years. This place meant nothing; it was a hole in which he had survived until he could no longer bear the evil of all that was happening. He opened the door and walked out into the complex, heading for the door to the main exit point.

He had to get word to Tremaine somehow though. Perhaps a trip to sickbay before he left wouldn't be that unexpected?

'Hey John! Where you off to?'

John turned to see Mark Trainer walking toward him.

'Got orders to report to Colonel James,' John said.

'Really? That's unexpected. I guess he must have liked the way you handled yourself this morning.'

'What do you mean?' John asked.

'Well, that little bit of information you gave me paid off. That fat bastard Handley might not be in charge around here for much longer. I'm telling you this in confidence … you understand?'

'Sure,' said John. Trainer was only confirming to him how bad things had got in MD59. It was all a matter of time before Handley got his just desserts. But who would make sure that James got his? John pushed down the thought. It wasn't his problem anymore. He was getting out. Right now.

'Shall I walk with you to the exit?' Trainer said.

'No. I'm good. Gonna call in to see one of my drinking buddies. Let him know I'm moving up in the world.'

Trainer nodded. 'I'm sure I'll see you again. Hoping to get my transfer through soon too.'

They shook hands and John moved on. With Trainer sniffing around him he couldn't risk going directly to Tremaine, he would have to trust the message to someone else.

Kerry.

John usually kept away from his sister, showing her the distain that the others showed their female relatives. It made him more accepted and hid his true feelings about the behaviour of his friends. But, as Tremaine's wife, Kerry was safe from being put into the female programmes … for now. Kerry had been through enough and she didn't need that.

He turned left and hurried toward the officers' quarters. It would not be too odd to let his close kin know that he was moving to another base. No-one would see this as a direct connection to Tremaine, he was sure.

He reached the checkpoint, explained to the guard there why he needed to see his sister, and passed through without any delay.

'Better do my duty and let her know I'm leaving …' he said.

The guard nodded, but was indifferent to John's comment.

That's the problem with this place, John thought. *No-one feels anything anymore. They might as well all be under hypnosis …*

At her apartment, Kerry answered the door. She looked flustered. She was hot and sweaty and not as neat and tidy in herself as usual.

'What's up with you?' he asked.

'Inspectors are due any time to make sure I'm keeping house properly.

I've been cleaning all morning.'

'Jesus. Controlling bastards …'

'Shhh …' she whispered. 'I'm never sure that we're not being watched. Or listened to. Come inside quickly.'

Once inside, John glanced around. The room was spotless and smelt of chemical cleaning products. It was a little plusher than John's own room, bigger, with better furniture, but still basic.

'So what's brought you over here?' asked Kerry.

'I'm leaving the base.'

'*What*? Where you going?'

'Orders from Colonel James.'

Kerry sank down onto her sofa, 'Oh. That's not good.' She glanced down at her bleach-sore hands.

'You know I have to go, right?'

'Yeah. You have to follow orders …'

'Kerry. Look at me.'

Kerry looked up. Her eyes were watery.

'I brought you here to keep you safe,' he said. 'I didn't know it would be … like this.'

'I know. And you've done your best for me, John. The doc is kind. He makes sure I'm okay. So don't worry.'

'I am worried. And … I'm not going to MD1. I'm getting the fuck out of here. Tremaine may feel he needs to do the same too. Things are going shits up here.'

'You want me to tell him? That's why you're here?'

'Yes. I want him to do what he can to get you out. I can't take you with me through the main gates. That would be suspicious.'

'I know. But I'll be glad to know you're out, John.'

John bent and kissed her cheek.

'Warn him. It's time,' John whispered.

Kerry nodded. Then she threw her arms around John and hugged him.

'Love you bro. Get away. Get far away and be safe.'

'Hopefully Tremaine will bring you to the rendezvous soon.'

With his new orders in hand, the base's front door opened for him and mask in place, John exited. He passed through the gate driving one of the jeeps used to convey soldiers between the two bases. MD1 was only a two hour drive away.

He turned in the direction he was expected to go, intending to take another detour once he was out of sight of the base. Coming out into Llanberis Pass near the former tourist information centre, John drove through the car park, which was full of abandoned and rusty vehicles, and took a right, beginning his descent of the long steep valley.

Just a few yards down, the jeep spluttered and stalled. John braked and pulled to a stop. He glanced down the hill through his windscreen, then secured the handbrake. He sat for a minute, heart pounding. He wondered if the engine had been deliberately fixed to break down on him. But no. That was paranoid and impossible. He'd had his choice of vehicles, and the attendant hadn't steered him to one or the other. This had to be a coincidental mechanical issue.

The fuel tank was full and there was no reason that he could gather from looking at the dashboard as to why the jeep had failed.

Just his luck.

The jeeps were usually well maintained and fully fuelled. John turned the key in the ignition once more, hoping it had been just a fluke, but the engine wouldn't spark. It was possibly an alternator problem, but he wasn't sure.

'Shit!'

He climbed out of the jeep, leaving the door open, then lifted the bonnet and looked at the engine. John wasn't much of a mechanic, but he thought he would be able to spot a loose connection. Something that would explain this sudden failure. But nothing was obviously amiss.

He slammed the lid down. He could hike downward or freewheel the jeep. Perhaps it would even jumpstart if he did.

He climbed back inside, slammed the door shut and took off the handbrake, moving the gearshift into first. The jeep was on a steep gradient and immediately began to roll. John let it gain momentum, then he turned the ignition once more and pumped the accelerator. The jeep coughed and fired, then died. He turned the key again. Nothing. The third attempt brought the engine spluttering back to life.

John experienced a momentary relief before he was grabbed from behind. Fingers dug into his scalp and tore at his ears. He screamed.

The car swayed from one side of the steep road to the other. John glanced in his rear-view mirror and saw the crazy that was clinging onto him – a rabid teenage boy, poisoned by the toxic atmosphere.

'Shit!'

He cursed himself for not doing the most basic of security checks: always check the back seat! The kid must have climbed in while he was checking the engine.

The boy yanked John's mask off.

John held his breath, trying not to breath in the venomous air. He didn't want to change into a flesh-eating zombie – and no matter what James and Handley called the drones, John knew better. That woman had been a ravening animal. Not human at all.

The kid bit into the back of his neck, tearing at his flesh. John screamed again even as he wrestled to keep the jeep under control. He couldn't help breathing in, but tried once more to hold his breath.

The jeep swayed, hitting the rock face on the left side of the car. The impact sent the vehicle spinning.

A red wall of anger came down over John's eyes as he sucked in the polluted atmosphere, unable to hold his breath any longer. He felt himself beginning to change – craving the blood and flesh and sinew of the child that now attacked him.

'No!' he cried through gritted teeth, spraying spittle onto the windscreen.

With the last bit of strength and control he had left, John turned the wheel of the jeep. If he was going to lose his soul, then he would be better off dead. With one sharp twist the jeep hit the rotted and worn barrier: breaking through on impact. For a moment the momentum gave the vehicle flight, and it soared upwards over the valley. Then the front edge dipped and John saw, through rage-filled eyes, the sheer drop beneath them. He closed his eyes, holding onto his humanity for as long as possible.

In the collision with the barrier the insane kid had been thrown back. Now he raged at John, clawing at the back of his head even as the car crashed down onto the cliff face below. The teenager was thrown forward, his head smashing with a sickening crunch into the skull of Private John Guilor, whose neck broke with the force.

The fully-fuelled jeep burst into flames and rolled down the mountainside, a ball of fire, setting light to everything in its path. The dried-out grass caught fire, the flames spreading across the valley.

As the jeep came to a halt in a raging torrent of fire and melting plastics, John's cindered body lolled through the hole that was formerly the windscreen. He hadn't felt the flames consume his chest, face and arms, nor had he been aware that his blood-filled eyes boiled in their sockets. The broken neck had mercifully ended his life.

10

'We've searched everywhere. The kid is nowhere to be found,' Harvey said.

'Not everywhere,' said Jas. 'She might have crossed the barrier.'

Caroline burst into tears, falling to her knees in the sand as she hugged Jamie to her. She had held herself in check for so long that her breakdown was complete, and it terrified the small child, who was not quite two years old.

'She's only a baby,' Caroline sobbed.

Jas picked up the frightened little boy from Caroline's arms. 'Will someone go to my tent and fetch Kale?'

Kat came forward from the gathering crowd to comfort Caroline.

'I'll get her to Doc Avery. He'll have something that will help calm her until we find the little girl.'

Jas bit her tongue to prevent herself from saying how they no longer needed the ministrations of a doctor. Here, magic was what counted. But Gerald's help in calming Caroline would be useful and would free up Kale for the search, so she let Kat take Caroline and Jamie away with the help of Sylvia. The two councillors were wisely being useful. Jas suspected this was because neither of them wanted to see the camp fall apart anymore than she did. It was important that they all stayed calm and hidden in their desert oasis for their own safety.

Harvey sent someone to fetch Kale, who arrived a few moments later. The mage frowned and appeared distressed when they told him what had happened.

'We don't know when, or if, Selene crossed the barrier,' Jas said. 'Can you help?'

'Yes, but she may have already been observed beyond my protection spell,' he said.

'Then we have to find her before the warriors can ...'

'You don't understand. If the child is beyond here, her presence may well have revealed *our* location.'

'But the shield is in place ...?'

'It is, but another of my order could sense something. The camp may stand out because they can't scan the area. It will be a void. Just as the mage's tent was to me,' Kale explained. 'But only if they get close enough.'

Taylor arrived with a small search party, but Jas and Kale did not tell them of the possible danger. There was no need to cause panic.

'Kale will search beyond the barrier,' Jas said.

Kale tapped his staff down three times and a beam of green light projected from the top.

'The green represents protection,' Jas explained to the others. 'He's searching, while attempting to remain invisible himself, and while maintaining control over the camp.'

'He is a force to be reckoned with,' Kat said behind them.

'Is Caroline okay?' Jas asked.

'She is sedated. She was hysterical. Sylvia has stayed behind with her and Jamie, because Caroline was acting weird about being alone with the doctor. What's going on with that?'

'I can only wonder …' said Jas.

'Anyway, I wanted to be part of the search party,' Kat said.

'All help welcome!' said Taylor. 'We'll head out across the barrier when Kale tells us which direction to go in.'

Kat joined the band of men and women that had gathered already by the barrier. There were seventeen of them in all. Jas recognised her former pupil, Andy: he had been the only one of the children in her care that she had been able to save five years ago. They had then spent a few years together, fending off other, more feral, survivors. For this reason, she and Andy had always shared a bond. Sadly, he hadn't been as welcoming or trusting when she had returned to Earth three years later. Jas hoped, now that all of his doubts and suspicions were put to rest, that his attitude toward her would change for the better. She realised, however, that she hadn't seen much of the young man since they had crossed the vortex to Emin, and so she waved, smiling warmly to show her affection. Andy saluted and smiled back in response. He appeared relaxed and happy, despite the circumstances that they now had to deal with.

Jas's eyes fell on Kat. The woman was standing looking out across the barrier, her hand shielding her eyes from the bright sun. She was clearly tense and worried about the missing child, as they all were, but something about her posture made Jas curious about her.

'What's her story?' Jas asked Taylor.

'Who?'

'Kat …'

Taylor shrugged, 'The same as us all, I suppose. She came to the Trafford Centre about a year ago. I assume she had lost everyone she cared about. She's generally very quiet. Although she took up a role on the council and makes very valid contributions.'

'I sense the child …' Kale said.

'Where?' asked Taylor.

'North. She's crossed the barrier. Probably couldn't find her way back through.'

The party, led by Kale, crossed the camp to the north. Taylor, Andy, Harvey, Kat and the others were armed to the teeth with the weapons they had brought through the vortex.

'Those are useless here,' Jas pointed out. 'It's swords, daggers and magic … When will they realise we aren't on Earth anymore?'

Kale glanced at Jas, frowning at her short temper.

'Sorry,' she said. 'I'm tense. I want Selene back, safe and sound. I can't bear for us to lose anyone else.'

Close to the barrier, Jas could hear the hum of magic and see the trace of the protection spell: a green haze in the atmosphere.

'Can the others see and hear this?' she asked Kale.

'No, Empress. Only we can.'

Jas turned to the search party. 'Okay everyone. We are about to cross the barrier. Kale will project a temporary protective spell over us. We don't want to become exposed and be a beacon for the enemy. Stay close together.'

The small band of soldiers and volunteers crossed the barrier, led by Kale, Jas and Taylor. Strapped to Jas's waist, courtesy of Kale, were a Jinx sword and two daggers. With her hand on the hilt of the sword, and Kale and Taylor either side of her, Jas walked through the barrier. She experienced a slight tingling sensation as the protection spell touched her face and head, and then she was through.

The rest of the search party passed the barrier to join them in the desert.

'That's weird,' said Andy. 'You can see the desert from inside the camp, but not the camp from this side.'

'I know. We're truly invisible,' Jas said. 'Now come on. We have to find Selene.'

Kale led the band out into the desert.

'I can sense her, but she's quite far away now,' he said.

'Poor kid! She must be terrified,' Kat said.

'I think when she passed the shield she probably just couldn't find her way back and kept walking,' Taylor speculated. 'But we'll find her. We have to.'

He moved forward, booted feet tramping on soft desert sand.

At the rear of the posse Jas glanced back behind them. Unlike Andrew and the other Earthlings, she could clearly see the camp and the barrier. She suspected this was because Kale allowed her to, or perhaps because she had some magical ability of her own that permitted her to see through the magic of others. If this was so, though, what was to stop one of the Sharik mages from also being able to do exactly the same? For the first time since they had arrived, Jas experienced real fear. She was afraid for the Trafford Centre survivors. They were all that was left of the world she once knew. If anything happened to them, humanity could become extinct. Any remaining survivors back on Earth would be too damaged; and, the way things were going, not around for much longer.

Reminding herself that Selene was in possible danger, Jas forced aside her worries for the future of her people. She pulled her mind back to the task in hand and hurried to catch up with the rest of the group as they walked across the desert. There was a job to be done and they would all do it. Whatever the outcome.

11

Earth, The Dawn Of Time

He stood on the pinnacle of the newly erected pyramid. His golden imperial robes flowed around his outstretched arms as a soft breeze picked up in the desert. This was his finest achievement. It had taken so little magic to raise this grand temple up from the sand, and Kil'n knew how to wield his power to his best advantage.

Below the pyramid his people gathered, gazing up in awe at this display of his considerable strength.

'There is a traitor among us,' Sulemen told him.

Kil'n did not ask who the traitor was, for he already knew. He felt the man's hatred flowing upwards toward him: Hren was at the heart of a quiet conspiracy to spread unrest.

Hren was a spiritual scientist. He believed that magic should not be used, because it had a negative impact on the universe. His belief was that magic might even destroy the world when held in the wrong hands. Kil'n knew that Hren believed **his** *were the wrong hands. Hren alleged that the Emperor was addicted to using his magic. There was a faction of people who shared this belief, and they gathered to talk about their scientific theories and listen to Hren's ravings about the Emperor.*

Hren had his own vanity too. His crowning glory had been to design the pyramid that Kil'n now stood upon. It was an intricate work of art that would have required thousands of men to raise it, and many years of work in the building of the structure. However when Hren had proposed the build at the senate, Kil'n had opposed it on the grounds that it would use up too much manpower; and the Emperor always had the final word, because no-one in the senate would go against him.

When Sulemen had revealed Hren's divergence, Kil'n had remembered the design, and using magic had regained full recall of the structure's size and interior layout.

'We'll need a public demonstration of the Emperor's inexhaustible strength,' Sulemen had said. 'Any further rebellion will be blocked.'

Kil'n had agreed. 'I'll raise Li's pyramid from nothing but sand. Show them all how unnecessary it is to put good men to work on something that is so easy for their Emperor to create.'

So Kil'n had made a decree that all of his subjects must attend, and there he had drawn a symbol of power in the air and the pyramid had risen from the ground under his feet with very little effort.

Now he looked down at his shocked people, arms outstretched as he celebrated his own magnificence.

'I give you the pyramid,' said Kil'n, and he felt no need to reveal the original architect of the design. He had built it with the power of his mind, and therefore was justified in claiming it. He had also modified the structure to be both temple and fortress for the royal family. Kil'n thought nothing of how he had inadvertently mixed magic and science with the wave of his hand.

His subjects bowed down and worshipped Kil'n. Their adoration made his power swell. Or at least it felt that way to Kil'n. His ego and pride were massaged more by this display than the real benefits of devotion for his magic.

*Standing in the crowd, Hren directed his hatred to the Emperor, and despite Kil'n's best intentions, his subjects did not honour him more than they had – they now **feared** him. For absolute power made good men turn evil, and reign by terror created hatred among those without authority.*

Kil'n was oblivious to all of this.

Instead his plans to wed ensued.

'Bring the females,' he ordered Sulemen.

Then Kil'n went down into the pyramid and to the newly formed throne room, where the nobility were already gathering. He took up his place on the new throne and looked out at his people.

'Henceforth this place will be our sacred room,' Kil'n said. 'Beginning with our first bonding.'

Ten pre-chosen noble females of marriageable age were brought to the throne room in the hope that one of them would be a match for Kil'n. Each of them had been prepared for the ceremony in advance, with weeks of tuition and advice. This much choice and preparation were given only to the nobles among them. Kil'n had never met any of the women prior to this moment, as they were never launched into their society until married, and so he looked at them all carefully as they were brought forward. He was curious. Which among them would be his match? For it was certain one would be. They were all dressed in identical robes in the imperial colours. Veiled. This was to ensure that none had any physical advantage over another. Not that it would make any difference. Magic would choose the right one, regardless of what each thought, or so they all believed.

'Come forward,' he said to the first, and the girl walked boldly toward the Emperor. Under the veil he could make out that she was smiling and attractive. Kil'n liked her but he did not test her. Another came forward and was rejected in the same way, and this happened four times until the fifth girl approached. She had long dark hair, beautiful glittering blue eyes – a rarity among his people – and the whitest

skin, as though it had never been touched by the sun. He held his hand up, palm outwards, and she responded by holding hers the same. A spark of magic flared between them.

His hand reached toward her, skimming the air over her aura, and her pale skin glowed like liquid moonlight in response. This girl, Kil'n soon learned, was Shamila: she was his perfect match.

Sulemen stepped forward and began the marriage ceremony, even as the other nine women were led away. Though each of them would return again and again to the ceremony until their own mate was found.

But only Shamila was a good enough match for the Emperor, so all noble eyes looked upon her and Kil'n with envy.

Kil'n's life became one of domestic bliss. His indulgence in his new bride took him away from his duties at the senate, although this was to be expected, as all new-bonded couples were obsessed with each other. The power of bonding magic could never be denied.

Later, as Kil'n lay in the pyramid chamber with Shamila while she moaned beneath him, their mutual virginity gone, he was overwhelmed by this new thing between them. Sex; passion; joy; love – sometimes pain – were born of experimentation.

Kil'n could barely leave Shamila alone, even when they were both exhausted. He became obsessed with the idea that he wanted to bring her definitive satisfaction. He wanted to see her face change as she writhed in pleasure beneath him. It was something that magic could not give him easily, only physical exertions.

Kil'n used all of the pleasure movements he had been taught in theory in advance of his wedding. Facing Shamila, he pulled her up onto his thighs and parted her legs around his waist. He breathed in as she breathed out, penetrating her as he did so.

But then, as their meditation deepened, a new knowledge, a magical symbol came into his mind. He knew it would change their passion for the better. Without hesitation he wrote the symbol in the air between them. When his release finally came, for the first time a pod burst from him, up into her womb, and sent shock waves of ecstatic pleasure through Shamila's body. They both writhed as Shamila's orgasm spasmed over Kil'n's cock, gripping him tightly in her rapture.

'What happened?' she gasped, falling down beside him, her body shuddering with aftershocks, sending her into continued excitement.

'Magic. I've changed us,' he said. 'Now we have ultimate pleasure.'

But the pleasure came at a cost. Yes, Kil'n had changed them; he did not know for some time the full extent of that change.

While Kil'n and Shamila indulged themselves, Hren was making his move.

'The Emperor does not work for the good of his people,' Hren told the other councillors.

A famine was upon them. Hren presented this as a sign of Kil'n's misdemeanour.

'He does not help revive the crops that are failing. For too long we have relied on the magic of a man who uses it only for his own gratification.'

'The Emperor is newlywed. This is normal,' argued one of the senators. 'If we bring the problems to his attention then he will …'

'I tried,' said Hren. 'He refused to see me. His council is no longer given in the throne room. All he does is eat and fornicate with his new bride. It is time we acted. Time we took back the power for ourselves. Man has always grown his own crops without magic. Nature is magic, and my science can help …'

'How?' asked another senator; an old man who remembered the old ways.

'Give me control over the farmers. I'll turn this scourge around.'

With the Emperor absent and unable to object, the council gave Hren the power he asked for. Kil'n and Shamila continued in their own self–indulgence, unaware that the science of Hren appeared to be saving the crops and averting famine without the aid of the Emperor.

When Hren went back to the council, some weeks later, they were ready to listen to all that he said. They were ready to act.

Warriors poured into Kil'n's and Shamila's chamber. The Emperor was seized and held. His hands were tied, preventing him from using his magical symbols.

'You are going to be tried,' said Hren, 'unless you and the Empress leave here and never return.'

'What sin have I committed?' Kil'n asked.

'Overuse of magic. Magic that is stolen from the universe will have dire consequences on our planet.'

'You're insane,' Kil'n said. 'Magic only helps us.'

'That is why you have been unaware of the deaths and famine in your land? Your magic caused this. My science has thwarted disaster.'

'That is untrue. Sulemen told me what was happening. I performed a ceremony. The crops you see revived are my doing.'

Hren laughed. 'You think the senate will believe that? You! Not making a public show of your magic! They have seen me work tirelessly, planting seeds with farmers, fertilising from the waste of our livestock. You have been hidden away, a sensualist, obsessed with your own sexuality. Just look at you!'

'Look at what?' Kil'n asked.

'You and your wife have been changed by the magic …'

Hren's warriors pulled Kil'n before the polished gold mirror and Kil'n then saw his changed state. His body was completely hairless, his chest no longer had nipples. He was taller too than all of the men. Taller than he had been earlier that day. So too was Shamila.

Shamila was wrapped in their bed sheets – the warriors had afforded her that dignity – so she could not see if her own body had altered, but she looked at Kil'n with fear-filled eyes.

What had his magic done to them? Was there really a price to pay every time he used it? For the first time, Kil'n doubted himself.

'We have your warriors and their families. They are swearing fealty to you, so you will not leave alone,' Hren said, as though he were being generous.

They pulled Kil'n out of the pyramid and up onto the top, where his subjects, pre-summoned, now watched on.

'Those of you who remain loyal to the Emperor may leave here with him unharmed,' said Hren.

Hren was surprised by the division, which was an almost equal split. Instead of one tribe they had now become two. Humans and Arrak Nah Tiamen, as Kil'n's people began to call themselves soon after.

Kil'n's loyal followers surrounded the pyramid. He realised then that even if his hands were free, he could not remain, with so many of his subjects now turned against him and Shamila.

'Where are we to go, Sulemen?' Kil'n asked his royal adviser.

'Search your magic, my Emperor. Take us out into the stars. Let us find a new home where the poison of science cannot taint the beauty of magic.'

'Release me,' Kil'n said. 'And I and my subjects will leave.'

Hren knew that Kil'n was a man of his word, and gave the signal for his warriors to untie the Emperor's hands. Then he and the rest of the traitors left the pyramid's peak.

Kil'n looked out over the desert landscape and he visualised another world, another planet. His eyes looked up into the night sky and he saw the moon glowing down on the pyramid.

'A moon,' he said. 'Far away from here. A place where we can survive this outrage and live once more as our supernatural nature dictates.'

The symbol came into his mind, and Kil'n drew it in the air.

A wave of magic surrounded the pyramid and touched all of his loyal subjects – his new tribe – and then the Arrak Nah Tiamen changed. Their Emperor gave them his pleasure magic as a gift for their loyalty, though none of them realised at that point that they had altered, beyond that they all grew in stature.

'We are no longer human,' Kil'n told them. 'We are Arrak Nah Tiamen, Warriors of Space, and we will leave this science-cursed planet and find a new world for ourselves. Henceforth we shall have our own language – the semantics of magic.'

Kil'n's subjects felt the magic the Emperor spoke of, and as it touched their tongues they cheered.

Kil'n raised his hand and drew the symbol that appeared in his mind. Then, in the blink of an eye, the Arrak Nah Tiamen found themselves, pyramid and all, on a completely different planet.

Arven opened his eyes and found Malachi standing over him.

'Emperor?' he said.

'I know how the split occurred between the two tribes.'

'Does this explain the curse we find ourselves under?'

'No,' Arven said. 'There has to be something more.'

'Emperor, I beg you be careful. We do not know what this tainted magic will do to you.'

'I'm fine,' said Arven. 'Better than I've ever been.'

Then he closed his eyes again and let himself be plummeted once more into the past.

Malachi, Prins and Elee looked on, but only the mage was afraid as Arven fell back down into a deep trance.

12

'Tell me again what John told you?' Tremaine said.

Tremaine had arrived back at their apartment minutes after the inspectors had left. Kerry was shaken up by the inspection, as she always was, but she had passed with few advisories.

'He said it was time. He was scared. Why was he so afraid, Richard?'

'There was an incident today in P Sector. Alan Kenney was killed,' Tremaine said.

'Killed?' How?'

Tremaine shook his head, 'It doesn't matter. He's dead and things are rapidly going to shit on the base. We *need* to get out of here.'

'They'll never let you leave here with me.'

Tremaine was quiet for a moment. Kerry watched his face change from worry to determination.

'Security on this base isn't as tight as you might think. We lost a lot of soldiers in the attack on the Trafford Centre. I've been thinking this through for some time. It's not going to be easy, but it can be done. There is a route out.'

Kerry listened while Tremaine outlined his plan. When he finished speaking, she knew exactly what she had to do. And Tremaine was right: it wasn't going to be pleasant, but this might be the only way out for them.

'I hate to ask this of you,' Tremaine said. 'But there's never been a better time to take advantage of some of the soldier's worst traits.'

'I know. But you've saved me so far. I can't see any other solution, and if what you say is right, this is the perfect, and only, opportunity we might have. Especially with the absence of the P Class women.'

Tremaine packed a small bag that contained essentials for them both.

'Yes. I'm counting on the soldiers feeling quite … desperate by now. They've had women on tap for years. Even the most unattractive among them hasn't had to worry.'

'Yeah. Disgusting really,' said Kerry.

'You sure you're okay with this?' Tremaine asked.

Kerry nodded. 'It's the only way. Besides, you'll be near. Won't you?'

'Of course! I'll get one of my colleagues to meet me at the med centre with outdoor clothing and gasmasks. There is also a document waiting for me on my desk. It's important and may give me information about the women we helped escape today, so I'll bring it with me.'

Tremaine went to his computer and sent out the coded message to all of the fifth columnists.

'Come on,' he said.

'Now?' Kerry answered.

'We have only a limited window of opportunity. James was here earlier, so it's unlikely he'll return today. I got word that Handley is out of favour, and he'll be doing whatever he can to cover his own back. What with the Trafford Centre fiasco and this morning's disaster, he'll have a lot of explaining to do. The base is still in chaos and a lot of the border detail has been seconded to search duty. They still think the P Class women might be on the base hiding somewhere, which is to our advantage, because there aren't any search parties going outside.'

'Okay. I'm ready,' Kerry said.

She stood up and pulled on her cardigan. Wives on the base were expected to dress conservatively and she had no clothing that wasn't something her grandmother would have worn. The theory was that no-one but their husband should find them attractive. That sort of girl was found only in the P Sector. Kerry wondered how they had become so puritanical on the one hand, but so corrupt on the other. It was an oxymoron of principles.

'When we get to the exterior checkpoint,' Tremaine said, 'undo a few buttons. You're an attractive woman, so I don't think it will take much.'

Holding hands, they left their residential sector and walked across to the nearest checkpoint.

'Hey, doc,' said the soldier at the first checkpoint. 'What can I help you with?'

'I'm taking my wife into the medical centre. We think she might be pregnant. Got to do the tests,' Tremaine said.

'Wow. Great news, doc!' the soldier answered, and he raised the barrier to let them through.

'Thanks,' said Kerry. 'I'm so excited. We've been trying for a while.'

The soldier saluted Kerry and she and Tremaine walked away at a leisurely pace, continuing to hold hands as though they were a truly devoted couple.

A few blocks from the checkpoint they reached the medical centre. They passed without going in. Then, as they approached the external checkpoint, Tremaine stopped and pretended to tie his shoelaces.

'Hey honey! You check on John. There's something I need at the Medical

Centre,' Tremaine looked through his long fringe and watched the soldier on the checkpoint glance over to them both. Then he stood up and turned away.

Kerry opened the first three buttons on her blouse and walked toward the checkpoint. She hadn't forgotten how to flirt, and now she swung her hips deliberately as she walked toward the soldier. She saw him watching and gave him her best smile.

'Hey there,' she said, coming to a halt in front of the barrier. 'I'm Mrs Tremaine.'

'Yes ma'am, I know,' said the soldier. He was in his thirties, but still had that appearance of youth, because his face was red with acne. He was definitely on the 'most unattractive' list that Tremaine had mentioned when referring to the soldiers earlier. And Tremaine should know, being one of the few secretly gay men that lived among them.

'Well, I wonder if you can help me …?'

'I doubt that, ma'am,' said the soldier.

Kerry hated him immediately. He was an arrogant little shit who clearly had no respect at all for women. But even so, she widened her smile.

'It's nothing much …'

The soldier's eyes ran over her. Kerry knew he was appraising her looks. In the old days he would never have even been able to talk to a girl like her – and he knew it.

'Ma'am, you really shouldn't be out here without your husband …'

Kerry suppressed a shudder as the soldier's cold blue eyes refused to meet hers. It said a lot about who he was that he was unwilling to treat her as an equal. He was obviously one of those men who agreed fully with what Handley and James were doing.

'Oh. He could be in the Med centre for hours!' Kerry said. 'He always forgets the time. I'm on my own a lot. It gets a bit lonely. *You know what I mean?*'

Kerry leaned on the barrier, and the neck of her blouse opened. She noticed the soldier glance at her cleavage.

'Yeah,' he said. 'Gets lonely being in this place, don't it?'

'He leaves me for hours. Days sometimes. Always looking after those … breeders. I never actually get his attention for long … And … a woman has needs …'

The soldier met her gaze then. His eyes narrowed.

'What're you *doing*?' he said.

'Just passing the time of day …'

'You said you *wanted* something?'

Kerry straightened up. Maybe she had read him wrong after all. A slight flush coloured her cheeks as she contemplated possible failure. She was supposed to seduce this creep. Perhaps she was *really* out of practice. A moment of panic flooded her chest, then she took a deep breath and smiled.

'I was wondering … what time my brother left? Private Guilor? He was called over to MD1. Reassignment I think.'

'Why do you need to know?'

'He promised to e-mail and let me know he'd arrived,' Kerry said.

'I'm sure he will. When he can.'

'Look. I'd be *really* grateful if you can help. He told me things aren't too … good … *outside*. I'm just a little concerned. I should've heard from him by now …'

Kerry leaned on the barrier again. The soldier glanced at Kerry's cleavage again. His stance had changed. He was looking less formal and his body language, despite the coldness of his words, had altered. He was interested. Yes indeed.

'I'd have to go and check. Over there in the guard-house. On the schedule …'

Kerry reached out and touched his hand. The soldier shuddered a little. She glanced down at his pants and noticed the obvious bulge.

'Could you?' she said. 'I can wait *here* …'

'No. I couldn't leave you here,' said the soldier. 'Not without anyone at the barrier … How long do you think your husband is going to be?'

Kerry leaned further forward, revealing that she wasn't wearing a bra. 'I could come to the guard-house with you. If that's allowed? My husband will be *ages* … half an hour at least. Maybe even an hour …'

'You're sure?'

'Yes. He has paperwork to do. Some test results to read. That always takes a while …'

The guard nodded, then glanced round. There was no-one but the two of them in the area. 'Look, I'm not supposed to … but, how *grateful* are you feeling?'

Kerry smiled again. 'I told you. *Very*. There's *nothing* a sister wouldn't do for her brother … you know …'

'C'mon,' the soldier said.

Kerry followed him to the guard-house, and as the soldier unlocked the door she made sure she brought up the rear and entered after him. Then she closed the door, but left the bolt unlocked.

The soldier smiled. 'Men have needs too,' he said.

'I'm hoping so,' Kerry said.

'And there's no P Class … Not since … It's been over a week since I was able to …'

'Yeah. I heard,' said Kerry.

The soldier unfastened his belt, then threw it and his set of keys down onto the workstation table beside a computer terminal. He pushed Kerry hard up against the wall of the guard-house. His hands were all over her, groping her breasts, diving between her legs. It crossed her mind that the man was behaving like he hadn't had sex in years, not merely one week. He was a savage.

'Hey, slow down,' she said. 'I want something out of this too. You said you'd check when my brother left.'

'Pay up first,' he said.

He kissed her. Kerry felt sick as he tried to push his tongue into her mouth. But she was saved that disgusting slobbering, because the soldier was impatient. He flipped her around to face the wall. His hand went up her skirt, and he began to yank her panties down. Kerry couldn't believe how brutal and desperate the guy was. It was as though he had totally forgotten how to treat a girl under normal circumstances. Even when she appeared to be willing.

Kerry closed her eyes and thought about the old days. How had these men become so brutal, so savage? Was it all because of Handley's new order? Or had they always been this way, hiding who they truly were when society wouldn't have accepted such bad behaviour in the past? Whatever it was, there was no protection for women anymore. No respect. Only this sort of scum who were affectively ruling what was left in the world.

'Spread your legs for me ...' he said.

With the soldier this close, a waft of stale sweat and piss reached Kerry's nostrils. Bile rose in her throat. The soldier was vile: like most of the men on the base. He was an unwashed, unclean animal. But she obeyed him and opened her legs while he fumbled behind her. She heard his zip and then he pushed his cock against her. She swallowed, feeling truly sick to her stomach. The soldier was clumsy though, and had trouble finding her. Kerry squeezed her eyes shut and waited for him to penetrate her. She hadn't realised how hard this would be and was beginning to regret agreeing to it. Where was Tremaine? He had promised he would be here in time ...

At that moment the guard-house door opened. Tremaine entered.

'What the fuck is going on here?' Tremaine said, playing the cuckolded husband as they had planned.

Kerry let go the breath she was holding and almost collapsed as the soldier released her.

The soldier fell back, shocked and confused, and began to fumble with his trousers, sticking his rapidly deflating cock back inside. Kerry recovered her equilibrium and used his confusion to grab the gun from the holster attached to the belt he had discarded. The soldier's reflexes were slow, and before he knew it he was facing Kerry, who levelled the gun with expertise directly at his chest.

As if in slow motion he watched her flick the safety catch off. It was obvious that she knew what she was doing. The sight of her, with her knickers around her ankles, holding the weapon with a look of disgust and determination, was enough to bring a strangled, nervous giggle from the soldier's lips.

'You're going to give us the keys to one of the cars. And you're *not* going to raise the alarm that we've gone,' said Tremaine.

'Like fuck I'm …' the soldier said.

'Yes you are. And just for the record, I would never have slept with you in a million years,' Kerry said. 'How you behaved then just showed what a savage dick you are. You and your friends. I'd happily shoot you in the crotch right now just to make sure you couldn't treat another woman that way, but I can't … as it would stop us getting away from here. '

'Slut,' the soldier said.

Kerry hit the soldier hard in the face with the butt of the gun. He crumpled into the chair by the computer station. When he tried to stand, Tremaine pushed him back down.

Kerry noticed that Tremaine was carrying a new holdall. He bent down and removed a roll of duct tape from inside.

The soldier kept his eyes on Kerry – he now had a bloody nose to add to the redness of his face. She kept the gun trained on him while Tremaine tied him to the chair and covered his mouth to keep him quiet.

'Where's the keys?' Tremaine asked.

Kerry clicked the safety back on the gun and stuffed it into her waistband. Then she picked up the soldier's belt from the workstation and passed the keys to Tremaine. She was calm.

'Good,' Tremaine said.

Tremaine searched the bunch of keys, trying them until he found the one that opened the cabinet above the workstation. Here he found more sets, each with a licence plate number attached. Not that plates mattered any more – there was no such thing as road tax since the old world no longer existed. But old habits die hard, and at least the plates separated one vehicle from another.

Tremaine took the keys belonging to a jeep. He pulled out an overcoat for Kerry from the bag. Then, as a last-minute thought, he picked up all of the other keys and dumped them into his holdall.

'That should slow them down if they try to follow us. Stay here, I'll bring the car to the barrier. Open the barrier and then we'll get out of here.'

'Okay,' said Kerry. 'Where's the barrier control?'

Tremaine pointed to a switch on the wall above the workstation and next to the key cupboard.

'Put the coat on,' he said. 'You'll need the protection outside.'

Kerry pulled the gun out of her waistband and waited by the door of the guard-house until she saw the car pull up to the barrier. She glanced at the soldier. He was seething behind the duct tape gag but wasn't capable of going anywhere. She hit him hard again across the temple. The soldier slumped in the chair unconscious.

'Serves you right ...' she sneered. She felt such rage that in that moment she wanted to kill the man, or at least beat the shit out of him, but she controlled herself.

She pressed the button and the barrier began to lift. Then Kerry opened the door, slipped through, and locked it behind her, leaving the restrained soldier inside.

She reached the car and climbed in beside Tremaine.

'Well done, Kerry!' Tremaine said. 'Didn't realise you knew how to handle a gun.'

'I was a cop. *Before.*'

Tremaine absorbed this information, feeling guilty that he hadn't actually asked her, in all of these months that she had been his wife, what she had done before the Jinx.

'Put this mask on,' he said, handing her a bag. 'The main door should open as we approach.'

Kerry took the gasmask and put it in place, as Tremaine secured his.

Tremaine glanced at Kerry to reassure himself she was protected, then he pulled the car across the check point and turned it out of the base.

'Where are we going?' Kerry asked.

'There's a rendezvous point. Hopefully when we reach it a few of the others will have got out too. And Harrington should be there with the P Class women by now.'

'And John,' said Kerry.

'Yes.'

'What about the others? Maybe they'd need cars?' Kerry mentioned. 'And we have the keys ...'

'I've hidden them on the base in a vent. It's where we passed things to each other, and it isn't far from the garage where the cars are kept. So, they won't be stranded, but Handley's soldiers won't be able to find them and use the cars. That's the most important thing.'

'You thought of everything,' Kerry said.

For the first time in years Kerry saw natural daylight as the main doors opened and the car left the base. The sky was cast with an orange muck that glowed – if dullness could be described that way – with an unearthly tone.

'What the ...?'

'Yeah. It doesn't look the same, does it?'

'What's happened?' Kerry said.

'James and Handley happened. They've been polluting the atmosphere to control any survivors outside.'

'Those sick fucks ...'

'Yeah ...' said Tremaine. 'They don't give a shit what they are doing to the planet. But don't worry. We've been planning an escape for a while. We have somewhere we believe is safe.'

'What about the remaining women? The breeders? The other miserable wives?' Kerry said.

Tremaine grimaced. 'Unfortunately I don't think we can help them anymore.'

Kerry grew serious. 'I can't believe what happened. Every day while we've been in there all I could do was keep telling myself it would all be fine. Once we escaped.'

'It won't be fine, but we'll carry on. That's the important thing …'

'Now all I think of is how I can't believe we survived in there so long.'

'You and me both,' said Tremaine. 'The things they made me do …'

'I'm sorry,' said Kerry.

'So am I. Especially for all of those women and children remaining.'

'Try not to think about it. Like you said, there's nothing you can do for them now, but maybe when we regroup, we can do something in the future. And who knows, those soldiers who have been helping might get a few more out with them today.'

'I hope so,' said Tremaine. 'I never realised what an optimist you are.'

Kerry smiled.

'For the first time in five years I have a reason to be optimistic. Hey! Look!'

Tremaine slowed the car down and they glided past a broken barrier that opened up on a deep cliff face. Below they could see a smouldering army vehicle and a charred body shape halfway through the windscreen.

'Oh my God!' said Kerry.

Tremaine pressed his foot down on the accelerator. 'Don't look.'

'It's John,' she said. 'I know it!'

'No-one could have survived that fall. That fire.'

The tears came then.

Tremaine could barely see to drive: he couldn't wipe his eyes with the mask in place. This was hell, and the enormity of it, the horror he had kept in check for this last five years, finally overwhelmed him. Tremaine thought he was drowning, but he choked it back. Glancing at Kerry sobbing, her mask-covered face in her hands, he knew he had at least to get her to safety. What else could he do? If he couldn't save just one of the women, then everything he had tried to do was worth nothing. And John had been his friend. He had to take care of Kerry. No matter what.

Tears flowing unchecked, Tremaine took a deep breath as they reached the bottom of the steep mountain road. At the intersection he turned left. They would head out of here, back toward the coast, where the sea breeze kept the air cleaner. At least, that was what he and the others hoped.

'We'll get there,' he said, more for himself than for Kerry. 'And Harrington and the women will be there, and so will the fifth columnists. We'll start our own survivor's colony. There will be a future … There has to be …'

Kerry sobbed silently beside him until the tears exhausted her, then she fell quiet.

There was comfort in the silence of the countryside as they drove through empty, winding country lanes, and it soothed both her and Tremaine.

They were out. They were free. No-one appeared to be following them. At least they now had control of their own future, no matter where that led them.

13

The survivors made steady progress with Taylor, Jas and Kale leading them. The desert was hot, but with Kale's magic in place none of them was suffering from the temperature. As always the air around them was perfectly moderated by the Jinx mage's energy. They had been following Selene's trail for almost two hours when Kale spotted a Jinx oasis ahead.

'Wait. That's a new one,' he said. 'Which means that there is another Al Kuzemen nearby who built it.'

They paused.

'Do they have Selene?' Kat said.

Kale searched cautiously. 'The camp is protected but I sense a human among them. It could be the child.'

'What do we do?' Jas asked.

'I think we need to use stealth and radio silence,' Taylor said. 'Can you help us with that, Kale? Keep us invisible? Give us some form of supernatural speed?'

Kale tilted his head and looked at Taylor. 'I have never physically enhanced anyone before. We don't use magic that way as a rule. But I *can* keep you hidden.'

'Could you do it? Enhance us? If you wanted to?' Harvey asked.

'It's against the Al Kuzemen code ...' Kale said, shaking his head. 'I'm not sure why. Unethical perhaps, to change our physical form. Just as making someone fall in love against their will can never work ... or would have consequences that aren't good.'

'Harvey ...' Taylor said. 'If Kale can help us, we'll go on recon ... Guys, it might be easier if you wait here. Less for Kale to worry about.'

Kale went with Taylor and Harvey as Jas stayed behind with the rest of the group.

'I hope they find her,' Kat said. 'I hate to think of any child out there on her own and captured by the Jinx.'

'If the Jinx do have her she'll be unharmed. They'll feed her, give her water. She'll be fine ...'

'Future brood stock?' said Margery beside them. 'They look after their animals …'

Jas rolled her eyes. 'She's a child. They won't hurt her. It's not their way.'

A short time later Taylor, Harvey and Kale returned.

'We have a problem,' Kale said. 'That's Elidon's warriors. They are the ones who attacked me. I doubt they are working under the Emperor's orders. They have Selene and another mage. We saw them both, though I couldn't *feel* them. The place is heavily cloaked and I have no way of testing whether the mage is friend or foe.'

'What should we do?'

'We're outnumbered five to one,' said Taylor, 'and this is Jinx home ground – they've got all of the advantage.'

'We'll have to wait until they decide to send her to Sharik,' Kale said. 'The warriors won't want to drag a child around with them.'

'What if she tells them where we are?' Margery said.

Jas took Margery's arm and pulled her aside from the rest of the group.

'Why did you even come with the search party?' she asked. 'You're not helping at all.'

'I don't trust the Jinx. Someone has to be the voice of caution,' Margery said. 'And I don't trust *you* either.'

'Stop it,' Kat said. 'As Jas says, this isn't helpful. We need to make camp here and watch until someone leaves with the child. Squabbling amongst ourselves is counterproductive.'

Duly cowed by Jas and Kat, Margery fell silent.

'Jas?' called Taylor. 'There's movement.'

Jas returned to Taylor and Kale and watched as two warriors saddled up two el lien mecks. Then they mounted and a third warrior came out of the tent carrying Selene in his arms. He passed the child to the first, who placed her in front of himself on the camel-like creature.

'They are moving her sooner than I thought,' Kale said. 'And we have no way of following on foot.'

'What do we do?' Kat said.

'We'll return to the camp, then I can open a small vortex to drop us down near Sharik. This close to their camp, I daren't risk it without revealing our presence.'

The party watched in silence as the two warriors galloped away from the oasis carrying the little girl with them.

'Are you sure they will go to Sharik?' Kat asked.

'It's the nearest place, and they are from there. So it makes sense,' Jas said.

'Let's get back to the camp. The sooner we travel to Sharik, the better,' Taylor said.

Jas held back as the others turned around and began the long walk back to their hidden camp, with Kale at the lead. As she watched, she noted Elidon and another warrior she didn't know, also mounting el lien mecks. These two warriors set off in a completely different direction from the others. Jas wondered where they were headed and why. A few minutes later the magic at the oasis began to revert.

'Kale!' Jas called and the party stopped and turned around.

Kale turned.

'Most unusual,' he said. 'Normally a new oasis would be left in place. For some reason the warriors want no-one to know they were here. Hence they are removing all traces of their presence.'

Then he watched as the mage he had seen earlier came out of the last tent before it collapsed and became sand once more. The mage now dropped the shield, and Kale tapped his staff on the ground once. A spark of energy, a mere sliver of light that only Kale and Jas could see, focused in the orb at the top.

'A truth spell,' Kale explained. '*Can I trust you?*'

His words seemed to whisper on the wind as they flowed toward the mage.

'His name is Dianede,' Kale said. 'We were colleagues and perhaps friends once. I'm testing his loyalty to the Emperor ...'

Dianede turned to face the hidden search party as though he could suddenly sense them.

Jas gasped. 'He can see us!'

'No. But he feels my magic and he will answer the question whether he intends to or not.'

At that moment Dianede turned to the remaining warriors and barked an order at them. An el lien meck was brought to the mage. He mounted as did the warriors. Dianede glanced once more in the direction of the search party, then he turned his mount and rode away. The warriors followed as though they were escorting the mage back to the town he belonged to.

'What happened?' Jas asked, letting go the breath she had been subconsciously holding.

'He didn't betray us. Whatever it was he had been brought here to do, I think he was under duress.'

'So. You *can* trust him?' Jas said.

'I think so. But I'm unsure if I should reveal anything to anyone yet. Not until we know what's going on here,' Kale said. 'Because something is wrong on Emin. I just have to learn what it is, and who is behind it.'

14

The damage done by the night beasts meant that the decision had to be made soon.

Kil'n's appearance was out of place in the restful haven of their chamber – his imperial robes had been replaced with armour. None of them went outside during the evening for fear of attack, and so they were preparing for war.

'Why must you go?' asked Shamila.

She was lying in bed, the curtains pulled around her while she rested. The baby was lying heavy now, and Kil'n suspected she would give birth soon. She was tired and was resting more and more.

'Our child needs to be born on our home planet, where he will be safe from pestilence,' Kil'n said. 'For this reason we need to take back control of our dynasty.'

Kil'n's mind flew back to their painful exile. But surely they had grown in strength since? His warriors had been training for the battle, and Kil'n's own powers were now beyond anything any Emperor had held before. Even so, he couldn't help recalling the indignity of his previous defeat. The rejection of more than half of his people still stung his pride.

'Your word was given,' Shamila said.

'I gave my word to leave without trouble, but did not promise to remain exiled.'

'That is just semantics,' Shamila said. 'The implication was we wouldn't *return.'*

'We can't remain here. This place is poison *to us,' Kil'n said. 'Every day there are more reports of sickness. And the bite of those things has killed old and young alike ...'*

'Then we go somewhere else. You did it once, you can move us again, Kil'n.'

Kil'n was silent for a moment.

'But how will we know if the next place is safe?'

'We won't,' said Shamila. 'But you named us Warriors of Space, *so we must earn that name. For every world we conquer, there will always be others waiting for us.'*

'You are wise beyond any other, Shamila,' Kil'n said.

'Oh!' she gasped.

'What is it?' Kil'n rushed to her side.

'The baby comes ...'

Kil'n summoned help, and their chamber was soon filled by the midwife and her handmaids.

The midwife pressed her hand against Shamila's distended stomach and smiled.

'I wish my sister was here,' Shamila said.

On hearing this, Kil'n recalled Neferia. She was Shamila's younger sister. He recalled now that she too had been presented to him at the bonding ceremony, next in the line before he had fallen for Shamila. The girl had stayed behind with her newly-bonded husband, a senator called Aris, who had betrayed Kil'n along with Hren.

'All is well. The child is ready,' the midwife reassured. Then she went to the Emperor, who stood helpless by the door. 'It will be many hours before the Empress gives birth,' she revealed.

Kil'n nodded. He turned and left, knowing his place was not in the birthing room. But he thought of Neferia now. Different from Shamila, but no less beautiful. Where had she been the night they left Earth? He summoned up the memory of every face that had been in the crowd. All of their subjects had been required to attend; where then had been Shamila's sister? Kil'n was certain she had not been there …

He pushed the thoughts of the other girl aside. What did it matter? Other than that Shamila felt she needed her … a tradition that could not in this case be continued.

Still in his armour, Kil'n returned to the throne room. He called a meeting with his most trusted councillors, and as they gathered around him, Kil'n's mind was brought away from Shamila and the birth of their child to the problem they faced on the planet.

'We must leave here,' said Miachi. Along with Sulemen, Miachi was a trusted adviser.

'Shamila foresees disaster if we return to Earth. I will erect a barrier around the camp. This should keep those beasts from us at night. I don't know why I did not think of this sooner. In the meantime, I will use my magic to find us a more suitable home.'

'But we may find ourselves in worse circumstances,' Miachi said. 'If we return to Earth, we know what we face.'

'There will be war,' warned Sulemen. 'Loss of lives on both sides.'

'Yes,' said Miachi. 'But the Emperor can persuade the others of the error of their ways. You can give them the pleasure magic. No-one would ever wish to lose such a gift once it has been received and experienced.'

There were murmurs of agreement from the other council members. They all loved their new reward, and the change in their stature. All of the Arrak Nah Tiamen were taller, stronger, and aside from the unfortunate pestilence that they had experienced on what would come to be known as the Eleventh Moon, they appeared to age slower and be in full health, which would indicate longer life.

'Our magic will only work for them if they too forsake science,' Kil'n said. 'The two beliefs cannot live side by side.'

'You'll persuade them,' Miachi said. 'But first you must take back the kingdom by force. Only then will you have their true respect.'

'Through fear?' Sulemen argued. 'That is not the way ...'

The councillors erupted into a heavy debate. Some objected to Kil'n's about-turn. The decision to return had already been made. Others agreed with Kil'n's caution and were happy to wait it out.

'The child is born!' said a voice, and the council fell silent.

Kil'n turned, he saw the midwife standing in the doorway behind the throne. She held the baby, wrapped in a robe of gold.

'A new heir to the throne,' she said, but her eyes were serious and the delighted cheers that erupted in the throne room were met by her stoic silence.

Kil'n went to her and gazed down at the child who lay sleeping in her arms.

'What's wrong?' he said.

'Your son has all of his fingers and toes, but ...'

'What? Tell me, I beseech you!'

And then the baby opened his eyes and looked at his father for the first time.

Kil'n took a step back in shock. The pupils of the child were not ... human. Magic swirled in them, and it was difficult to look directly into the shifting pattern for long.

'Your magic has changed us more than you know,' the midwife said sourly. 'I hope this does not impact on our humanity.'

Then she turned and took the baby back down the corridor to his mother and their chamber.

Amid the cheers and celebration, Kil'n stood silent and solemn. He did not know how to react to this news or how he could face Shamila. What had his magic done to his son? What did it mean for the future of the Arrak Nah Tiamen?

Wine was brought out and the councillors toasted the Emperor and Empress and their child: the first to be born in their new world. Kil'n drank several glasses before he had the courage to go to see his wife.

'Tonight will be a celebration of new birth in our new world ...' Kil'n said. 'I erect a barrier of protection around our town. For the first time we will be not be plagued at night by those bloodthirsty beasts.'

Kil'n thought for a moment, then raised his hand and drew a symbol of power in the air. The throne room erupted with colour; the air was filled with glittering particles of golden light, and the councillors gasped in wonder. With a wave of his hand, the throne room doors burst open and the golden particles left the space with a whoosh. In the antechamber the magic gathered, and then Kil'n waved his hand once more and the main door opened.

Outside the townspeople were scurrying for shelter. For on the Eleventh Moon, night and day were not on a regular pattern. Night came unexpectedly, and so it was again. But as this time, as the night creatures began to fly, Kil'n's magic poured out like pure, burning sunlight.

'Look!' shouted a woman who hurried with her child back to her home. 'The sun *has found us!'*

The sky lit up. Kil'n's magic reached into every corner of darkness and even found the lair of the beasts. The flying creatures burst from the shadows, and as the magical light hit them, promptly burst into flames.

'Ooh!' shouted the onlookers in unison as they paused to watch.

Kil'n and the councillors came out of the pyramid and gazed at the spectacle.

'All praise the Emperor,' called Suleman. 'And the new son that was born to him this night!'

The crowd cheered, as much for the birth of a new heir as for the destruction of the awful creatures that had tormented them.

15

They had come away from Llanberis, passed through Betws y Coed and hit Llandudno. There they joined the A55, and now, with the sea to their left, Tremaine drove the jeep down the empty coast road.

'There're no cars,' Kerry said. 'Not even abandoned ones. This is so weird.'

'The military took care of it before we went underground. People were ordered to stay in their homes – under threat of incarceration. It was a good way to keep the highways clear and stop them all running. They promised that they would be safer from the Jinx at home. The truth was, leaving them out there alone made them a distraction that the military needed while they were moving their own people around. And anyone who didn't listen, I guess they did get arrested. Perhaps the women were put into the breeder programme or P Sectors. There were 60 bases to fill, after all.'

Kerry blinked, taking this information in. 'That's a *lot* of women imprisoned! Oh god! This is so awful ...'

It was as though Kerry had only just fully understood that others had been suffering even more than she had: Kerry had been one of the lucky ones, protected by her brother and by Tremaine.

'I suppose all remaining vehicles,' Tremaine said, changing the subject, 'any that could be drained of fuel, were confiscated. I've heard that there are car graveyards that they use for parts. But I have no idea where they would be.'

'That bastard James has a lot to answer for. I thought *our* small little world was all there was ... That and James's base,' Kerry said. Then she fell into her own thoughts, shutting out the world around her, even Tremaine.

As they continued down the former 'A' road, past Colwyn Bay, Tremaine spotted one such car graveyard just off the road.

'See that?' he said.

'The rumours were true, then,' Kerry said, coming out of her fugue.

Tremaine turned his eyes back to the road. 'The rendezvous is in Prestatyn. There's a hotel, near the beach. Those on the team who had access to the outside have been preparing it for the last three years. It's not a million miles away from the base, but we figured the air would be cleaner near the sea. Plus Handley and James would have no reason to look for us there. They'd expect us to run as far away as we could get.'

'I had an aunt who lived in that area,' Kerry said. 'I suppose … John … suggested it?'

Tremaine nodded, and the mention of her brother and Tremaine's fallen friend reduced them both to silence again.

But as they came off the motorway at Rhyl, Kerry perked up and looked around.

'I remember this place …'

The old seaside town had been not the best holiday resort. In the past it had attracted all of the 'wrong sorts' and been a place to avoid. Now Kerry regretted her old snobbery and wished for a return of the days when families roamed the arcades and shops.

As if he understood how she was feeling, Tremaine turned the car down the promenade. They looked at the bleak, ruined children's rides; the abandoned and looted shops; the empty arcades – lights long since burnt out, silent as the grave.

To their left they saw the tide was in. It rocked hard against the manmade buffers, wearing them down as the sea tried to reclaim this piece of land as its own. Kerry's eyes were round with wonder at the devastation. Was it only five years since the world they knew had ended?

'There's someone standing on the pavement ahead,' she said.

Tremaine slowed the car to a snail's pace and looked where Kerry pointed, but as they drew closer, and the figure came into view, it became apparent that this was no living person. It was a man, and he had been tied to a lamp post – left for the elements, or any roaming beasts to feed on.

Kerry gasped and turned her face away from the corroded face that leered with a skeletal grin as they passed. A warning to trespassers, perhaps …?

Tremaine pushed down on the accelerator, not wanting to risk being prevented from passing through if there was a feral gang in the area. Though the place felt completely empty, he doubted it. And the fifth columnists that had access to the outside had been making a point of clearing away any insane trash they had come across: killing them was a mercy. This body might be the only evidence of occupation left.

'The world has become a brutal, desolate place,' he said. 'I'd heard there were feral leftovers of humanity left. I won't deny that our future will be hard, but at least we'll be free.'

Kerry didn't reply, and when Tremaine glanced at her, he noticed she still had her eyes closed behind her gasmask. Maybe she couldn't take any more just now? Or maybe their flight had exhausted her and she slept. He hoped it was the latter.

At the end of the promenade Tremaine followed the road to the main route from the town. With clear roads ahead and nothing to slow their progress they reached Prestatyn within a few minutes. Tremaine took a left turn and headed down a road toward the small beach. There he pulled into the front entrance of a hotel. The sign above the door said 'THE BEACHES'.

There was a metal grille across the door, and all of the windows in the hotel were boarded up. Someone wanted to keep something out. Or maybe keep it in …

Kerry opened her eyes and looked around as the car came to a halt. There was no-one around and no reason to feel the irrational fear she was experiencing now that they had reached their destination.

'Come on,' said Tremaine. 'Harrington should be here with the girls. And maybe some of the others have arrived too. But he'll need our help with them, I'm sure. The drugs I gave him to keep them calm won't last, and then we'll have to counsel them all through the aftermath.'

But Kerry wasn't taking in anything Tremaine said. Illogical terror gripped her, and she experienced an agoraphobic reaction to leaving the car. The thought of placing one leg outside, touching the pavement, walking to the door, and passing that secure grille – terrified her. Where had her earlier bravery gone? She couldn't summon the will to move.

'I … c … can't …' she stuttered.

'What's wrong?' Tremaine asked.

'I'm *scared*. Scared of what's *in* there …'

'Kerry, what you're experiencing is perfectly normal. You've been cooped up inside the base for five years. Never leaving, having your life fully controlled. You didn't like it, but it was the familiar, and now we are entering unknown territory. And a future of which you are less certain.'

Kerry was breathing too hard into her mask.

'You need to calm down or you will hyperventilate,' Tremaine warned.

'I can't breathe,' she said. Her hands clawed at the mask.

'No!' gasped Tremaine. 'It isn't safe, and this stuff in the air … it's very bad …'

Tremaine's sharp cry reached home. Kerry pushed her trembling hands down onto her lap.

'I'm all right,' she said, forcing her breath to slow down. 'It's just … all too much …'

'I know. But I promise you'll be safe here.'

'Okay … Let's do this,' Kerry said. The trembling continued, but Tremaine had to admire how strong she was; how quickly she had herself back under control. Not easy in the circumstances. At least he had been out before, sometimes travelling between bases, in the early days. How must she feel, outside for the first time in years, and now facing a new, unknown inside?

'Stay here. I'm going to go and open the door. Then we'll hurry you straight in. Is that okay?'

'*I can do that,*' she said.

Tremaine climbed out of the car. He looked around, though this seemed an over-the-top precaution. The silence was punctuated by the occasional crash of the sea against the buffers on the other side of the hotel. Kerry concentrated on the sound. Then she noticed the lack of seagulls. But then, what would draw them inland when there were no people to drop food that they could scavenge …? Had the birds all died?

Kerry's hands were stone cold, yet sweat peppered her brow and, even with the mask in place, she could smell the stench of her own perspiration. The fear hadn't left her; she was just holding herself tightly in check. Wasn't that what she had been doing for the last five years anyway? She could do it for a few more minutes, and then, safely inside the hotel, with friends, she would break down and sob her heart out for everything she had lost.

'Come on. You can do this,' she murmured.

She opened the window as Tremaine walked to the hotel door, but the air that came in was clammy and stung the exposed skin on her wrists and neck. She quickly put the window back up.

Tremaine glanced back at the car, then he pressed what appeared to be an intercom on the side of the grille. There was a loud 'buzz' and then, the grille and the main door unlocked and opened.

Tremaine turned back to Kerry and waved for her to come to him.

She froze for a moment, then swallowed her fear back down.

'You've got this!' she told herself. 'Come on Kerry – think about all those crooks you faced back in the old days. You had fear, but you did it anyway … Move your arse!'

The pep talk to herself was all she needed. Glancing around, she opened the door, climbed out, slammed it shut and ran to Tremaine.

'There's an airlock system here. After that we can remove the masks,' he explained.

'Oh, thank God!' Kerry said.

Tremaine took her hand and led her inside. The grille gate closed and locked behind them as though someone was watching through a hidden camera and knew they were safely inside. Then, the airlock door shut and Kerry and Tremaine found themselves in a small enclosed space with no apparent door on the other side. A whoosh of air burst around them. Then the blank wall ahead began to move in front of them. Following Tremaine's lead, Kerry removed her mask.

16

'I'm coming with you,' Kat said.

'No offence, but you're not a soldier, Kat,' Jas said.

'I'm not, but I need to see this Jinx Town for myself. I can report my findings back to the council. And you said we'll move through unseen.'

'I see no harm in this woman coming along,' Kale said. 'If something does go wrong, and we need to fight our way out of there, then she can take charge of the child, leaving those who can fight free to do so.'

'Nothing is going to go wrong, right guys?' said Taylor.

'No,' Jas answered.

The search party had returned to the survivors' town, and now a small band of soldiers, which included Andy, Harvey and Taylor with two more men, Jas, Kale and now Kat stood at the barrier.

'Come,' said Kale. 'I'll channel the Empress's power as an extra precaution to ensure our arrival is *unseen*.'

They crossed the barrier, and walked a few feet into the desert.

'We know where the child will be taken,' Jas said. 'There is a holding tent for orphaned girls. They are cared for and educated in the ways of the Jinx until they are at bonding age.'

'Like a harem?' asked Kat.

Jas shook her head. 'Just an orphanage and school really. Last time I was there, Mallory was running things. She had an arrangement in place with Arven that the girls could not be bonded until they were 18 or older. She was not only educating the girls, but also the Jinx on how to do this all … *nicely*, I guess. But the girls were very well looked-after, and Arven approved everything Mallory recommended. She was pretty powerful in the town, and although I didn't always agree with all of her methods, I did actually think she was doing the best she could for the girls.'

Kat looked at Jas. 'By educating you mean brainwashing, right?'

Jas laughed. 'It was more – this is how we live now … these are the new rules, really … But I guess *you* would see it that way. I did too, so I don't blame you!'

'But you don't now?' Kat said.

Kale rapped his staff down on the sand three times, bringing everyone to his attention and saving Jas from any more of Kat's intense questions. Jas moved to stand at Kale's side and let him take her hand.

'Ready?' Kale said.

Jas nodded. Kale raised the staff and muttered a few words of power in the Arrak Nah Tiamen tongue, then he tapped his staff down once more.

Jas felt the magic surge down her arm and into her fingers and then pass into Kale. Reality blurred around her as the power bounced back and around her body as Kale manipulated it, taking only what he needed. Then the world righted itself and the strange sensation receded.

The wind picked up, and a small vortex opened before the group. Kale and Jas entered, followed by the others. The air eddied around them at dizzying speed as they stood on a still platform inside. The small group settled themselves in, and then the vortex closed. They were encased in swirling matter, then, in the blink of an eye, the void reopened and they found themselves looking out at slightly different terrain.

With Jas's and Kale's power combined, the vortex had been held steady, which meant that there was very little disruption to the sand around their landing point. Though they were still in the desert, they could see Sharik was a mile ahead of them.

'This is as close as we dare go,' Kale explained. 'We need to walk the rest of the way to remain undetected.'

The party left the vortex, and as Kale and Jas exited, the swirling wormhole-like mass shrank to a pin-prick and then vanished.

The group turned to look at the Sharik skyline. The town was huge, a black shadow of uneven-height tents against the glow of Emin's two moons that hung in the distance over mountainous sand dunes. The sight gave them all pause.

There wasn't one among the human survivors who did not feel slightly intimidated by the thought of walking right into the world of the Jinx.

The rescue party entered Sharik via a pathway between two rows of tents.

'This *feels* like *suburbia*,' Kat observed.

'It is exactly that,' said Jas. 'It's a town, just like any we would live in. There are bakers, butchers … shops, if you like. Guilds of magicians who later become mages. The only difference is that they use magic to fulfil the needs of the population. For example, they don't make clothing, furniture or anything like houses. As you know, they live in tents. And that's all summoned up by the mages. Also the agriculture is all magic-driven. No need to tend it, though the Jinx do harvest it.'

'That explains the bathroom,' Kat said. 'How the water just purifies itself and you, when you're in it.'

'Exactly,' said Jas.

'Utopia, under other circumstances,' Taylor said. 'Especially to us, because we've lived so hard these last five years.'

The group fell silent and halted when a Jinx male and his human wife came out of a tent to their left.

'*Ai ki'am mare,*' said the woman.

'*Ik var'a doon,*' replied the man.

Then they walked hand in hand down the moonlit street like any married couple might. The woman was smiling and laughing as they chatted, casting the male flirty glances. The Jinx male smiled back at her and put his arm around her waist. They halted in the street, turning to kiss, the Jinx male bent down in order to accommodate their different heights.

'They look … ' said Taylor.

'… happy,' finished Kat.

'I believe they are,' said Jas.

She remembered how it felt to be with Arven. Bonding was a powerful magic that she now knew couldn't be broken – except by death.

The couple reached another tent. All the tents were in complete darkness, and so when a human female opened the flap and welcomed the couple inside, it was a surprise to see the light pouring out onto the street, and sounds of music from within. As the flap dropped back down, silence and darkness fell again. The tents were like mini vacuums. They contained their occupants, giving them ultimate privacy inside. Just as a brick-built house would.

'Friends visiting friends …' said Jas. It was good to see this, even for her. She had not appreciated what was really happening in the town with the ordinary men and women. Now she could see what appeared to be an idyllic life.

The group fell silent again as they passed the tent, not because they could be heard or seen, but because each of them was absorbing what they had witnessed of the normality of the town.

'The orphan tent is just on the next row,' Jas said, breaking the silence. 'We'll enter unseen, find Selene, and then get out of here as soon as possible.'

The tent loomed above and beyond the others, almost as large as a circus big top.

Jas and Kale now stood side by side while the others fanned out around them.

The tent was silent, and no light shone out through the canvas, just like the smaller tents. Jas walked forward and pushed open the flap, and light and the sound of childish chatter wafted out to the group.

Jas jerked her head to indicate that they should follow her, which they did – even though they felt vulnerable entering the tent.

After they were all inside, Jas dropped the flap back in place, shutting out the street. Then turned to see a small group of teenage girls sitting on cushions on a plush rug. In the middle of them was a low table, from which they were eating bread and cheese and drinking a fruit-juice-type drink from small chalices. Selene was not with them, but the chatter – all in the Arrak dialect – indicated to Jas and Kale that there was a new girl brought in and they were curious about her.

'They all speak Jinx,' whispered Kat.

'Of course they do,' said Jas. 'These children are from all corners of our former Earth; the Jinx language is common ground for them now. And – there's no need to whisper. We're cloaked. They can't hear or see us.'

She then explained what the girls were saying.

'It seems Selene is in the dormitory. I think it's this way …'

The group followed. Andy, Taylor, Harvey and the two other soldiers remained quiet, keeping their guard up at all times.

Raising another flap at the far end of the room, Jas led them through to another area.

'This is the dormitory,' she said.

'Each girl shares a room with one other, so that they aren't ever alone. There are seven rooms on each side of this corridor. I'll check this side, Andy – you check the other.'

Andy nodded. Then, without hesitation, he raised the first flap.

They were halfway down the row when Andy found Selene.

'She's not alone …' he murmured.

Jas hurried to the doorway, and there she saw Mallory and the two warriors that had taken the little girl from the Jinx oasis. Selene was sitting on the bed. The child looked terrified, and was too afraid to even cry or speak.

'Drop the curtain,' Kale warned. They did as he said. 'We'll have to wait until the warriors leave.'

Just then one of the warriors raised the flap and looked out into the corridor as though he had heard something. He cast his strange, swirling eyes up and down the corridor; then, satisfied, he turned back to the other warrior. He spoke, but Jas couldn't hear what he said, because the tent flap fell down and swallowed the sound. Both warriors came out of the room shortly afterwards. They appeared relaxed and unconcerned as they walked back down the corridor to the common area. Jas hoped they were leaving the tent and Selene with Mallory.

Jas stepped forward and reached a hand out to the flap, but before she could touch the fabric the door opened and Mallory stood in the frame.

'I know you're there,' she said in English.

Mallory's eyes cast over the corridor but didn't rest on Jas, Kale or the others. Perhaps she had seen the flap being raised earlier and had realised that someone had come to rescue the girl.

Jas glanced at Kale. 'Let her see and hear me,' she said. 'But keep everyone else hidden.'

Kale sighed. 'Are you sure this is a good idea?' he said in his native tongue. 'She *betrayed* you, Empress.'

'I know. But her heart has always been in the right place where the children are concerned. She won't want to see Selene orphaned when she knows her mother is alive and needs her child back.'

Kale tapped his staff down lightly. There was a shadow on Jas that none of the group had noticed until it now dropped away from her.

Kat glanced down at her own arms to see the shadow still sitting on her skin, then around at the soldiers, who were doing the same thing. All were in shadow, as though they were ghosts rather than beings of substance. A fact that Jas's exposure now showed them.

'*You!*' Mallory gasped. 'Come inside, quickly.'

Jas entered Selene's room, leaving the flap open so that Kale and the others could hear their conversation.

'I've come to take her back,' Jas said.

'Who is she to you?' Mallory asked.

'A friend's daughter … Her mother is missing her.'

'I shouldn't be so surprised to see you. They were questioning me about you,' Mallory said. 'Plus the bonding would always make you bounce back to Arven …'

'Do you know where he is?'

'Who?'

'*Arven?*'

'*He's not in Sharik?*' Mallory said, surprised. 'He's been refusing to see me, but I thought it was because …'

'Because?'

'Never mind. If he's not here, he must be in one of the other towns.'

'He's not on the planet. I can't find him anywhere,' said Jas.

'That explains a lot,' said Mallory. 'His two most trusted warriors aren't *available* either. One of them, Prins, is a … *friend* of mine. It is unusual that he hasn't been around to see me.'

Jas digested this information before asking, 'What did the warriors want?'

'They wanted to know if I had seen you or Kale. They said he'd been sighted outside another town. Then they found the little girl and wondered where she had come from. I told them she was one of mine who had gone missing. Fortunately neither of them can speak any English. Their jabber terrified the poor kid into silence.'

'Good,' said Jas. 'Then they don't know anything.'

'What is there to know?' Mallory asked. 'It's obvious to me, however, that you brought a group of survivors back with you.'

Andy stepped forward, bowie knife in hand, as though he intended to kill Mallory in order to keep their presence secret.

'No need for that,' Taylor said, catching Andy's arm.

'I'm not sure I trust you enough to keep my presence secret,' Jas said. 'There are more lives at stake than mine.'

'Then listen, and maybe I'll persuade you,' said Mallory. 'Something is going on here. Since you left we have a new mage, Prestin. He refuses to have an audience with me, and a new decree came from the Imperial tent saying that all girls over the age of 15 are to be moved to the marriage tent. So far I've been able to put them off, but I have three teenagers who are approaching that age soon. I think they are too young, and Arven agreed to the 18 threshold because he knew I was right. I've not prepared them enough for an adult future. That would involve three more years of growing up ...'

'He *wouldn't* go back on that,' Jas said, casting a look over her shoulder to the group who were still invisible to Mallory.

'No. He wouldn't,' Mallory agreed. 'He's a man of honour. Which is what made your betrayal so hard to understand.'

'I'm not interested in talking about that. I have sworn to protect my friends, and I can only do that with Arven's help. You really *don't* know where he's gone?'

'I'd tell you if I did. We need him back *here*. I don't have time to explain more, but there are rumblings in the council. And Councillor Marlin's constantly spreading dissent. Your behaviour has played right into his hands.'

'Don't worry. You'll have plenty of time to tell me what's been happening. There's only one thing we can do,' Jas said. Then she turned and looked at the others. 'We take her, and the other orphans, back to the camp with us. That way she can't tell anyone we were here, and the girls in her care will be safe from premature bonding.'

'*You're not alone!*' Mallory said, and then Kale dropped the shadow from all of them and Mallory found herself face to face with the mage with whom she had once shared a kind of friendship and trust – until, that was, she had betrayed both him and Jas to Arven.

It will require an unshielded burst of magic, Kale said directly, and secretly to Jas. *But I can still make our destination untraceable with your help, Empress.*

'Do it,' Jas said.

'Do what?' Mallory asked.

Jas took Kale's hand and, with a tap of his staff and blinding flash of light, the entire tent was teleported out of Sharik and landed with a bump behind the barrier of the Earthlings' newly-formed town.

17

Kil'n stumbled into their bed chamber. He removed his armour, noisily dropping it onto the floor beside Shamila's dressing table. Then he climbed between the fresh sheets beside his wife. He was drunk. A combination of drowning his sorrows combined with the high of becoming a father.

'Have you seen **him***?' she asked.*

'Yes,' Kil'n said.

'He'll be ridiculed,' Shamila said.

'No. It just shows that we are all still evolving,' Kil'n said. 'I have found a spell to destroy the pestilent beasts ...'

'The servants told me,' said Shamila.

'We are safe here for now,' Kil'n said. 'We will not return to Earth, but move onwards, as you so wisely suggested.'

'Good.'

Shamila closed her eyes and slept. Kil'n knew she must be exhausted from the birthing of the babe and needed her rest. He lay awake beside her, thinking about the peculiarity of his son's eyes. The wine relaxed his brain, fuelled his sleep, and he drifted off, dreaming of symbols of power that could right the balance, make his son's appearance the same as everyone else's.

The next morning he found Shamila surprisingly revived. Her figure had returned to the svelte shape it had been before the pregnancy and she looked and behaved fully recovered.

'This must be a beneficial side-effect of the magic,' Kil'n said as he watched her dressing without the aid of a serving girl.

'I don't even bleed,' she said. 'It is as though I have never even been with child.'

But as Shamila glanced at her image in the mirror she made a small shocked gasp.

Kil'n leapt from the bed and hurried to her side, fearing that she had hurt herself by leaving the bed too soon.

'What is it?'

'What have you done?' she said.

'Nothing ...'

And then he saw. Shamila's eyes had also changed. They too swirled and writhed with magic that coiled around her pupils like a snake waiting to strike.

'Yours too!' she said.

Kil'n looked at himself in the mirror.

It wasn't long before they learned that they weren't the only ones affected. Everyone of the Arrak Nah Tiamen had changed. And this time, there were more changes. The women themselves no longer had nipples, but smooth pert breasts, on long-limbed, slender frames. Their skin was a golden hue that reminded them all of the desert landscape they had not long since left. All except for Shamila, who retained her alabaster skin tone and whose eyes were filled with lavender swirls, showing her talent for foreseeing the future.

'How will I feed our child?' she had worried.

But this was not a problem. When they had left, they had brought with them beasts of all kind to breed in their new land. Now the milk of one beast was taken to feed the child and for the many new births that soon followed. The Arrak people had evolved in another way. Women were no longer tied to their brood for the practicality of breast feeding. All reported rapid recovery from their birthing too, and the Arrak Nah Tiamen, though having lost one element of who they used to be, still had cause to praise Kil'n for what they had now become.

They were stronger than before. How could they object to this change?

A year passed and Kil'n's and Shamila's son, Kisha, grew strong and healthy. His size and abilities were those of a three year old child. This unusually rapid growth was seen among Kil'n's subjects also. Teenagers became adults in that year, and then their physical development halted.

'Maybe I have made us immortal?' Kil'n wondered.

'No,' Shamila said, gazing into space as one of her trances took over. 'We will live long lives. The Arrak Nah Tiamen have centuries, as opposed to humankind's mere three score and ten ...'

Kil'n listened to his wife's words. All of it was good. All of it justified everything he had done. They wouldn't live forever, but ageing would be far slower.

The flying beasts were no longer a cause for concern. Every night, when the darkness suddenly fell on the Eleventh Moon, Kil'n's magic would ignite and the light show would begin. The children watched in awe until the nights arrived when no more of the evil creatures came out of the dark to their destruction. And now that the Eleventh Moon was clean of the devils that had once plagued them, they were free to live their lives here. They could build an empire that would be greater than they had ever known.

In the back of his mind, though, Kil'n was afraid. He still recalled the night of Kisha's birth, and the strange dream he had had of the symbol of power that could change them. Sometimes, flashbacks to that dream would haunt him. He imagined climbing drunkenly from the bed and, staring at his own image in the mirror atop Shamila's dressing table, drawing a symbol of power that he could no longer remember. And not remembering the symbol also meant he had no understanding of what the side-effects were.

In view of this, Kil'n had a new phobia about using his magic. He was afraid to trust the mysterious symbols that often came into his head when he needed to resolve a problem. He feared the hidden elements of magic now. The unseen price that the Arraks must pay whenever he used it.

For this reason Kil'n encouraged the physical building of their new city. And although some of the council members questioned this, they accepted his argument that it was unhealthy for their people, strong as they were, to remain idle. Building the structures was seen as a form of physical training for their warriors, and the town sprang up strong, white, and sterile. The buildings lacked the imagination of the pyramid. They were simple, square and perfectly serviceable. They protected Kil'n's subjects from the weird sandstorms and cold weather that came up unexpectedly. Weather that Kil'n could change, but was afraid to ...

But their world was otherwise perfect. A spiritual awareness was born from the warrior training, and an untainted peace had descended over them. They were all happy. Until another pestilence hit the Arrak children.

'Emperor, I must seek your counsel,' Sulemen said as he entered the throne room.

Kil'n was surprised to see that only his advisor was in the room. Even the royal guard was absent.

'This is most unusual,' Kil'n said.

'I did not wish the guard to hear our conversation. There is a problem,' Sulemen said.

And then Sulemen told the Emperor what was happening outside of the pyramid.

'Blindness strikes as suddenly as the flying beasts once did,' Sulemen said. 'Affecting only children. One minute they see, the next the swirling motion stops. Their eyes whiten and vision is no more ...'

'I must use my power. Find a cure ...' Kil'n said.

'Thank you!' Sulemen said.

'Bring all of these children here,' Kil'n said.

Sulemen opened the great doors to the throne room and gave the order. Soon Kil'n's warriors rushed to obey, and all of the children were brought into the pyramid.

As their parents lined up with their offspring, it became apparent that the only ones suffering the affliction were those born on the Eleventh Moon. Kil'n was all too aware that Kisha had been spared this. But why?

But as the children breathed in the air in the pyramid, a miracle occurred. The whiteness in their eyes faded away. Their swirling pupils reappeared and each of them slowly regained their sight.

Within seconds the people were hailing Kil'n. But he knew he had done nothing to save them. Was it possible that the walls of the pyramid had become infused with his magic?

'Thank you, Highness,' the people praised, bowing and worshipping Kil'n as they left once more.

But as the final family departed, cries of fear went up outside. The people pushed back inside the throne room in terror. Kil'n's warriors could barely contain the panic.

'Silence!' Kil'n roared. 'What is this commotion?'

'They can't see. Outside. They can't see!' wailed one of the mothers.

It was true that the children were struck blind on leaving the pyramid, but as they returned they could all see once more. This meant that they could see only inside this space.

Rumours began to abound that this was due to the changes to their physical form. The happiness and faith in the future the Arraks had, changed quickly to fear and hatred. Maybe they had been wrong to follow their Emperor? Perhaps his magic was evil?

Kil'n was aware that fear made people dangerous.

The blind children had to stay inside the pyramid or their condition returned. This upset parents who wanted them home, but it also raised questions as to why it was happening. Kil'n had no answers to give.

'I could use magic to fix this,' said Kil'n.

'Perhaps we should wait until we know what is the cause, Highness ...' his advisors said.

'It is not the magic ...' Shamila said, entering the throne room. 'It is this place. The Eleventh Moon is poison to us.'

'But why then are we not all afflicted?' asked one of the council members.

'The newborns have never been to Earth,' said Shamila. 'They are besieged by the pestilence of this place because they do not have our previous immunities. Something that I believe, despite our changes, we originals carry within us.'

'But why are they all right inside the pyramid?' asked Sulemen.

'The pyramid came from our planet with us. It is clearly a source of protection and holds strong magic. All of the other buildings around us were made from the fabric of this land.'

The council debated this, but could find no flaw in Shamila's reasoning.

'Then we go back to Earth, as we had planned over a year ago ...' Miachi said.

Kil'n's magical eyes swirled with excitement at the thought of return. The thought of a battle that would win them back their homeland brought forth all of his resentment of those who had exiled them.

'We must not return to Earth,' Shamila said. 'There is another place for us that will resolve these issues and where magic fits better in its environment.'

But the council refused to listen to Shamila this time. There was only one future they could see and it involved going back to punish those who had rejected them. They wanted blood. They wanted revenge. They wanted desperately to go home. And no amount of logical reasoning could change this view. Therefore the die was cast again, and Kil'n and Shamila were outvoted. The Arrak Nah Tiamen would return to Earth and take back their kingdom. Only then would their future and children be safe.

18

'What have you done?' Mallory said.

With the sudden return to the oasis, Kale dropped the shield completely from the soldiers, Kat and Jas. Selene, who had been sitting silently on her bed, looking at Mallory as she appeared to be talking to no-one, now came out of her stupor and began to cry with the shock of her experience.

Kat moved into the room and picked up the small child.

'Come on. Your Mummy has been worried sick!' she said. Selene buried her head into Kat's shoulder and sobbed with relief. Then Kat nodded to Jas and took the little girl out of the room and back down the tent corridor.

'I need to see that the girls are okay,' Mallory said. Pushing past Jas and Taylor, she too hurried out into the corridor, where she was greeted by the young girls leaving their dorm rooms and the small group of older ones who had been socialising and eating in the common area.

'What's happening?' they all asked, rushing to huddle around her.

'We aren't in Sharik anymore,' Mallory explained.

'Where are we?' asked one of the older girls. 'Who are these people?'

'They are from Earth,' Mallory explained. 'They are … survivors.'

'You'll all be fine,' Jas said, and then the girl recognised her and began to chatter in Arrak dialect again as she bowed to her Empress.

'We want to go back home …' another girl said.

'Earth is …' Jas began to explain.

'Earth? No … *home*. Sharik!'

Jas looked around at the frightened girls in surprise.

'You see, they are fully integrated …' Mallory explained. 'They know nothing but Sharik now.'

'It's just as well,' said Jas. 'Earth is lost to us. But I'm afraid Sharik is also no place for you all right now. Not unless the Emperor returns soon.'

The girls were struck dumb by this announcement, and they followed Jas as she led them and Mallory out of the tent.

'It's time you met the people I brought,' she said.

Mallory blinked and looked around. The survivors had been drawn from their tents by the sudden arrival of the orphanage in the middle of the camp.

'My God!' said Andrew Petch as he came from his tent. 'Where did …?'

His eyes fell on the young woman that stood beside Mallory. She was a girl of around 14, one of the teenagers who had been socialising as Jas and the others had entered.

'Bryony?'

The girl looked over at Petch. 'Yes. That's my name. *Andrew*?'

'My god! Bryony!'

'You know her, Andrew?' said Sylvia.

'She's my sister. Taken by the Jinx.'

Bryony ran into Petch's arms, and the former pastor hugged her.

'It's a miracle! You're alive. You're here!'

'It seems Bryony is no longer an orphan,' Jas said. 'Andrew, maybe you should take you sister and be reunited?'

Bryony went willingly with Petch as the other girls gathered around Mallory. They stared out at the growing mass of survivors. Jas wondered if there were any more surviving relatives among them to take charge of the girls, but no-one else came forward, despite the obvious scrutiny of the people in the crowd.

'How many of you are there?' Mallory asked.

'About five hundred,' said Taylor. 'We haven't really counted. These are family units mostly. But a few single survivors and some more orphans too that we've been taking care of.'

'Then we must gather them all together here,' said Jas. 'Mallory … will you join us in this camp until Arven returns? Will you help the survivors learn about the Jinx?'

'But … why? I don't understand …' Mallory said.

'Because, I'm hoping we'll all eventually become part of Sharik. That human and Jinx will learn to live together.'

'The women among them would be welcome …' Mallory said. 'But Jas, you *know* what they'll do to the men …'

'Not if Arven is here …'

'But we don't know where he is …' Mallory said. 'You said so yourself.'

'Or even if he's coming back …' said Taylor.

Jas shook her head in denial of this obvious concern. In the deep recesses of her mind, this was her own secret fear. But she couldn't face it.

The front row of the survivors overheard this exchange, and soon the information that Arven was off planet spread to the rest. There were panicked cries and shouts, the first of many fears being expressed since they had arrived on Emin.

'The Jinx will kill the men, imprison our women …' someone said.

'We have to leave …' another cried.

'The Jinx leader isn't here …' yelled another.

Jas faced the crowd, but she didn't know what she could say to ease their concerns. They all had a valid point. What could she tell them that would reassure them now? She didn't know where Arven was, so what could she do?

Then the baby inside her kicked. Jas's hand flew to her stomach. She glanced down. The bump on her stomach, that she barely noticed, was now beginning to show.

She held up her hand to silence the ever-growing restlessness and panic, but the survivors were too afraid to notice she wanted to speak. She tried several times to get their attention but to no avail. Then Kale slammed his staff down on the sand and a booming noise echoed across the camp, drawing all of their attention to the front of the orphan tent.

'The Empress *will* speak ...' he said, and his voice carried everywhere. Not just to those who were outside, but to the people who had remained inside their tents. 'Speak,' he said to Jas. 'Everyone will hear you.'

Jas looked out over the eager faces, realising that each and every one of them wanted words of hope and reassurance. She was not given to public speeches. Had never had to 'rally the troops' – that was more Taylor's forté than hers. But now, as her eyes fell on the captain, she realised that even he needed to hear something that would give them back their brief peace of mind.

'I've come a long way,' Jas began, 'from the person I was five years ago when the Jinx arrived. Even then, though, I was unhappy with our world. Our way of life was killing us. We all know how it was going down ... we are just too afraid to admit it. Or maybe, because things got so bad after the Jinx, we like to remember "before" as better times. They weren't. We are deluding ourselves.'

A few cries of disagreement came from the back. But they all fell silent when Kale tapped his staff down once more.

'We *never* lived in a perfect world. But this, right now, is the best it's been for a long time,' Jas continued. 'Yes, I know you're afraid. You don't know what the future holds. But when did you ever? No-one can predict what will happen.'

'But the Emperor isn't here ...' someone in the crowd reminded her. 'How can you protect us?'

'I know that. And I'm scared too. But I also have faith that wherever Arven is, he's on an important mission. He's doing something for the good of his people. That is how he is.'

'What mission?' another voice called.

'You left him to return to Earth. How does he feel about that?' said the same male voice who had mentioned his absence.

'I should think,' said Jas, 'that he's pretty pissed at me. But when he returns – and I do have faith that he will – we'll sort out our marital discord and everything will be fine.'

'How can you be so sure? What if he wants a divorce?'

Jas peered out in the direction of the voice. There she saw Gerald Avery, and knew that the doctor was deliberately stirring the pot.

'Divorce doesn't exist in the Arrak culture. Family is everything. And, I have every reason to believe that Arven will welcome my return. He loves me in a way that I didn't understand until I experienced it. Bonding is not like our marriages, our love. It is an unconditional meeting of mind, soul and body.'

'But what happens if he doesn't return?' Gerald called. 'Surely your bonding with a dead man will mean nothing. You can't protect us without him. Can you?'

Jas glanced at Kale.

Tell them, he thought. Jas caught the telepathic link and nodded.

'He will. But if he doesn't – it won't matter. The Imperial throne is a birthright but, as Arven's consort, I will have control over the Jinx. I will make it so that you can live together.'

'How will they respect you? You can't go back right now without him there. You've just admitted that. So there's reason for you to be afraid. Without him, you'll have no control,' Gerald continued.

'Dr Avery,' Jas said. 'I've never liked you. I don't trust you. But I'm glad you're shit-stirring right now.'

Gerald fell quiet.

'And I'll tell you why. I will have control over the Jinx. Like I said, the throne is a birthright. And if Arven doesn't return, I'll be devastated, because he's my husband. But, it won't make any difference. This is because … I am carrying *his child* … the future heir to the throne. None of the Jinx could refuse my claim as the consort and mother of the future Emperor or Empress. You see, they follow their leader as though he or she were God.'

Beside her, Jas heard Mallory gasp.

'Gerald?' she whispered.

Jas glanced at Mallory, then back at Gerald. Gerald had moved forward from his heckling place at the back. He was going to challenge Jas further, but then he saw Mallory.

'Mal?' he said.

Jas looked from one to the other of them.

'You know him?' she asked Mallory.

Mallory nodded. Her eyes were wide with shock, but the expression changed from surprise and turned cold with hatred.

'Oh yes. I know him all right.'

'Mal! You're alive,' Gerald said, rushing forward.

But instead of running into his arms, Mallory backed away.

'Stay the fuck away from me,' she said.

'Mallory?' Jas said. 'Who is he to you?'

'He's my husband.'

Mallory turned away and pulled the orphan girls back inside their tent. But before she dropped the flap over the doorway she turned back to look once more at Gerald.

'Keep him away from me or by God, I swear I'll kill him.'

PART 2

The Curse

1

'What did you see?' asked Malachi as Arven came out of his trance.

The old chamber was cold and dark, but as the Emperor awoke, the torches lit and a tray of food and wine appeared on Shamila's dressing table.

'*Emperor?*' gasped Malachi.

'You're cold,' Arven said. 'I could sense it. And hungry. We must regain our strength before we leave here.'

'Leave? Then you have the answer you seek?'

Arven sighed. 'Yes. I know why we were cursed.

'Then please … tell me so that I may find a way to dispel it.'

'Eat. Elee and Prins, and you too, Malachi,' Arven said. 'There will be time enough on Emin for explanations.'

The warriors did not wait to be asked twice. They were sick with hunger and cold, but the torches were warming the chamber now, and the wine and food were welcome. They all gathered around the platter of cheeses and fruit and soft sweet cake as though it was the most magnificent feast they had ever seen.

'I have to think this all through first,' Arven said. 'This place is too corrupt for you to use your magic. Therefore we will not be able to raise a vortex here to take us home. So we must return to our point of entry, where you can once again reconnect with your magic and I will let go of this borrowed enchantment.'

'Of course! We will eat and leave immediately,' Malachi said.

'No. Your bodies are exhausted. You'll all rest, and tomorrow we'll return.'

The warriors and the mage were indeed tired, and as soon as Arven said it, they felt weary in every part of their bodies. Arven used the borrowed magic to create three extra sleeping areas and, after they had eaten, they all lay down.

Sleep came to the mage and warriors quickly. But Arven sat on the bed his ancestor had shared with his wife Shamila and thought about all that the magic had shown him. Now that he had seen what he had come to see, touching the sheets and pillows no longer induced a trance-like state.

His heart was heavy. This burden was indeed difficult to bear. Kil'n, driven by his lust for power, had used his magic to change the Arrak Nah Tiamen into what they were. They had once been *human*. Just like Jasmine and the other women from Earth. It was no coincidence then that they were compatible. But then, Arven had always known, deep down, in some indistinct inherited memory, that this was in fact the case. Earth was the Arrak Nah Tiamen's past as much as it had been their future.

He sighed.

What would Jasmine think of this?, he wondered. *She has said we are brutal. Savage. Inhumane.* So how, now, could he share this curse with his wife? And how could he wish it on his unborn child?

He glanced over at Malachi. The mage was fully asleep, and Arven knew he needed it, and so he resisted the temptation to wake him up to talk through his fears. Until he had bonded with Jasmine he had not known what fear was. Then, she had changed him – he had hoped for the better – but if the curse came to fruition, what difference would it make?

What have I done?

His mind was full of Kil'n and Shamila. He saw them both now with his and Jasmine's faces instead of their own. They may well have been reincarnated, as their ancestors once believed possible. But to what end? To make the same mistakes over and over again?

He closed his eyes, allowing that fateful moment of revelation to reform behind his eyes.

'We promised never to return,' Shamila said. 'And now you've brought a curse upon our heads that is bigger than the one your overuse of magic wrought!'

Kil'n's wife had ended up despising him. Arven couldn't bear the thought that one day Jasmine would feel like that about him too.

Thinking of Jas, his mind sought her. He had power now. At least while he remained in the pyramid. And so he searched for her in the last place he had known she would be. *Earth.*

His mind opened up, reaching out across the dimensions that filled time and space. *Jasmine …*

Then he saw … Devastation. The abominations! Vile creatures feasting on human flesh. The Trafford Centre under siege and Jas, Kale and many more humans hurrying into a vortex, which promptly vanished. Then he plummeted back into his own body with a thump.

It took him a moment to realise that he had projected himself from his body, as Jas had when she had returned to him, even though she was on

Earth. Then the reality of what he had seen began to sink in.

'No!' he gasped. *Where? Where had they gone?*

He closed his eyes and focused his mind again. He tried to follow the magic trail left by the vortex, but his untrained mind, although power-filled, was not adept at controlling the magic, or interpreting what he saw.

Jasmine and Kale were gone, and what surprised him more than anything else was that Jas had been the stabilising influence for the vortex. She was a mage in her own right. It explained how she and Kale had been able to leave Emin without the aid of another mage. But, how had this come about in the first place?

Kale must have trained her ...

Arven sat up, swung his long legs over the edge of the bed and stood. He paced the room, though quietly, for he didn't want to disturb his loyal companions when he knew how exhausted they were. He had energy, however, and the magic he had just used coursed through his veins. It was intoxicating.

He forced his mind back to Kil'n. Remembering his ancestor's mistakes steadied him. It would be foolish to cling on to this addictive power. But he could use it wisely while he had it.

Kil'n had made many mistakes that Arven was certain he wouldn't.

'We are going back to Earth. We will take back what was ours,' Kil'n said.

'Don't do this!' Shamila begged. 'I had a vision ...'

But Kil'n didn't listen. He and the warriors returned – pyramid and people, all in one go.

Arven saw the wreckage caused by that return now, behind his mind's eye. Kil'n's former home had become a bloodbath, and the Emperor had been filled with battle rage. He had killed indiscriminately, taking down the former senate and Hren, his enemy, until there was nothing left but wasteland. It was the end of the first tribe: the murder of an entire race of people.

Kil'n returned to his pyramid to find Kisha on the floor of the throne room. Shamila sat beside him, holding the small boy's hand tightly.

'I wanted to save the children!' Kil'n said. But around him the children lay dead.

It transpired that Earth's atmosphere was poisonous to the newborn, and Kisha was among those who died.

Seeing this all through Kil'n's eyes, Arven knew the guilt and pain the Emperor had felt when he realised what he had done. While his son was dying, Kil'n had been out destroying his enemies.

After the slaughter, the Emperor had looked around at the remnants of his fallen former people. The humans hadn't stood a chance against the might of the Arrak Nah Tiamen. All they had been able to do was pray to their many deities – prayers that had gone unanswered. Despite his power, Kil'n had been no god, merely a demon sent to torment them. How then could they ever have wished the humans to worship him again?

They had returned to the Eleventh Moon, leaving the survivors to pick up the pieces of their lives. There Shamila had told Kil'n the vision she had of the future.

'The only way you will ever atone for this is to give away your magic,' Shamila said. 'This power you hold is too much for one person. You must share it.'

And so the Guild of Mages was born. Kil'n's trusted advisor, Sulemen, was the first to receive the magic. When Kil'n wished it so, the power left him and sought out the worthy among them. They were named Al Kuzemen – wise men – and they were dedicated to the careful use of magic.

Laws had been put in place that Arven recognised. These things had become the Al Kuzemen code, and those wise men, like the priests that had served in the old world, had devoted themselves solely to the service of the people.

Unlike Kil'n, they could not summon up symbols in order to create, but they made thoughtful spells and rituals that could be used when needed. All of them had a focus for their power: a staff topped with a rare jewel that acted as a conduit. This prevented the mages from being seduced by the magic. For without their staff, or the right spell, they could rarely focus the energy at all.

Arven understood now, more than he ever had, where their power had come from. And as the magic continued to bubble inside him, he understood why it had needed to be fragmented and shared amongst the others. Shamila had been right. This power was too much of a weight for any one person to carry. He would be glad to return home and give the burden back to those that could handle it.

With this thought deeply embedded in his mind, Arven returned to the bed. The restlessness he was feeling abated.

His mind flew to Jas as he lay back down. His heart fluttered with anxiety about where she and Kale had ended up. He determined that on his return he would get his mages to find her. Enough was enough. She was coming home. It was time – and they would face the aftermath of the curse together.

He searched around for that place where he felt her inside of himself, a feeling that had been there since they had bonded. There was warmth growing in the pit of his stomach. There. There she was. *Alive …*

Jasmine was safe – he knew that at least. He closed his eyes and, for the first time since they had arrived on the Eleventh Moon, Arven slept.

2

The airlock opened onto the former lobby of the Beaches Hotel, and Michael Harrington was waiting on the other side. Tremaine threw aside his mask and fell into his lover's arms. They hugged and kissed. Glad finally to be able to do so without being judged. It brought tears to Kerry's eyes, and she found herself sobbing along with the two men.

The scale of all they had lost and now would have to fight to regain, and keep, hit Kerry firmly in the chest, and she fell to her knees, gasmask still clutched in her fingers.

Aware of her distress, Tremaine and Harrington let go of each other and went to her.

'Kerry?' said Tremaine.

Kerry couldn't speak. But tears leaked from her eyes as she let the men help her stand.

'Come on,' Harrington said kindly. 'Let me show you around. That'll make you feel a bit better.'

Kerry wiped her eyes with the back of her hand. She noticed she was still holding the gasmask. She held it up, bemused, not sure what to do with it.

'I'll take that,' said Tremaine.

He prised it from her fingers, bent and picked up his own discarded mask, and placed them both in a box beside the airlock door.

'Come and see the girls,' Harrington said.

He led them away from the reception to the right, and into another room that looked as though it were the former restaurant or perhaps a function room. Kerry had a sense of unreality as she took in the chintzy decor before noticing its occupants.

The P Class women were sitting at the former dining tables. Each had a drink and a bowl of food in front of her. Some were eating. Others just stared into space, while one of them picked the food out of the bowl and lined it up on the table as though she were creating a piece of art. It was as though they had just walked into an asylum ward, where all of the occupants were on lithium. Kerry stopped crying and stared. She forgot her own pain as she looked around the room. These poor creatures – God only knew what they had been through.

'I didn't expect you to get here so quickly,' Harrington said. 'Shit happened, huh?'

Tremaine nodded. 'John and Alan are dead.'

'*Jesus.*'

'John did have chance to send out the warning though. So, I expect more of us to arrive soon,' Tremaine continued.

'You'll have to fill me in,' Harrington said. 'But for now maybe you can help with the injections. I didn't have time to administer the second batch. I just bundled them into the waiting truck and got out of there. Obviously, we've been here only a few hours ourselves. I didn't even have time to allocate them rooms.'

'Yeah. That was the right thing to do. The joke is, Handley's lot still think the women are somewhere on the base. But let's hold off on the injections. I have a file in the car that tells me what they did to the girls to brainwash them. I need to read it before we give them anything else.'

'But your contact … I thought this was the right stuff …'

Tremaine pulled Harrington out of earshot of Kerry and the P Class women.

'One of them killed Alan …'

'Impossible! They aren't capable of anything other than taking instructions …'

'Not right now they aren't. But I found traces of the second injection in her. And she was tainted by the toxin. My feeling is that in this case it wasn't a cure but an accelerant of …'

'What happened?'

Tremaine shook his head. 'I don't know exactly, but she turned into one of those *things* …'

'A drone?'

Tremaine nodded. 'Then she … attacked him. He was …'

'Oh God! Alan gave her that jab to bring her round! Then he realised something wasn't right and took her back inside with him. Shit. He saved all of our lives by doing that … Can you imagine her freaking out in the back of the truck while I was driving?' He glanced back at the P Class women. 'They wouldn't have stood a chance, would they?'

'None at all.'

'Let's go and get that file,' said Harrington.

'Kerry?' Tremaine called. 'You okay if we nip outside for my bag?'

Kerry turned her face to meet his eyes.

'These poor girls,' she said. 'I'll make sure they all eat properly.'

Then Kerry sat down at the first table and picked up one of the bowls. She scooped some of the food up onto a spoon and began to feed the nearest girl as though she were a baby unable to fend for herself.

Harrington and Tremaine returned to the airlock.

'Is Kerry okay?' Harrington asked.

'Yeah. She's been through a lot. And unlike the P Class girls, she wasn't doped up through it. Hopefully when they come round they won't remember much.'

'That would be a mercy,' said Harrington. 'I'm so glad you're here, Richard … When I left, I didn't know if I was ever going to see you again.'

They embraced again. Tremaine's lips sought Harrington's and they kissed, long and passionately.

'I'll pop out and back again,' Tremaine said. 'You stay on the door.'

Harrington stroked his arm. Then squeezed his hand before reluctantly letting go. He turned and picked up one of the gasmasks out of the box by the door and passed it back to Tremaine.

Tremaine placed the mask over his face and re-entered the airlock. The door closed behind him and air rushed in. Not the filtered air from inside but the polluted outside atmosphere. Tremaine felt it sting his skin. He would need a shower after this at the very least.

Outside he glanced around. As before, the street was empty, but the vacuum of people made him feel paranoid and he rushed to the car, yanked open the back door and grabbed his holdall. Then he turned and ran back to the airlock. At that moment he heard the sound of a vehicle coming toward the building.

'Let me in,' he yelled through the intercom. The grille and door closed again behind him. The airlock flowed in purified air. Then the door opened back on the reception. Tremaine was shaking by the time he got inside.

'What's wrong?' asked Harrington.

'Army vehicles headed our way!'

Harrington returned to the intercom, examining the screen to see who had arrived.

'Jesus, Rick! You're jumpy. It's friendly! *It's our guys*! Looks like they made it out all together!'

Tremaine came to the viewer. He saw all familiar faces exiting from the trucks.

'Thank Christ! Sorry. I am jumpy …'

'Go check on the girls,' Harrington said. 'I'll get them all inside. Then we're going to have to hide the vehicles.'

'Why?' asked Tremaine.

'Because Handley and James will send out scouts. Maybe even a helicopter or two, once they realise they have soldiers going AWOL. And they *will* notice.'

Tremaine went back to the dining room and saw that Kerry had worked her way around half of the room. The thirty girls seemed to be coming around a little. He didn't know what to do about the injections. A source had told him they would help bring them round. Now he wasn't so sure that source was reliable.

He found himself a quiet corner and an empty table and sat down.

Opening the bag he extracted the file on the P Class conditioning, and began to read.

'Hey!' Harrington said as the last of the soldiers, some with wives and children, passed through the airlock. 'Great to have you guys here!'

He directed them all into the hotel's former bar and noted that not all of them had managed to get away. They would do a roll-call later to see who was missing. Maybe more would follow, but they had no way of knowing if the others had tried and failed to get out. He hoped that they had just decided not to take the risk … Anyone caught might be tortured and could reveal their location. But Harrington didn't want to worry about that for now. All he wanted to think about was now, and this feeling of freedom – long may it last.

'This is a fully-stocked bar,' yelled one of the wives.

'Help yourself,' Harrington said. 'You all deserve it, especially today! Though we will have to ration food and drink.'

The fifth columnists and their families had been doing that for the past few years anyway. During the time they had been planning escape the hotel had been secured. Then the air filtration system had been installed. Shutters had been added to the inside – blocking all of the windows, making everything airtight. All this had been done as the soldiers had surreptitiously stolen the equipment they needed. It was just as well that there were engineers among them.

Once they were sure no-one could get into the hotel, the fifth columnists had begun to donate drink rations as well as non-perishable foodstuffs for the larder. The kitchen was as full as possible and the hotel had become their escape bunker. They would be fine here for some time; but they would still have to be careful. Hopefully they would fall off Handley's radar, and the atmosphere outside might improve once the military rounded up their drones and stopped pumping that shit out into the air. Then they would really be able to think about the future.

'Can't believe we finally did it …' said Jack Garrity. 'You gonna join us for a drink?'

'Not yet. Another vehicle just arrived outside …'

Harrington went back to the viewer, and there he saw another familiar face. This one was Enoch Parry. He was one of the newest fifth columnist recruits. But he had someone with him that Harrington didn't recognise.

'Hey Jack!'

'Yeah?'

'You know this guy?'

Jack peered into the viewer, 'Yeah. Enoch.'

'No, the other one.'

'Shit! That's Donovan. Haven't seen him for years. He was part of Taylor Arch's team.'

'Yeah. I remember him now. Wasn't he ... one of the Trafford Centre prisoners?'

'Yeah,' said Mack. 'Let 'em in.'

Harrington pressed the release button and the airlock opened on the other side. He and Mack waited for Enoch and Donovan to pass through.

Donovan was in handcuffs as they came out of the airlock. Enoch removed his mask and undid the manacles. Donovan had been beaten by Handley's thugs, and had a black eye, bloody nose and split lip.

'Where am I?' Donovan asked, confused. 'Is this James's base?'

'No, and count yourself lucky it was me assigned to take you there,' Enoch said.

'What's going on?'

'You've been rescued, mate,' said Jack. 'We've all flown the MD59 nest.'

It was then that Donovan learnt about the fifth columnists, and despite his injuries, he began to feel better than he had in days.

3

'I'm not going to ask you about him. But if you want to talk, I'm willing to listen,' Jas said.

Mallory was sitting on a stool in the orphanage common room as Jas followed her into the tent.

'He's an evil man,' Mallory said.

'I don't doubt it …'

Mallory looked at her sharply. 'What's he done to you?'

'Water under the bridge, but clearly not as much as he did to you. And I suspect to other women in this camp. That's another story … But they felt they needed him since he's the only doctor we have.'

'Are my girls safe here?' Mallory asked. 'If not I'd rather we were returned to Sharik.'

'You're safe. No-one will come near you. These people value life, Mallory. They've seen enough death. And, all any of them want is to be free of fear. When you feel that way you don't bring pain and suffering to others.'

Mallory burst into tears. Something Jas didn't expect, as she had always found Mallory to be composed – serene even.

'I've been happy here,' she said. 'I don't want anything to spoil it. But there's corruption in the council now. And I'm afraid again. Afraid for the girls. Afraid what will happen. My life was shit on Earth, even before the Jinx. *He*. That *thing* out there …'

She cried again. Sobbed into her hands. Jas put her hand on Mallory's shoulder and sank down beside her.

'You don't need to revisit it …' she said.

'But I have to. It's all come flooding back. He was a good doctor. *I thought*. The villagers loved him. I loved him. But then … he changed. He became this person I didn't recognise … I think it started when we learnt we couldn't have kids. *I* was the problem. And he never let me forget it. I suggested adoption, but he shunned the idea. Then … the Jinx came and Gerald … he got worse. Started acting weird. Loved the power he had over the village. He was the only one who could care for the sick. But one by one, raid by raid, we lost everyone. The men were killed. Women taken.'

Jas nodded. She remembered those times.

'Gerald was our saviour ...'

Mallory paused. Then she explained how Gerald had used that power. How he had manipulated them all. Drugging her, assaulting the other women while they were also drugged. And all because of some awful power trip.

'He'd lost his mind. I'm sure of it. Maybe he felt weak and that was the only way he could feel strong again. I'd never realised what a sociopath he was. How nepotistic his behaviour had become. Even before ... All those traits were there, they just became more obvious once there was no law. No rules to make him behave. He just became who he really was because he no longer had to hide it.'

'What did you do once you found out what was happening?' Jas asked.

'I had to save the women he was hurting. I tackled him. He threatened to kill us all. He was *insane*. And so, we handed ourselves over to the Jinx. It seemed the lesser of the two evils.'

'Oh my God,' Jas said. She glanced at the tent door, remembering her own sacrifice for Andy. She had gone with the Jinx to save the boy's life. It had been the only thing she could do too. 'I guess you and I are more similar than you think.'

Mallory rubbed the tears away from her eyes.

They talked for a long time, and an hour or two later Jas went to the tent door and raised the flap.

'Stay here. You need to feel safe here. I can't allow any other scenario.'

Most of the other survivors had been dispersed by Taylor and his men, back to their individual tents. They had to establish some normality to the camp again as soon as possible, for everyone's sake.

She saw Taylor talking to Harvey as the last of the survivors went about their business.

'Taylor,' Jas called. 'I want you to arrest Dr Avery. Kale will help you secure him ...'

Taylor looked at Jas in confusion.

'*What?*'

'You!' Jas said, stopping one of the other soldiers. 'Find Doc Avery and arrest him.'

The soldier was unused to taking orders from Jas and didn't react immediately. He just stared at her blankly as though she were speaking a language he didn't understand.

'Get Doc Avery!' Taylor said, realising that Jas wouldn't have made such a demand without reason. 'Bring him to see me. Now!'

The soldier ran off in the direction of the doctor's tent. But soon returned.

'He's not there,' he reported.

'Then find him. And quick,' Taylor said.

They searched the camp from corner to corner, but by then it was too late. Gerald had vanished.

'I want security on the orphanage,' Jas said. 'Mallory and the girls are to be protected at all times.'

'What the hell has he done?' asked Harvey.

'What I always suspected him of … but worse,' said Jas.

Taylor pulled his most trusted men together and told them.

'Andy, I want you and Marshall to be on the first duty. You're to watch over the orphanage. No-one goes in there without my permission or unless Mallory is happy to welcome them. The rest of you … we need to find Avery. He's done some terrible stuff. Some of it we knew he was capable of, but we thought we needed him. He's not to be trusted and I don't want him anywhere near that tent. Or alone with any women on the camp. Is that clear?'

'What do we tell people if they ask? There were questions when we were searching …'

'Nothing at this point. Except that we just want him for questioning. He has to be hiding out here somewhere. Only a lunatic would go through the barrier and leave this camp,' Taylor said.

'Don't expect him to be rational,' Jas said. 'He's dangerous. And no matter how plausible he seems, don't be taken in.'

The soldiers saluted in uncharacteristic formality and went to renew their search.

'Empress?' Kale said coming to Jas's side.

'You haven't found him?'

'No.'

'Then he must have crossed the barrier …'

'No-one could survive that desert on foot. It would be suicide. Where is he going to go?' said Taylor.

'If you're right, we won't have to lock Avery up. He'll be dead and no longer our problem,' Jas said.

'But what if he isn't? What if he reaches one of the towns?' Taylor said.

'Without our protection … they'll kill him,' Jas shrugged. *Good riddance.* 'I need to go and talk to Caroline about Avery too,' Jas said.

'You think he did something to her too?' Taylor said.

'Yes. She insisted he not be left alone with her when Sylvia asked him to administer a sedative. And you need to speak to Dawn …'

Taylor blinked twice but didn't answer immediately.

'I've been suspicious of him ever since she demanded he stay away from her and Lucy,' he said. 'I've asked what was wrong but she wouldn't tell me. Perhaps you …'

'You know she won't tell me anything,' Jas said. 'She hates me. She wanted to kill me. I think it best she and I stay out of each other's hair.'

'Maybe you're right,' Taylor said. 'And perhaps she'll tell me now. When I go back and explain what happened with Mallory.'

Jas nodded. 'Worth a try. It will be good for her to address it. First step to putting it behind her.'

Jas left Taylor then and, heading to Caroline's tent, she found that Kat was still there, and so was Sylvia.

As Jas entered the tent, Caroline came out from behind the bed curtains. She threw her arms around Jas and hugged her.

'Thank you! You have no idea what you've done for us.'

'Is Selene okay?'

'Sleeping. Her little adventure has worn her out. I think there was a lesson learnt today for both of us. I can't let Donovan's loss make me neglect the children …'

Jas hugged Caroline back. 'You're a good mother. This wasn't your fault.'

'Thank you. But it is hard to forgive myself for this …'

'I need to ask you something …' Jas said. 'Kat, Sylvia … perhaps …'

'We'll go,' said Sylvia. 'You all need your rest anyway.'

The women hugged Caroline and left.

'Sit down,' Caroline said. 'What is it?'

'Gerald Avery …'

'Oh.'

'I'm sure Kat told you all about the rescue?'

'Yes.'

'Mallory, who was taking care of her, was married to Gerald. Before the Jinx …'

Jas told her Mallory's story.

'Oh,' said Caroline again.

'When Taylor found you. You and Dawn and the other women … Where were you before Prestwich?'

Caroline thought for a moment. Then she said, 'Over the last few days the memories have been returning. Gerald Avery was working with the military. He was part of a group of doctors who were *conditioning* us.'

Then Caroline told Jas the awful tale of her capture and the brutal hypnosis that she and Dawn had been put through.

'We were both put out in the field to attract other women that were hiding themselves. The plan was always to have them taken into one of the bases. But then, Taylor's soldiers answered our call and found us. We went with the flow as we had been conditioned to do. I remember arriving at the Trafford Centre, seeing Gerald and knowing he'd been placed inside your camp to keep an eye on Taylor's men. James and Handley didn't see them as a threat, but they certainly didn't trust them either.

'When he could get us alone, Gerald gave us new orders. He fed us the drugs that made us forget what we were.'

'What were you?' Jas asked.

'Sleepers, I guess ... Ready to be activated when the military wanted to use us.'

'So you were spies in the camp too? As well as Avery?'

'Yes. But Dawn and I didn't know. We met our men, fell in love. Had our kids. We didn't *know*! Can you imagine that? Living a life like that? Completely with this other personality inside you?'

'So how did you start to get your memory back?'

'Somehow I missed a dose of the meds. At the same time, so did Dawn. We both began to remember what they'd done. It was like a nightmare but we were living it awake. Handley, James and even Avery. They used us ... in every way. Once I was clear of the drugs I began to avoid him. By then, you were there and Gerald was edgy. His days were numbered and I guess he knew it.'

'Listen. I want you to be careful. Avery has gone missing. We think he's left the camp, and if so – his days are indeed numbered. Either he'll die out there alone or the Jinx will kill him if they find him. I doubt they'll wait long enough to even ask questions. But be alert at all times. Just in case.'

'I will,' said Caroline. 'And if that bastard has the nerve to come here, I'll kill him myself.'

'Okay. But just to be on the safe side I'm going to get a guard detail assigned here.'

Once she was sure that Mallory and Caroline were being protected, Jas met up with Kale and they returned to their tent. Julia was waiting for them and was proving to be quite domesticated, because she had food prepared.

'You two must be exhausted,' she said.

'Where did this come from?' Jas asked, pointing to the small dining table off to one side of the sitting area.

'I asked Kale to make it. I like to sit at a table when I eat, and frankly I don't think sitting cross-legged on the floor is good for you in your condition. Talking of which, I heard your speech ...'

Jas sat at the table and Kale joined her.

'There wasn't any choice. It's the only thing I could think of to use to reassure them,' Jas said. 'I hope it worked.'

'Well, it was going to become pretty obvious soon anyway. Just look at that bump. You wouldn't have been able to hide it much longer.'

Julia placed a bowl of stew down in front of them both. Then she fetched one for herself and sat down next to Kale.

'We caught some chickens today,' Julia said. 'So it's a change from the fish.'

'Chickens? We have chickens?' Jas said, surprised.

'Well, not *exactly*, but it's the closest thing to them I've seen. They are birdlike, make a weird clucking noise and can't fly. So, I'm *calling* them that,' Julie said. 'Hopefully they'll lay eggs too ...'

Jas smiled at this. And why not? The animal, whatever it was, had to have a name, so why not 'chicken'?

They were both hungry, not having eaten much, what with the search and rescue of Selene, let alone the stress of Mallory's and Caroline's revelation and, of course, Gerald's disappearance. All of which they told Julia about now.

The food was delicious. It didn't taste exactly like chicken but the texture was similar. Perhaps a little more gamey than the chicken they were used to, but Jas enjoyed every bite, and the stew was thick with Emin vegetables. Rich, fulfilling and tasty.

'This is nice,' Julia said when they had finished their recount of the day.

'Nice?' said Kale, surprised. 'It's been a most unpleasant day.'

'Not the day's events. *This*. Us sitting here talking. Like a real family,' Julia said. Then she reached out and took Kale's hand. They looked at each other, and became quiet. Lost in the moment.

'I'm tired,' said Jas, taking the hint. 'I need to slow down a bit. This baby thing is starting to have an impact ... Night, you two.'

Jas smiled when their mumbled goodnights didn't distract her two friends from each other's company.

She got up from the table and went to her curtained cubicle. As she turned to close the curtain around the bed she saw Julia lean over the table and kiss Kale's lips. The mage froze in confusion, then he stood, pulled Julia up and took her in his arms. They kissed again.

This isn't a Jinx thing, Jas thought. *It's all happening the human way. Boy meets girl and they fall ... Wow.*

Jas dropped the curtain back down, giving Kale and Julia complete privacy. As was the way with their magical partitions, Jas could hear nothing now from the room outside.

She removed her clothing and climbed into the bed in her underclothes, regretting briefly that she had taken her leave so suddenly. Now she couldn't go out again and go into the pool, to clean off the grime of the day. But she hadn't lied. She was tired – emotionally as well as physically. Almost losing Selene had caused her tremendous stress, even though she always had to appear strong to the group. But seeing Mallory again, and learning about Avery's sordid past, had not helped at all.

She turned on her side and the baby protested, kicking her hard in the ribs.

'Ouch! Little blighter!' she said. 'I think I have a warrior in there. Just don't put your armour on until you come out, okay?'

Jas stopped talking as she realised this was the first time she had ever spoken to the child. For the most part she had tried to ignore the pregnancy. Being a mother wasn't something she had really wanted. Plus she had been so wrapped up with everything else happening around her – survival always being top of their priority list – that she hadn't really had time to think about it.

Now she pushed back the covers and stared at the small bulge in her usually flat stomach. How far on was she? She had no idea. But she thought that it had to be four or even five months now.

What was it Mallory had told her of Jinx/human pregnancies … *They normally take longer*. Almost a year, wasn't it? She couldn't remember. But certainly the growth was slower in the womb, but quicker out … or was she getting confused with something else? A story, or a dream she had once had …?

Jas drifted off to sleep.

She thought she heard music. The strange disjointed sounds of a gramophone – not unlike those she had heard coming from the tent of the couple they had seen in Sharik. Yes, that *had* been an old gramophone, she was sure of it … Glenn Miller …

4

Arven could hear music as he began to wake from a deep dreamless sleep. He felt the tug of the bond and jerked. Jasmine … he could *see* Jas … She was in bed, sleeping. He hung onto the vision: she was lying with the sheets pushed back. His ethereal eyes examined her face. How beautiful she was in sleep! Her hair had grown since he had last seen her, and now it flowed around her shoulders like a black shawl. She moved; her hand absently stroked her abdomen. He saw then the signs of their child growing. And much faster than normal for the Jinx babe in the womb. All of this he knew, because the magic gave him insight. Just as he had felt the exact moment when he had impregnated her.

Now he could almost see inside her … There … an anomaly again! He looked closer. It was true! Not *one*, but *two* children.

This was not something a Jinx female had ever done. Arven wondered what it meant as he drifted in his half sleep closer to Jas now than he had been in some time. Two babies.

He heard movement but tried to stay in the place between their two worlds.

'*Emperor?*'

He snuggled back down in the bed, refusing to be disturbed. He wanted to remain with her. If he woke she would be gone.

'*Highness?*'

A hand touched his shoulder and shook him gently.

'We must leave,' Malachi said.

Arven opened his eyes. Jas slipped away, far from his grasp. The vision of her faded too quickly as reality returned. He was angry at being disturbed, and then … he let that anger dissipate.

He sat up quickly, rubbed the sleep from his eyes and looked at Malachi, Elee and Prins as they waited, eager to leave.

'Yes. We need to get going,' said Arven.

He drew a symbol in the air and summoned up breakfast for the men, and a full flask of water each.

'We'll eat on the move,' Arven said.

'But how do we leave here?' Malachi asked.

'That is no problem now,' said Arven.

He drew another symbol, and the torches lit. Taking their provisions, the four of them followed the path of light back to the throne room, where the doors stood open to the outside world.

As they drew closer to the exit, Arven paused. He ran his fingers over the mechanism. He felt a surge of energy that made his heart race as it swooped up through his hand, into his arm and then over the whole of his body. Was this the last time he would feel magic coursing through him?

When they crossed the threshold, the pyramid closed up behind them. They stood for a moment in the reception area before stepping out into the barren desert. It was still murky outside, and Arven knew that it never really got light on the Eleventh Moon, because the sun it once orbited had long since burnt out – soon after the Arraks had abandoned this planet. It had been decaying ever since.

Arven expected a loss of the power as he crossed the threshold, but felt no difference as they began their climb back up the edge of the sand dune.

As they reached the pinnacle, a spark ignited in Malachi's staff. Arven nodded at the mage: this was the point where his power would drain, then, and Malachi's return. All was as it should be: he felt no regret.

Once they were out of the shelter of the pyramid the sand whipped up around them. The four Arrak men walked side by side and, head down to ward off the wind, pushed ahead. It was hard going and they knew their journey would take many hours. Their legs ached as they moved on through the soft sand.

As they reached the bottom of the dune, having effectively walked over the pyramid peak, there was a crack of thunder from the sky. Malachi and Arven turned, and there they saw the pyramid-dune collapse down into the surface of the planet.

'What's happening?' called Arven above the noise.

'I think,' said Malachi, 'it had been waiting only for you. You gained the knowledge you needed. The magic is gone. The planet is finally able to break the structure down.'

They watched the pyramid and white buildings dissolve into sand before turning away. Their journey would now be much harder but they had no choice but to carry on: the pyramid and the town no longer offered shelter of any sort.

Some hours later they reached their arrival location, though it was difficult to recognise as such, and all other parts of the planet looked the same. Awash with the charred sand, it was barren and desolate. Malachi stopped. He looked around, trying to find that spark of magic that would lie in the precise point of their entrance. A storm was brewing again on the planet and they would soon be caught in it. He had to raise the vortex and get them out of there as soon as possible.

Malachi tapped his staff down three times and then channelled his mind, reaching out to Taenan, who had been his anchor back on Emin. But Taenan didn't respond to his call.

Malachi tapped the staff again. A spark came from the gem. His magic was working, but for some reason he couldn't get through. It was as though Taenan and Emin didn't exist.

'What's the matter?' asked Arven.

'I can't open the vortex without Taenan,' Malachi said. He explained what was happening. 'There's a void. As though Emin is being cloaked. We're cut off.'

'Maybe your power hasn't fully returned?' Arven said.

'It seems in order. I'm just …' he tapped his staff down again on the ground, 'being blocked …'

'Blocked? By whom?'

Malachi shook his head.

The storm began. Malachi tapped his staff down once and a tent rose from the planet's surface. The four Arrak men gathered inside and were immediately protected from the pummelling of the sand. This time Malachi's power had also given them chairs to sit in.

'We'll wait the storm out and try again,' said Malachi. 'It could be the weather that is interfering. You see, I am at full strength once more. Far away from the pyramid.'

Arven sat down and opened his flask. The water inside was cool and clean, and he drank some to swill the sand from his throat.

'We must be patient,' he said. He opened up the parcel he had of food and they shared it around. The food was good, fresh and fulfilling. It made them all feel stronger and calmer. They had waited this long that another hour or so would make little difference, and soon all of them would be sleeping once more in their own beds.

'At least we won't starve while Malachi is able to raise such good provisions,' Arven said.

'These were your provisions, Highness,' said Prins, 'and we thank you for them.'

The storm ended just as abruptly as it had begun, and none too soon, as the men were beginning to get restless.

'Time to try again,' Arven said.

They left the tent in place and, after doing a small location spell, Malachi found the point of entrance once more. This time he didn't just channel the energy to his staff, but he stood directly on the place in order to amplify the enchantment. He sent out his call once more. There was a flare of recognition but the magic was pushed back down again.

Malachi tapped the staff harder. His concentration was now focused on Emin. He called to Taenan, saw the mage as though he stood before him. Taenan turned, hearing the call, and then Malachi felt a huge surge of power slamming into his staff. The rush of energy ran up his arm and flooded his body. Malachi's staff burst into flames and flew from his hands.

The mage fell to the ground.

Arven rushed to his side. Malachi was severely injured. His skin was blackened, as though the power was so hot it had burnt him from the inside out.

'Malachi!' Arven said.

'A traitor ...' murmured the mage.

'Heal yourself ...' Arven said. 'Quickly ...'

'Too late ... Emperor ... Listen ... your life ... your child ... *danger.*'

'Rest until you've healed,' Arven said. 'Prins, pass me his staff.'

The warrior ran to retrieve Malachi's staff. He brought the charred and damaged stick and handed it to Malachi. Arven pressed the staff into his hand. 'Heal ...' he said again. But the staff didn't spark.

'Let's get him into the tent,' Arven said.

Elee and Prins lifted Malachi, but by the time they got him inside, the Al Kuzemen mage was dead.

'What can we do, Highness?' Elee asked.

'Lay him down here. Rest the staff across his chest,' Arven said.

Arven watched the men carefully lay Malachi down on the floor as he had commanded. Then he collapsed back into one of the chairs. He was in shock but didn't wish Elee and Prins to see his fear. The fact was, without Malachi they couldn't leave the Eleventh Moon. Furthermore, without the mage's magic, they would soon run out of provisions.

The pyramid was gone, and so too was the borrowed magic that Arven himself had been able to use there. With no way back, and no way to leave, he could see no scenario that could enable them to escape.

Which meant only one thing: they were doomed.

5

'We found this *human* in the desert,' Elidon said as two of his warriors dragged Gerald Avery inside the Emperor's tent.

Marlin was sitting on a plush ottoman with a table of fruit and a chalice of wine before him. Since Prestin had told Marlin of the Emperor's failed attempt to return, the councillor was feeling more secure. He had blatantly taken up residence in Arven's tent and was administering justice as though he were already in possession of the throne.

'I'm surprised you didn't kill him already,' said Marlin.

'I thought he might know something,' Elidon said. 'After the orphan tent vanished, and we found that strange little girl … But that Mallory told my men she was already one of her orphans. She obviously lied. A trait of human females, it seems.'

'Get one of the human women who can speak our language in here to translate,' said Marlin.

A few minutes later Elizabeth was brought in. She was only young, just turned 18, and newly bonded to one of Elidon's warriors. She had been on Emin for three years though and spoke fluent Jinx as well as English.

'I can only help if he's English …' she said in the Arrak tongue to Marlin. Then, addressing Gerald: 'Where did you come from?'

Gerald was terrified and didn't answer. Then Elidon kicked him, and the doctor began to blubber gibberish.

Elizabeth folded her arms across her chest. She didn't like to see the brutality that Elidon dished out, nor did she like his friendship with her husband, Reylin – who was always kind to her. She had put the history of her arrival in Sharik behind her. She didn't want to think about the world before, and how she had been snatched from her home and brought here. Even so, she had been happy ever since. Acceptance wasn't such a bad thing when you had met and married the one person who was always meant for you.

Although she had seen the murderous side of the Jinx, it was always calm in Sharik. Elizabeth felt safe. Safer than she ever had at home. There was no rape or murder to speak of, though there had been some crimes recently. But Elizabeth knew that was just men being men. And the ones who weren't lucky enough to have a wife yet were sometimes agitated. It was understandable once you knew what it was that they were missing by not being bonded. But yes, she was safe here, or so she had believed, until recently.

Elizabeth had seen that change since Elidon and Marlin had arrived at Sharik. The two of them swanned around town as if they owned the place. She didn't care for either of them, and was thankful that Elidon hadn't bonded with her. She recalled him being there, in the tent, his arrogant head held high as though he were the one rejecting her, not that the magic saw them as a bad match. It had been her and ten men, so the odds were stacked that one of them would be her soul mate – as she liked to think of it, since she was of a romantic disposition. Fortunately that had turned out to be Reylin.

Elidon shook Gerald, bringing Elizabeth's mind back to the present.

'Hey! Stop that!' she said. 'Or I won't help you. You'll get nothing from him if he's scared half to death.'

Elidon raised his arm as though to strike Elizabeth for daring to speak to him. The girl stepped back in shock. No-one had ever threatened to hit her before. Not here! Not in Sharik!

'Elidon!' Marlin said. 'Leave us …'

Elidon glared at Marlin, then left the tent.

'Come, my dear,' said Marlin. 'You need to persuade this human to tell us what he knows. I'll let you into a little secret, my dear. The Emperor is missing. This man may have information regarding his whereabouts.'

'Oh no! You think he hurt the Emperor?' Elizabeth said. She worshipped Arven, as all of his subjects did.

'Who knows?' Marlin said. 'But we must find out, mustn't we?'

Elizabeth kneeled down beside Gerald and began to talk to him slowly.

'Don't worry. I won't let them hurt you. Can you tell me your name?'

'Ger … ald.'

'Good. Now. Where did you come from?'

'Earth. In a vortex.' Elizabeth relayed this to Marlin.

'Who brought him?' said Marlin.

'Kale and the Empress,' came the answer.

'Where are they now?' Marlin wanted to know.

'A camp in the desert,' Elizabeth said. Then added, 'Isn't that *wonderful*? That the Empress has returned?'

'Ask him where the camp is. To give its *precise* location …'

'He doesn't know. He was walking for miles until he was found,' Elizabeth explained.

'Then he's useless to us. Call Elidon back in. We'll have him executed.'

Elizabeth was appalled by Marlin's words but had no power to stop them from doing precisely that. Marlin was so cold. So calculating. She could see this awful energy around him and knew instinctively he didn't care about the lives of others.

Elidon came in with another warrior. They began to drag Gerald away.

'Help me!' begged Gerald, realising that this was the end.

Elizabeth was horrified by his rough treatment and didn't know what to say to prevent the inevitable.

Then she heard what Gerald was saying.

'*Wait*! He says he has important information.'

'What?' asked Marlin.

'Your Empress ... Jasmine ... is pregnant,' said Gerald. 'And if you want her back, then you'd better keep me alive. She is sure to come looking for me ...'

'A royal baby!' said Elizabeth. 'What wonderful news!'

'Silence!' Marlin said, cutting off the girl. 'You may leave us. But should I hear that you have revealed anything of what you have learned today then there will be consequences ...'

'Not even to my husband?' she asked.

'I'll kill him if you do,' Marlin said. His voice was mild, and this made the threat all the more sinister.

Elizabeth felt cold. She believed he would do it, and probably kill her as well. She saw that swirl of darkness around Marlin again. He was evil. She just knew it.

'I won't say anything. To anyone,' she promised, really afraid for herself and Reylin now.

Elizabeth was sent away, but she was trembling with shock and fear. Who could she turn to but her husband Reylin at a time when she was afraid? But she loved Reylin and would not risk his life, which meant she would have to keep this fear, and Marlin's secrets, to herself, no matter what.

As Elizabeth walked away from the Emperor's tent, she began to feel agitated. Angry. She had been promised safety in Sharik, so long as she forgot her old life. And she had been willing to do so. But this Marlin was a bully – which went against everything she had been led to believe about the way the Arrak lived. He had an attitude that didn't fit in with the loyalty and respect that others of their race had for the Earth women. And why had he taken up residence in the Emperor's tent? Surely that was not permitted?

Elizabeth returned to her tent, head buzzing with information. The need for secrecy and nagging suspicions rattled around inside her head. She was fanciful by nature, she knew that, but there was something very wrong now in Sharik, and Marlin and Elidon were at the centre of it.

Fortunately Reylin was out on some patrol that Elidon had sent him on, so there would be no questions about her absence. It wouldn't be difficult to avoid saying anything at all about the incident. She wondered if Reylin had been chosen deliberately for this task in order to get him out of the way.

Under normal circumstances, Elizabeth would have wanted to tell Reylin everything that had happened. Especially Elidon's move to strike her ... *Why is he such an evil dick anyway?* she wondered. She didn't know. She was certain, though, that Reylin wouldn't like it if he knew.

There should be laws about that sort of thing in Sharik, she thought. If there were, though, no-one had ever told her of them. Violence toward women wasn't something that generally occurred here, at least not that she had ever heard of. Consequently there might be no adequate punishment in place to fit the crime.

Elizabeth paced around their small tent until her legs ached. They didn't have much, as Reylin was a lowly warrior. It would mean years of working hard before they would qualify for something better. When they had children they would be given more room. But Elizabeth did like the small open-plan layout. At one end of the tent was the living space, the other the sleeping space, with those discreet curtains that ran all around the four-poster bed. Beds had to be large, though, to accommodate the Arrak stature, and Elizabeth found theirs comfortable.

Unable to think or worry anymore, Elizabeth decided to retire. She went first to the poolroom and stripped off her clothing. But as she entered the water, the flap between the bathroom and the living area opened. She turned, expecting to see Reylin returned, and was ready to welcome him into the water with her. Instead she saw Elidon standing in the doorway.

She covered her breasts quickly with her arms.

'What are you doing here?' she said.

'Councillor Marlin wishes you to return ...' Elidon said.

'Why?'

'He wishes to speak with you. About what you heard ...'

Elizabeth's heart began to pound in her chest with anxiety. What did this mean? Was Marlin going to make sure she was silent ... forever.

'I need to dress ... Please go away.'

Elidon remained where he was. He leered at her, in the way men from Earth might have, but she had never seen a Jinx behave this way before. It made her feel sick and vulnerable.

'Get *out*,' she said. 'Or I'll report your behaviour to my husband.'

Elidon laughed, backed out of the room, and dropped the curtain back down.

Elizabeth took a deep breath to steady her nerves. Then she hurried from the pool and pulled on her clothing as quickly as possible. She didn't want Elidon to change his mind and return before she was fully dressed.

When she entered the living area of the tent, Elidon was lounging in her husband's chair with his back to their bed. His position in the room made her feel doubly uncomfortable and afraid. There was very little space between the chair and the bed, so she had to pass in front of him in order to leave the tent. Taking another deep breath, Elizabeth tried to ignore Elidon as she hurried toward the door, but as she passed, the warrior reached out with his long arms and grabbed her. Pulled her onto his knee.

'Get off me!' she said in English. 'You arrogant dick!'

Elidon's hands were all over her.

'Stop it!'

As his hand touched her breast, Elizabeth lost her temper and slapped his face. Shocked, Elidon pushed her to the ground. He stood up, knocking the chair aside, and then delivered a stunning backhand blow across her face.

Blood burst from Elizabeth's nose. Her head snapped back and her skull cracked hard against one of the beams of her four-poster bed. For a moment Elizabeth knew what it meant to 'see stars', and then, mercifully, she blacked out.

6

'I tell you I *felt* him,' said Jas. 'I was asleep and then I dreamt that he came to me.'

'Like you travelled to him when we were on Earth?' Kale asked.

'Not the same … I *really* came back. He wasn't physically here. More *spiritually*. Like a ghost. But not dead.'

'That would mean the Emperor had entered the astral plane. Leaving his body while his spirit came to you. It isn't *possible*,' Kale explained. 'Only a mage could do that, and not all of us are adept at it. The Emperor has never shown any ability in that area. It's not his calling.'

'Then what was it? What did I feel?' Jas said.

'It might have been a dream. Maybe you summoned him to you? You are showing a great many abilities. Did this dream tell you where he is?'

'No.'

'Then there is nothing we can do,' Kale said.

'I feel like all we do is wait,' said Jas. 'I need to *do* something.'

'I understand that feeling,' said Julia. 'Try to keep calm though. It's not good for the baby.'

'I must go and check the barrier,' Kale said. 'I'll be back soon.'

Julia smiled at him. There was a moment of awkwardness when they stood next to each other and Julia waited, as though expecting a wifely kiss goodbye, while Kale, knowing nothing of this convention, merely looked at her.

'See you *soon*, then,' she said finally, and turned away to pour a hot cordial into a clay cup.

When Kale had gone, Julia looked up to see Jas smiling at her.

'What?' she said innocently.

'Did somebody *get some* last night? Only enquiring minds want to know …'

Julia blushed.

'We kissed a bit …' she admitted. 'It's a little awkward and new.'

'Then boy have you got a treat in store for you …' Jas grinned.

Julia's blush deepened.

'Believe me, I'm just commenting because I'm jealous. I can't wait for Arven's return for more reasons than just him saving us.'

Julia giggled at this revelation. 'I take it … he's *good* in that department?'

Jas laughed. 'Just wait. Just wait.'

Julia picked up the clay mug and sipped the cordial. 'Nice – like camomile or something,' she said to hide her embarrassment.

'I'm sorry. Didn't mean to tease,' said Jas. 'I'm happy for you both.'

Then she hugged Julia.

'I'm just going for a walk. I want to check on Pastor Petch and his sister Bryony. If only we could reunite everyone with a family member.'

When Jas was gone Julia began to have doubts about what she had started with Kale. Surely all she had been through at MD59 was enough to put her off men for life? It was odd how, since she had arrived on Emin, none of that seemed to matter anymore. It was a lifetime away and she felt at home here. As though she knew Emin, and had always lived there. One thing was for certain, she was finding it easy to adapt to this new life. But then anything was better than her previous incarceration, wasn't it? Now she was free … or the potential to be so was there.

She put down her empty mug and went to the tent door. Picking up the flap she looked outside at the camp – or town, as she was now beginning to think of it. The place was bustling, and the noise from outside came in only when the flap was open. Peculiar how that worked – but right too. Although she wasn't adept in any way, Julia was beginning to understand and appreciate magic more all the time. She wondered how they could have lived without it for so long. Wouldn't the Earth have been an amazing place if they had lived as simply as they did now? No conspiracies, no murder or rape and no people like Handley. Plus – no hunger or thirst?

She saw a group of children playing in a park that Kale had made, summoned from the memory of one of the parents. A little girl was being pushed by her mother on the swing. A small boy climbed up the slide and slid down, arms up in the air with excitement. There was a roundabout, and a teenage girl was spinning it for two little boys who clung onto its centre. There was a see-saw also, currently unused. Good old-fashioned play in a protected environment.

Safe.

Seeing the children made Julia think of those babies forced on her at the base, and then cruelly taken away as soon as they were born. Five of them. One for every year she had been in MD59. What was happening to them now? What were they called? Were they boys or girls? She hoped boys – the thought of what became of girls on Earth was too much for her to bear.

The momentary flash of memory brought back her melancholy and doubts. How could she begin a relationship with Kale with all of this bad stuff in her heart and mind? She was a mother to five children she would never see. Could she move on from that and start again? Could she even have a child with Kale? Tremaine had said she *shouldn't* have any more. Her body had been through too much already.

But then, that was before Kale had 'healed' her, wasn't it?

Since then, the caesarean scar had completely disappeared. There wasn't even a silver scar line to remind her of the trauma her body had suffered. She was fresh and strong now that she no longer had to breathe in the poisonous Earth atmosphere. But the damage wasn't only to her body – there was a lot of harm done to her mind during those years. That was the part of her that really needed time, not magic, to heal.

Her mind fell back to Jas's teasing about sex with Kale. She was curious about 'bonding'. From what Jas had said, you didn't choose your partner, the magic chose for you. What if she and Kale entered this *marriage tent* and it didn't happen? What then? Plus, Kale was a virgin: Jas had all but told her that in her explanations of how the Al Kuzemen don't marry and are committed solely to their work. She wasn't sure how the whole 'sex-with-an-alien thing' would really go, or if she would be brave enough when the time came. Could Kale have sex without bonding? Julia knew she could, and thought perhaps they should try before commitment. But then, that was the old way of life, wasn't it. And Emin and the Arrak Nah Tiamen lifestyle were the new, even if monogamy did feel old fashioned.

'Juleeaa,' Kale said.

Julia turned to see Kale in the doorway of their tent.

'We need to talk …' she said.

'Do we?' said Kale.

'It's not an easy situation …'

'What isn't?' Kale said.

Julia found herself smiling at him. *Maybe Jinx men aren't that different from human ones after all*, she thought. Either Kale was deliberately playing dumb or he was oblivious to their new, complicated status. And if it was the latter, what did it mean? Had she read too much into the kiss? Did it mean nothing at all to Kale?

'I liked our … kissing,' he said, taking her by surprise. 'But I *am* confused. Al Kuzemen are not supposed to … *feel* … like this.'

'I know,' she said.

Kale took a step toward her, and Julie found herself embraced again.

'We're alone right now,' she said. 'Want to try it again?'

They kissed some more, and the blood ran up into Julia's cheeks as well as into all of her erogenous zones. Her nipples tingled as she pressed against Kale's chest, and a surge of almost uncontrollable lust rushed into her loins.

What was happening? She had never felt so turned on.

Kale pulled back first. Julia wouldn't have been capable. 'I want you ...' he said.

'It's mutual,' Julia pressed her lips on his until he couldn't help but respond.

She didn't want to stop kissing him. She opened her mouth, but when Kale's tongue didn't explore her, she pushed her own small tongue between his lips and raked the inside of his mouth. She pressed her whole body against him then, and feeling the pressure of his cock against her stomach, knew that he too was experiencing this overwhelming attraction.

Julia's hand ran over his chest and down his stomach, then because she couldn't resist the temptation, lightly over the bulge in Kale's robe. So the Jinx weren't *just* tall ...

Kale groaned against her mouth as she stroked him through his clothing. 'Juleeaa ...'

All her earlier doubts flew away in the heat of the moment. Who knew what the future would hold? Spontaneity was not something either of them had ever been good at. But life had tested and changed them both.

'I'm ready ...' she said. 'I'm not afraid. What about you ...?'

Kale pulled out of their kiss once more and explored Julia's face with his gorgeous eyes. For once they weren't swirling and she could see that they were a warm brown. She thought it must mean that his sex drive was suppressing the magic: he looked at her with a wholly human and very male expression.

Julia was breathing heavily. She felt powerful in her seduction. Kale needed guiding, and this made her brave enough to take the lead. She was the one with experience, after all. She stepped backwards, taking Kale's hand, and drew him over to her own bed cubicle.

'It's been a while,' she said. 'But I haven't forgotten how.'

She led Kale to the bed, and pressed him down until he was sitting on the edge. Then she drew the curtains around them.

She began to unbutton Kale's robe, then stopped as she noticed him floundering. He had a deep frown on his brow and his hands were clasped together in his lap as though he were trying to hide that he was trembling.

'How about, you take a look at what's under my clothes first?' she suggested.

Kale nodded, and his eyes grew round as she stepped back from the bed. She was wearing the Jinx clothing that Kale had created for her with his magic, and now the top and pantaloons fell to the floor. What remained was a short camisole and boxer style briefs in white cotton.

Julia took Kale's hand and placed it on one of her small pert breasts.

'Just so you know, I enjoy having my nipples stroked. Like this.'

She dropped the strap of the camisole from one shoulder, and pulled it down so that Kale could see the curve of her breast and the erect nipple.

'That's happening because I feel … *aroused*,' she said. 'Being with you excites and pleases me.'

She began to peel off Kale's robe and he didn't resist, even though he had probably never been in this situation before. As his Al Kuzemen robe fell away, Julia was momentarily surprised to find the smooth, nippleless chest beneath. The Jinx mage was surprisingly hairless too. He wore Arabic style pants underneath the robe, held together with a drawstring. Julia untied it and then pulled the trousers down.

Kale glanced down at his own erection, and appeared confused. Julia felt sure he must know that this would happen if he was stirred up, but his behaviour suggested he had never been hard before; that he didn't know what an erection was; only that it was pleasurable. Had he ever masturbated?

He was big, but not monstrous. *Thank god!* And Julia was not overwhelmed as she feared she might have been had he been bigger still. Blood rushed down to her sex as she observed him. She went down onto her knees and looked up at him, before taking the swollen head of his cock into her mouth.

Kale groaned, and a pained and fear-filled expression crossed his features at the touch of her wet mouth. She ran her lips and tongue over him with excruciating slowness.

'No …' he gasped. 'We shouldn't …'

Julia let him go from her mouth and stood up, realising this might be too much too soon. He wasn't an ordinary man, after all, and he had never indulged this side of himself before.

'Let's hold each other,' she suggested. 'Lie back on the bed and I'll lie down with you.'

Kale did as he was told. Julia could barely believe he was being so compliant. But she could also feel his fear and insecurity. He was out of his depth for the first time in his life. She didn't ask those questions she had asked herself earlier, she just wanted to go with the moment and *feel*. She lay down beside Kale and wrapped her arm around him, resting her head on his chest.

'How's that?' she asked.

'Nice,' he said.

They lay together for a while until Kale moved and said, 'I want to touch you …'

'Okay.'

Julia lay on her back and Kale rolled onto his side, head supported by his arm. His eyes ran over her body, then his free hand followed. He explored her breasts, observing how they reacted to his touch. It pleased and fascinated him. His hand ran over her flat stomach. He explored her navel with some absorption, before going lower.

'Yes, there …' Julia murmured. She opened her legs slightly as Kale's hand moved toward her sex.

As his fingers lightly touched her, she moved again to help him find the right place. His finger brushed against her clitoris and Julia groaned, her hips moved against him. Curious of her reaction, Kale moved closer. He was aware of how engorged his own penis was feeling. Just the mere touch of it against her hip brought shivers to his spine. And it was all because of this beautiful place between her legs. Yes, this was the centre of everything.

'Please, Kale … Come to me,' Julia shuddered.

Kale looked into her eyes and she knew that even though he had never made love, he was a fast learner. She parted her legs, opening to him as he lay over her, instinctively holding his own weight off her small body.

Kale positioned himself between her legs. Julia felt his cock brush against her and shuddered again. Then she reached her hand between them and guided the head into place.

'Kiss me,' he said. 'I like it very much.'

And although he dwarfed her, Julia tilted her head and found his lips. Then she wrapped her legs around his hips and pushed upwards as Kale lowered his body.

He entered her to the shock of them both. Half buried inside her, Kale found his cock surrounded by the hottest, most exciting sensation. He paused half thrust.

'Oh g … od,' Julia gasped.

She moved her hips back and re-thrust, encouraging Kale to move again by pressing her hands on his buttocks. This time he hit all the way home.

'Again,' Julia said. 'Keep doing that …'

Kale thrust into her again, harder this time.

Julia moaned, 'Oh! Yes Kale!'

But instruction was no longer necessary as lust was coursing through Kale's veins and the sensation he was feeling brought a pounding to his chest that he had never experienced before. He matched its pace to the thrusts and soon Julia was crying out beneath him, thrashing, her face contorted in the most striking expression of sheer and raw pleasure.

She almost swooned for a moment and Kale stopped moving, fearing he had hurt her.

'Don't stop,' she gasped. 'I came … an orgasm … *Christ* you'll understand soon if you *just don't stop* …'

He began to move again, drumming into her until she was crying and gasping and swearing under her breath as she came again. Kale realised how much he enjoyed seeing her reaction and how it heightened his pleasure. He watched her face as she writhed against him and then he felt something build inside him. There was a delicious emotion that was focused not just in his penis but also in the pit of his stomach, and with each thrust Kale began to understand that he was heading toward what Julia called an 'orgasm'.

A cry erupted from his lips as something spurted from his cock on a final thrust that brought him crashing against Julia's cervix.

Then Julia learnt what Jas had been hinting at. Something came from Kale. A pod – Julia knew it was that – and it burrowed into her womb, bringing with it the most exquisite pleasure she had ever felt. She screamed at the top of her lungs, body jerking and twisting against Kale as she came hard again with greater intensity.

'Ohmigodohmigod …'

Kale collapsed over her, ecstasy altering his face as he spasmed inside her until they both lay gasping.

When he had recovered he propped himself up on his elbows, looking down at her with wonder. His cock was still swollen and inside her, but that intense itch that he hadn't known at first how to scratch was satisfied for the moment.

'I love you,' Julia said. Then she bit her lip. How stupid to blurt that out just because of great sex.

But something altered between them, and Julia noticed that Kale's skin was glowing with a golden hue.

'You're glowing,' she said. 'What does that mean?'

'So are you,' Kale said. 'It means … We've bonded.'

'Bonded?' Julia said.

'Yes. In human terms, you are now my wife …'

'But how?'

'Because we are meant to be together …' Kale said, but it was clear that he was just as surprised as she was. 'And love, real love, is what I feel for you also.'

Julia quelled the rush of tearful emotion that threatened to overwhelm her. She swallowed, then took a deep breath and forced a smile back onto her lips.

'Well,' she said, using her usual bravado to take back her self-control. 'Would you like to "bond" with me again? After all, that amazing thing between your legs isn't going down …'

7

'Bring me the Earth man,' said Prestin.

As Marlin gave the order, a warrior scurried away to fetch Gerald. A short time later the doctor was brought in. 'Sit down,' Prestin told him.

Gerald took a seat in a chair facing Prestin. He was trembling with fear, but somewhat reassured by the thought that they must need him or they would surely have killed him already. He was being well looked after, and so, even as a captive, he was clean and well-fed.

'You speak English?' Gerald said.

'I have cast a spell so that we may communicate,' Prestin explained. 'And I am hoping to get more information from you about the Empress. You see, we would like to have her returned … *safe and sound.*'

Gerald's eyes narrowed. There was something about the way the Jinx mage talked about Jas that made him suspicious of his motives. But the doctor didn't care. That bitch would get whatever was coming to her anyway. Gerald knew what he would like to do to her, given the chance. Though he thought that very unlikely.

'I'll help if I can …' Gerald said, 'If you promise me I'll be safe in your town. I'm a medical doctor; I may be of some help to you.'

Prestin laughed. 'We have no need of your science here. But yes, Councillor Marlin assures me that if you cooperate, we can come to some arrangement for you continued … *safety.*' Prestin did not add, *If not, then you will be put to death.* But the threat hung in the air like a punctuation mark.

'All right,' said Gerald, growing in confidence, because he knew he would tell them anything to ensure his own future. He had no loyalty to Jas or the survivors; they had all been a means to an end to him. He had entered the vortex and travelled with them only because he'd been dragged along with the crowd. All he wanted to do was return to Earth and to James's base, where he would take up his rightful place.

'How can I help?' he said.

'I need to look into your mind,' said Prestin.

'Look into my … I don't think …'

Prestin's eyes met Gerald's. The mage's swirling pupils quickened. A searing pain started up between Gerald's eyes. He tried to fight it but the pain grew worse. He fell forward off the chair onto his knees before Prestin. The mage reached out and lifted Gerald's face with one large hand, and as their eyes met once more, the Al Kuzemen's magic burrowed into his brain.

There was no escaping the eyes as they twisted and turned and writhed, as though he was looking into a pit of venomous snakes. A warm wet patch of piss stained the front of Gerald's trousers as his mind was invaded by Prestin. He tried to hide, tried to block the mage from seeing into the darkness of his soul, but Prestin tore him open with no finesse. Then the Al Kuzemen plundered Gerald's mind, taking every scrap of information he wanted.

Prestin recognised the woman Mallory in the forefront of Gerald's memories. He saw the doctor administering drugs to women in his care, and then doing vile, unspeakable things to them. He ripped through these hideous memories, searching for the one thing he needed now, but his Al Kuzemen magic absorbed everything that was inside the doctor's head. Even his science, his lack of belief, his total, callous disregard for the women of the planet, and last of all his dealings with the military there ...

It seared Prestin's mind. He had never seen such horrors as this man had committed in the name of ... what? Greed. Lust. Obsession.

He pushed and pulled and tore this filth all aside nonetheless.

When Prestin finished there wasn't much left of Gerald. The Al Kuzemen had given him no place to hide inside himself. Without his natural ability to suppress all conscience, Gerald was forced to face his sins. They moved in a loop to the forefront of his memory, over and over, never ending. It was a perpetual hell inside his own skull, for Prestin had taken away all of the sick pleasure that Gerald had gained in those moments. Now all he saw was his own pitch black soul against the suffering of the innocent juxtaposed with the violation he had suffered at the hands of the mage.

He whimpered and cried, cowering with an overwhelming feeling of desecration from the way his mind had been raped.

Prestin could have fixed all of this, but when he saw *what* Gerald *was*, he considered it a fitting state to leave this disgusting man in. Even though Prestin's own slate was far from clean, Gerald revolted him. The things this human had done to others of his kind – to women ... It was unimaginable. And those images would remain with the Al Kuzemen for as long as he lived. In some ways it justified all that he was doing in the name of saving the Arrak people: at least his men were not like *that*.

Gerald was unable to stand, so the warriors dragged him away, back to the tent he was being held in. The Jinx had no prison, but Prestin had put a ward around the small tent to prevent Gerald leaving and to stop Kale from finding him in Sharik.

'What did you learn?' Marlin said, entering after Gerald had been removed.

'Some very interesting information,' Prestin said. 'This man knows of many other females still alive on Earth. In some place that his brain calls a "base". There are 60 bases. But he didn't know the locations of them all, just some.'

'That *is* useful. What about the Empress?'

'She arrived with around 500 other humans. They are in a hidden town in the desert, a few miles from the oasis just outside of Sharik. I have the location in my mind and can take you there. But, the place is protected by Kale.'

'I'll gather the warriors. We'll attack tonight when they least expect it. Elidon will lead them.

'Yes, councillor,' said Prestin.

Elizabeth woke. Elidon was gone. She was alone and lying on the floor where she had fallen. She had no idea how long she had been there, but the arm under her body was tingling with pins and needles, which suggested she had been unconscious for some time. She wondered why Elidon had just left her there for Reylin to find.

Elizabeth struggled into a sitting position. She rubbed her arm to restore the circulation. It hurt a lot, and cramp shot up her forearm and into her shoulder. It was so painful that her stomach roiled with sickness and her head ached. She was bruised and dizzy, and as she tried to stand, a wave of nausea threatened to overwhelm her. She sank back down, swallowing bile, and waited while the feeling abated. Then she pulled herself up off the floor using the bedpost as a hoist. She held onto the post for a moment until she steadied and then staggered to her small dressing-table, where she sank down onto the stool. Her face was distorted and blurred. As though she were looking into a pool of moving water and not glass. She realised this was because her body was swaying in rhythm to the dizzy spell. It was like being seasick, except she knew she was on land. She forced herself to be still. She saw the damage then. She was deathly pale, and dried blood smeared her nose and mouth. She touched her nose gingerly and discovered that although it was bloody and swollen, it didn't feel broken. She was badly bruised though, and one of her eyes was swelling and was certain to blacken.

Her head hurt the most. Elizabeth raised her hand and felt along the back of her skull. There was blood in her hair from where she had cracked her head against the hard wood. But, as with her nose, the wound had stopped bleeding and didn't appear to be very serious. Even so, she was sure she had concussion.

I'm lucky to be alive, she thought. The blow could have killed her. *But then I've always been quick to heal.*

On the dresser were a wash bowl and jug, and Elizabeth poured some of the tepid water into the bowl. Immediately the water warmed. She dropped her wash cloth into it, then squeezed out the excess before wiping her face, washing away the blood.

She could see the injuries better now. Her nose was puffy, filled still with congealed blood, and her eye was already bruising. She would heal, it was just contusion and discolouration, but there was no way the injuries would disappear before Reylin returned.

Elizabeth couldn't keep this incident a secret from him. And – she didn't want to.

The problem was, if she said anything to Reylin, Marlin would have them both killed.

I need to go to Mallory, Elizabeth thought. *She'll know what to do. And she has the ear of the Emperor.*

But then she remembered what she had overheard. Mallory and the orphanage were gone. Vanished into thin air the night before. The Emperor was gone too, and Marlin was in his tent – *He's running things now!*

Elizabeth found her way back to the bed and sat down on the edge. Her stomach was still rolling, illness induced by fear as well as the trauma she had experienced at Elidon's hands. The man was a brute. She began to tremble, feeling cold and scared. So she pulled one of the covers off the bed and wrapped it around her shoulders. She remembered some advice about not going to sleep if you have concussion, so she didn't lie down for fear that it would be a bad thing.

Elizabeth looked around her little tent, no longer loving it but hating all she saw. This was not how her life was supposed to be. She had been promised security, happiness. She didn't feel happy, she had been violated, and her home was no longer safe when a warrior could just walk inside and abuse her.

A drop of fluid fell onto the back of her hand where it lay on her lap. Elizabeth looked down. Only then did she grasp that she was crying. The realisation surprised her, but once the tears came she couldn't stop the flow. Maybe it was shock, or maybe it was because she couldn't shake the replay of Elidon's hand as it swung towards her, juxtaposed with a memory from the day she was taken brutally from Earth and her two brothers and father were killed in the process. Both images kept looping around in her mind, as though they were one and the same thing. She saw herself falling back in slow motion, heard the loud crack as her head connected with the bedpost, and then recalled the blinding blaze of pain. But that was nothing to the feeling of loss she experienced now with the memory of her dead family. And little Georgie ... oh God! How had she forgotten Georgie?

A flash of memory showed her the four-year-old boy being sliced in half at the waist by a Jinx sword. In her mind's eye, she saw Elidon's face hidden behind his helmet and face shield.

Elizabeth shook her head; she was trying to dispel the memory but succeeded only in giving herself more of a headache.

Before that day she had hated and feared the Jinx … so how had she so easily forgotten what they had done afterwards? How had she merely settled for this? Her lack of loyalty to her family had led her here, she knew that. She had never let herself grieve for them, had she? Fear had prevented it … but fear of what?

For the first time, Elizabeth cried for her dead siblings. George and Jake … poor little boys who had never done anyone any harm. It didn't matter that they had once been annoying, as brothers were. They had been hers, and no-one but God had had the right to end them.

Elizabeth cried harder. The tears fell until she had nothing left. And then her thoughts drained away. What remained was a cold emotionless void. A state that made her see her life far differently than she had just a few hours earlier. She told herself that she didn't love Sharik. She didn't love Reylin. *They* had brainwashed her with their pitiful romance. She despised them all now. Especially the warriors, one of whom she had married. *Him* she despised the most for it was his companions who were responsible for the destruction of Earth and her brothers. She would see them dead, all of them, if she had her way, and the only way to end Elidon – that hateful murderer – was to tell Reylin what he had done.

Maybe they would kill each other … then she would be free.

It wasn't long before Reylin returned.

Elizabeth was waiting in the dark, still sitting on the edge of the bed, when she heard him enter. He would be tired from his patrol, but Elizabeth knew he would want her all the same. He *always* wanted her. The thought of their coupling sickened her now, but Jinx magic bound them to each other more fiercely than any human marriage could. She heard him stumble around, though, as though he were trying not to wake her this time. She leaned over to the side of the bed and lit the lamp, illuminating the tent.

'I thought you slept,' Reylin said.

She saw him approaching and her heart missed a beat. Yes, she enjoyed looking at him. But was this love or just Jinx magic that she had been happy to accept as love? The emotions made her feel confused again and not as certain as she had been that she wanted revenge. Maybe she *did* love Reylin.

'What *happened?*' Reylin said when she raised her head, pushing aside the hair that hid the damage Elidon had done.

She didn't speak for a minute, and then the tale poured out. The way she had been called to translate. Her treatment by Elidon. The threat to Reylin's own life if she told him.

Elizabeth watched the range of emotions cross Reylin's face, none of them being fear for his own safety: all of them showing rage at her mistreatment. One minute she was elated by his concern, the next she was cold to his feelings. Her mind went back and forth as though it were caged in her own skull. *But ultimately,* an inner voice said, *nothing matters beyond revenge.*

'I'll kill him!' Reylin said.

'He's your superior, isn't he?' Elizabeth said.

'It doesn't matter. This is not our way. We do not beat women.'

'Elidon was jealous of you,' she said. 'He *wanted* me. In the way that only you do.'

'Then I'll end him, for the good of all women,' Reylin said.

He removed his sword from the scabbard that hung at his waist.

Elizabeth felt a small thrill then. Reylin would avenge her. Elidon *must* die. He was right, it was the only thing he could do. Yes, Reylin did love her if he would risk all for her honour!

'Kill him,' she said. 'Kill him for *me.*'

She remembered reading stories of men taking vengeance to protect the reputation of their women and saw Reylin as her knight in shining armour. A fitting image as he still wore his Jinx armour and sword. Yes, he would kill Elidon and thus prove himself to her.

'But no,' Reylin said, throwing down his sword as sanity returned. 'We must bide our time. If what you say is true, and the Emperor is not on Emin ... then I am powerless. Marlin is vying for control. He would kill me and you'd be left alone and unprotected.'

Elizabeth gasped at this instant about-turn.

'You coward!' she cried. 'You'd wait for the Emperor to do your dirty work? Elidon hurt me! He attacked me! He wanted to *rape* me ... Then he left me unconscious on the floor. I could have died. Doesn't that mean anything to you?'

'Of course it does. But we must be wise ...' said Reylin. 'Elidon has friends in high places. You know this ...'

'No. You don't love me. It's all a lie. We humans are nothing to men like Elidon. We are just a means to repopulate your land.'

'That's not true! You know how I feel about you. And if I could I would cut him to pieces right now.

'Then do it or stay away from me.'

Reylin sighed, 'What are you talking about? We are bonded. You cannot resist me, nor I you. We are forever.'

Elizabeth stood up from the bed and turned her back on Reylin.

'I want nothing more to do with you.'

She pulled the blanket tighter around herself. *She would leave here and return to the shelter of the marriage tent. That would teach Reylin not to stand up for her.*

She walked past him to the door of their tent, intent on leaving, but as she opened the flap she found herself face to face with Elidon.

Elidon blinked. He was surprised to find her at the door. Or maybe he had thought he *had* killed her? Elizabeth saw all of this pass over his face before his expression froze and his emotions closed down.

'Where's Reylin?' said Elidon, as though nothing had happened.

Elizabeth stared at him.

'Did you hear me, woman? Get your husband, he's needed.'

Elizabeth backed off, terrified.

'Reylin!' she cried. 'He's there. At our door. *Help me!*'

Reylin heard the distress in her voice and picked up his sword from the rug where he had discarded it. A red rage came down over his eyes. He couldn't bear to see Elizabeth's fear or feel the sting of her anger. And there was his enemy before him. Yes, he would protect his wife at all costs. No-one must ever hurt her again.

Reylin rushed at the door, sword raised, shocking Elidon, who had not expected Reylin ever to stand up to him.

Elidon had no time to draw his sword before Reylin's razor-sharp blade smashed down on his shoulder, cutting through flesh and bone all the way through the side of his body until it lodged deep into his pelvis.

Elidon pulled back, staggering away from the tent. Blood bubbled up into his mouth and splashed down the breastplate of his armour. Reylin held onto his sword as Elidon fell backwards, and the weapon came free as though it had merely passed through water. A pool of blood streamed out into the sand around the warrior as he fell to the ground. Reylin raised his sword again. Elidon raised his arms to cover his face. Then Reylin brought the blade down hard on Elidon's throat. In one blow the sword sliced through Elidon's neck, severing his head from his body.

The impact sent Elidon's head rolling, and it came to rest at the door of Elizabeth's and Reylin's home.

Then and only then did Elizabeth realise the enormity of what Reylin had done. He had killed another of his kind in what would appear to be cold blood. Would the courts of Sharik even consider Elidon's own bad behaviour before they condemned her husband to death?

Elizabeth looked into the dead cold eyes of Elidon and screamed.

Others came running then, and there was no place to hide for the young couple as their neighbours examined Elizabeth's injuries and heard her horrific story.

'What is going on here?' said Councillor Marlin, pushing through the gathering crowd.

'Elidon attacked Elizabeth,' said one of the Earth women. 'You promised us safety!'

'Reylin was right to kill him,' said the woman's Jinx husband. 'I'd kill anyone who hurt my wife.'

Marlin glared at Reylin. He was angry, but he was playing the long game. He wanted the support of the warriors and the mages, and that meant also the happiness and safety of the men's wives.

'Amnesty of course is granted to Reylin,' he said. 'I would not be doing my job as a leader of this community without saying that Elidon's behaviour was unacceptable.'

Appeased, the crowd quietened down, and some of the warriors took Elidon's body away.

'I don't feel safe,' said Elizabeth. 'I cannot feel safe until my home is secure.'

'What can we do?' said Marlin.

'A spell,' said Elizabeth. 'To make it possible to block our door from those we do not wish to invite inside. Even the mage who creates the spell. These are our homes, we should be able to lock our doors and feel secure inside.'

The other women took up their agreement with this request, wanting the spell to be on all homes from now on. Marlin was backed into a corner that he couldn't get out of without agreeing. He didn't like the idea. It meant that he or his warriors could be barred entry at will. This could be a problem if his coup were to be a success.

'I'll ask Al Kuzemen Prestin to arrange it,' he said. 'Now, please, return to your homes. There's been enough upset for one night.'

8

Following Elidon's death Marlin was unable to order the immediate attack on the Earth camp. The warrior's body was burnt the next day in the standard Arrak burial ritual. However he was not given the honours that accompanied a normal warrior funeral; a detail that pleased the masses, but not Elidon's former colleagues.

Later some of the men drank to him, but the crime Elidon had committed gave pause for thought even to his former friends and the warriors who had ridden with him.

'Elidon only did what some of us have wanted to do,' said one of the warriors, an Arrak called Baulin; he had been Elidon's right hand and the closest to him. He disliked the lack of honours at the funeral, but had taken the promotion offered by Marlin. He now filled the role of Head Warrior in Marlin's private army. Reylin had been transferred out of the group because of the general hostility the others felt toward him now. *Besides,* Baulin thought, *he has never really been one of us.*

'We have to bide our time, my friends,' Marlin had told the men in a private meeting. 'We need to seize control in such a way that it will not be questioned.'

'We'll avenge Elidon,' Baulin said. 'When the time is right, just as Marlin said.'

'But he shouldn't have attacked someone's wife,' another warrior said. 'That's not our way, whatever else happens.'

There were general mumblings of agreement among the men, and Baulin realised he had to win them over to his way of thinking, or the mission Marlin wanted them for would fail.

'Reylin wasn't one of us as soon as he bonded with that human ...' Baulin said. 'Elidon knew that the women were inferior. He only went into the marriage tent to prove his point. He told me that harridan had thrown herself at him. He hit her because she wouldn't accept "no".'

This story was untrue – Elidon had not spoken to Baulin or anyone else about the attack – but the lie fell with ease from Baulin's lips. He had seen

Elidon do this form of manipulation many times and had learnt from it.

The men mumbled again. Some believed, others didn't – not all of them had liked Elidon, but they had known him well: he had thrived on the raids on Earth, enjoying the bloodshed. It had been he who had grumbled the most at the lack of women. Elidon had thought the women inferior, that much was true, but he would have been happy if one had fallen his way in the marriage tent. But no matter, Baulin talked Elidon up and soon they were remembering the fun of the raids, his strong leadership and the many drunken post-victory celebrations. Elidon had been good in that way – always an Arrak's man.

'We have a mission,' Baulin finally said. Then he paused and waited while the men crowded around him. 'The Empress is back on the planet. Marlin says she is hiding in the desert and we need to bring her back. Prestin has given me the location. It'll be cloaked, but we need to trust what he says.'

'Why hasn't she returned to Sharik?' one of the warriors asked.

'Who knows what goes on in the mind of the Earth women,' Baulin sneered. 'She didn't return alone. There are others with her. Among them plenty of other females …'

Despite his derogatory comments about the Earth women earlier, Baulin knew what impact this information would have on the warriors. All of whom were single.

'Maybe the Empress went to fetch us more females …' one of the warriors commented.

'Well, whatever the reason, this is a fresh influx. And Marlin says we'd all get first chance as a reward. A mass marriage, like in the old days. Bonding is almost guaranteed.'

'When are we going?' said one of the warriors at the back.

'Tomorrow morning, before dawn,' said Baulin. 'But we need to be discreet. No-one must know we have the Empress.'

The men absorbed this information, and Baulin was surprised that none queried the need for secrecy. Of course, Baulin did not add the other part of this plan, that Marlin intended to keep Jas captive until he could play his hand. When the councillor revealed the demise of Arven to the council, Baulin would be there to enforce Marlin's coup, and what happened to the Empress after that was not his, or his men's, concern.

Jas woke from a strange dream. She thought she had heard Arven's voice. He was calling to her from a great distance, asking for her help. The words were unclear, and as she roused, they slipped further and further from her comprehension.

The baby was kicking again and she was uncomfortable.

She climbed out of bed and pulled on a robe over her long chemise night gown. Then she drew back her curtain from around the bed and glanced out into the sitting area. It was hard to tell what time it was inside the tent, because no natural daylight leaked in, but as Jas looked around she noted that Kale's bed had not been slept in. She glanced over at Julia's cubicle, noted the firmly drawn drapes, and smiled. So they were finally together. She was pleased.

Julia would be embarrassed later and Jas intended to tease her – but only a little.

But first, she wanted to speak to Kale about her weird dream. Every night for the past few days she had been getting visions of Arven, all in the shape of dreams. Although they were hard to read, the echo of this last one wouldn't leave her, Even so, she didn't want to disturb Kale and Julia. What she had to talk to him about could always wait.

In the living area she poured herself some water from a carafe on the table. Then sipped. Thanks to Kale's magic the water was always cold and the carafe self-refilling. She looked back at Julia's cubicle once more. Even if they were awake she could hear no sound of it through the curtains. Patience wasn't one of Jas's virtues. When would be a decent time to disturb them?

She went to the tent door and looked outside. Dawn was still a way off but she could see a glimmer of the first Emin sun on the horizon.

Pulling her robe tighter around herself Jas left the tent. She was so restless that it made sense for her to take a walk and rid herself of this excess energy. Then, when she returned, hopefully Julia and Kale would be up and about.

As was becoming her habit, she followed the barrier perimeter, checking in with each of the night watch guards. The men and women on watch were tired, and Jas knew they couldn't wait until morning.

'Not long now,' she said to encourage one yawning woman as she passed by her post.

The next post she came to was being manned by Andrew Petch. The former Pastor looked less tired than the previous sentinel, and he smiled and waved as he saw Jas.

'How are you, Andrew?' she asked

'Ready to call it a night soon,' he said. 'But happy. The last few days have been unbelievable. I'm so thrilled to have found Bryony.'

'Me too. I only wish we could reunite more of our people.'

'All it takes is faith,' Petch said.

'I thought you had stepped away from your former beliefs,' Jas said.

'I had. But this has gone a long way to restoring my conviction. You see, I think it was no accident that you came back to us, and then saved our lives.'

'You know, Andrew, I hope you're right. If you are, it means someone divine *is* looking out for us. I like that thought, and we need all the help we can get.'

'I'll pray for that,' Petch said. 'I'm planning to start a Sunday sermon again.'

'I'm glad,' said Jas. 'I like calling you "Pastor". Give Bryony my best. I'll call in to see her again later.'

The ground beneath their feet began to shift, and the soft grass of the oasis split, spitting up sand through the cracks.

'Earthquake?' Petch asked.

'Can't be,' Jas said.

They looked around, and then across the barrier out to the desert.

'I don't like the look of this. I'll go and fetch Kale,' Jas said.

But as she turned to head back toward her tent, a vortex opened up before her. The ground tore open, Jas stumbled, and then she found herself face to face with several Arrak warriors.

With Prestin's aid, Baulin and his warriors left just before dawn. Without knowing it, Gerald had revealed the guard change-over times, and Prestin knew this was when the humans were at their weakest: the night shift was tired, the day shift still drowsy. They also knew exactly where the Empress slept.

'Kill Kale,' said Marlin. 'That will leave them defenceless. Then, once we've taken the Empress, we can go back and take the rest of the women at leisure.'

Baulin nodded, but he had given some of his men instruction to capture as many women as they could this time around. He would personally take care of Jas.

Shielding the warriors from other mages, Prestin led them into the vortex.

This close to the Sharik, Prestin hadn't thought he needed to call in the help of another mage to stabilise the void. If Kale could take this leap unaided, so could he. But as the portal opened inside the camp, he found himself struggling to keep it steady. He was not as good a mage as he thought he was, and it angered him to realise that Kale would have been easily able to do this.

'I can't hold it for long,' said Prestin, regretting his vanity.

'Then we'll have to be quick,' said Baulin.

At that moment the vortex opened on the camp, and Baulin couldn't believe his luck. There was the Empress, as though she had been waiting for him to come for her. He wasted no time: he leapt from the void and caught hold of her. But Pastor Andrew Petch wasn't willing to let Jas be taken so easily. He drew the sword that Kale had given him and swung it hard at

Baulin. The first swing missed, but carried by his own momentum, he swung again. The sharp edge was forged so that it could cut through Arrak armour, and now the blade connected with Baulin's arm, slicing the warrior's hand clean off at the wrist. The hand clung to Jas for a second and then fell to the floor.

But Baulin was a hardy warrior, and he grabbed Jas with his uninjured hand, pulling her back toward the void.

'No!' shouted Petch.

By then the noise and disturbance of the vortex had drawn the attention of the other sentries, who were heading their way. Several men had run from their tents wielding swords.

The few Jinx warriors, expecting an easy victory, were outnumbered. Baulin saw that capturing other women would be impossible at this point. He focused on his mission, bundling Jas into the vortex, despite the fact that she fought and kicked with the strength of a man.

Baulin threw Jas down into the centre of the vortex, then turned to see the foolish Petch entering in an attempt to rescue her.

Aggrieved by the loss of his hand, Baulin barked one order that his men rushed to obey. 'Kill him.'

A sword swirled above Jas's head. She tried to stand, but Baulin was holding her down with his foot, and she watched with disbelief as the sword of an Arrak warrior pierced Andrew Petch's belly.

'No!' she gasped. 'Oh God, *no!*'

Petch's body jerked on the sword as he was held pinioned in the air. Then the warrior brutally threw his body out of the vortex.

'Return,' barked Baulin.

Blood was seeping down his armour and he was beginning to feel the loss. His normal robust colour drained from his face, but Prestin had no time then to deal with the warrior's injuries. He reacted to Baulin's order, slamming the vortex closed with a tap of his staff.

A few seconds later it opened again in the location they had prepared in advance: an oasis some distance from Sharik.

The warriors exited the unstable void quickly and Prestin closed it down. Around them the land was whipped up; sand flew into the air as the aftermath of the unstable wormhole damaged the area. Then the destruction stopped.

Two other warriors held onto Jas, as Baulin was no longer able to. She looked up to see a large tent, and was powerless to stop herself from being pulled inside.

The tent was bespelled. The idea had come to Prestin when he had fixed the spells requested by the town's women to ensure that no-one could enter their tents without their permission. This spell worked in the opposite way and was focused on just one person. The tent was a prison, and it allowed any of the guard to enter and exit, but not the prisoner. Not without Prestin permitting it. And that prisoner was Jasmine Regis, their Empress.

After they pulled Jas inside the tent, Prestin used a spell to staunch the flow of Baulin's blood and give him immediate pain relief. He also cast a healing spell that would help the warrior regrow his hand in the next 24 hours.

'You murdering bastard,' Jas said. 'It's a shame he didn't cut your throat!'

'Really Empress! Is that any way to speak of the warriors who risked their lives to rescue you,' said Marlin.

Jas turned to see the councillor sitting in a chair at a table laden with food.

'You must be hungry after your ordeal,' said Marlin. 'Please join me.'

'What are you playing at, Marlin?' Jas said.

'As I said, we rescued you.'

'I didn't need rescuing.'

'Well, Highness, you haven't been very good at making your own decisions of late, have you?'

'The Emperor will hear of this …' Jas said. 'When he returns he will …'

'The Emperor won't be back,' Marlin said.

Jas looked at him sharply, saw the coldness in his expression, and a chill threatened to ripple up her spine.

'What have you done?'

'Me? Why, nothing. The Emperor chose to go off planet. Prestin here merely made it impossible for him to return.'

Jas glanced at Prestin. 'You would betray your ruler?'

'For the good of my people I felt I must,' said Prestin. 'You see, there is no decree in force to deal with an inadequate ruler. The only way to end his reign is his death, and then to ensure that there is no-one left in his blood-line to claim the throne.'

'I see,' said Jas coldly. 'Then you have brought me here to execute me.'

'No,' said Prestin. 'One of my order could never condone such an action. But I feel the time is right for change, and Marlin put forward a good argument as to why he should be allowed to rule.'

'Why would you even listen to him? That's treason!'

'Because,' Marlin said, 'Prestin discovered that the Emperor's actions have brought about another curse.'

'What curse?'

'I don't know the extent of it yet. But I'm certain it is because he brought you Earth women here.'

'We didn't ask to be kidnapped,' Jas said. 'But I know that our presence ensures the survival of the Arrak race.'

'Not quite so. This whole experiment is destined to fail. You are too different from us.'

'Not much we can do about that …' Jas said.

'Oh, but there is,' said Marlin.

'We can't alter our differences, but we can work to meet in the middle,' Jas said. 'Wasn't that always obvious?'

'We accept or … we invoke ancient magic,' Prestin said.

9

Another dream, and Jas was still too far away. And then a thought occurred to Arven … What if he could still access the magic from the pyramid? The idea came into his head as a whispered suggestion from his inner voice. Arven questioned it. Was the magic trying to seduce him after all? He reached out, trying to focus his mind. But he couldn't find the magic so easily. Yet, having touched it, he knew it was still within his capability.

The staff, that inner voice murmured.

Arven walked over to Malachi's body and looked down at the charred staff as it lay over him. He bent down and retrieved it. As his hand touched the wood, the gem sparked.

Through experimentation, Arven managed to summon enough residual magic to use Malachi's staff as a conduit. He recalled enough of Kil'n's power to know how to do this, but it took practice. But holding it, even though it was damaged, did help. Now he concentrated on his connection with Jas, calling to her through her dreams.

He managed to get through, then felt her wake up. He cursed. The link seemed to work only when she slept. He attempted to centre his energy through the staff again. He saw Jas, and then the energy dropped and he lost his connection again.

Where was she? He tested the power and the link, establishing that Jas was indeed on Emin. He found himself looking through her eyes as she walked through the camp, just before dawn. He realised then what she and Kale had done.

In his mind's eye he could see the camp and the survivors, and he had to applaud her audacity and resilience. For taking the people back to Emin had been the best course of action. Although he couldn't at this point share why with his two warriors.

Then, something interfered again with his connection and Jas was lost. This time he couldn't get the images back.

'It's no good,' he said now, placing down the staff. 'I've lost her. I only hope that my last message got through and that she will tell Kale we need his help. They are our only chance of getting off this place and back home.'

'Rest,' said Prins. 'You are exhausting yourself, Highness.'

'Kale once told me that no Al Kuzemen is born with magic. They are adept and become active in their teenage years. After that, it takes years and years of hard work and focus in order to develop the ability to channel the power. Just two days ago I had more power at my fingertips than any of them will ever achieve in a lifetime of study. I still feel it there, but without the pyramid it's harder to use.'

'Prins is right,' Elee said. 'You need to rest awhile. Then try again.'

But time was not on their side. The limited amount of food and water they'd had was almost depleted, and the planet appeared to have grown even more unstable. With the aid of Malachi's staff, Arven learnt the horrifying truth: his ancestor had left enough power intact to deliver the crucial message that Arven had received, but now the planet was collapsing in on itself. Now that the magic had done what it was intended for, it was only a matter of days, perhaps even mere hours, before the planet imploded. If they weren't off by then, Arven and his warriors would be killed.

'Eat,' Prins said, offering his last ration to Arven.

'I don't need it,' Arven said. But he took a small sip of water.

The air was dry, even inside the tent, which was so far holding off the ever-growing storms. The sand outside whipped mercilessly against the canvas. Malachi had weaved a strong spell, but Arven knew it would never hold against the destruction of the entire planet. His warriors were right: he needed to rest. But, despite being exhausted, he didn't have time to stop. He had to find a way to get them all off the planet, or die in the attempt.

'I'm going to try something else,' said Arven. 'I'll reach out to Kale directly. I have Jas's last known location and I could feel Kale nearby, so this might work. '

He stood once more, pulling the staff upright before him. Then he closed his eyes and thought of Jas again. He cast his mind sideways and felt for the Al Kuzemen mage's essence. Kale had been in the cubicle next door.

As he looked beyond the Eleventh Moon, focusing hard on Emin, his tired mind forgot to channel the energy through the staff. He slipped into a trancelike state, reached up into the air and drew a symbol of power. Suddenly Arven's magic fixed. He *saw* Kale and a woman lying in bed together, naked and wrapped in each other's arms. The surprise of this sudden revelation almost made him lose his concentration, but Arven pulled his mind back to their dire circumstances and focused harder.

Kale, he called. *Wake! I need you!*

Kale stirred. Arven called to him again. Somehow he knew he was in a place where the mage's half sleeping state allowed him to see into different realms. Arven heard shouting. His astral body turned and saw people entering the tent. Kale leapt from his bed, pulling on his bottoms. He did not see Arven, though the Emperor saw and experienced everything the mage did, as though he were linked to him through the astral plane.

'What's wrong?' mumbled Julia.

'Someone just came into the tent,' Kale said.

Julia roused and pulled the covers around herself before Kale opened the curtain to find Kat standing in the living space.

'Kale, we need you. Jas has been taken!' said Kat.

'How?' asked Kale.

'A vortex appeared inside the barrier. One of the Jinx warriors grabbed Jas and stabbed Andrew Petch in the stomach.'

'Without knowing our precise location,' Kale said. 'I wouldn't have thought that possible.'

'Well somebody must have given it to them,' Kat said.

'Is Andrew still alive?' Kale asked.

'Yes. But barely. He needs some of your healing magic. *What's that?*'

Kale turned to look in the direction Kat was pointing. Arven realised that the woman could see him.

'I don't see anything,' Kale said.

'There's someone there. In your shadow ...' Kat said. 'He's gesturing. Trying to talk to you ... He says his name is ... *Arven.*'

'Highness? Where are you?' Kale said, addressing the area in the tent that Kat indicated.

Arven spoke to Kat directly then. She was hearing him clearer now, and his facial features were becoming more distinct.

'The Eleventh Moon,' Kat told Kale.

'Highness,' Kale pleaded, 'I have to save the Empress. Can you focus any more?'

'Yes,' he said, and this time Kale heard him.

Prins and Elee both gave a startled cry as they watched Arven's body beginning to fade.

'Highness! Don't leave us!'

On hearing their voices Arven was yanked back into the tent with them.

'I almost made it through,' he said. 'But it doesn't matter. I won't go without you, my trusted and loyal friends.'

He explained to them what he had been able to do. 'I must be getting better at using the staff,' he said.

'No,' Elee said. 'You dropped it to the floor and ran your hands over the air. Like you did in the pyramid.'

Arven recalled the symbol, and he knew it was true. But this mark of power would take him through to Emin only on the astral plane. He needed to get all three of them back there in reality as soon as possible.

'Someone has taken Jasmine,' he told his warriors. 'I have to get back. I have to protect her.'

'Then go, Highness. Leave us and save the Empress!' said Prins.

Arven shook his head in refusal. 'I know there is a symbol that will take us all there. I just have to call it forth.'

Arven concentrated. He remembered the symbol that Kil'n had used to move the pyramid and all of his people to the Eleventh Moon. But this was specific to location. He closed his eyes and thought of Emin.

The power rippled once more through him. A shape formed in his mind. He analysed it. The answer presented itself in the form of a symbol, and then he knew the formula for this spell. It was to do with something that exclusively linked a planet in a particular place.

Arven had little understanding beyond the basics of astronomy; this was something he had always left to his mages to control. Now he *saw* Emin for the first time in the way that a mage might – a planet with two moons on one side, two suns on another, and the stars aligned around it in a certain way.

Arven raised his hand and drew Emin in the air as he saw it, then added the symbol that Kil'n had attached to his location symbol. This was the binding magic to create the move. Then he took the hands of his warriors and watched as the symbol lit up in the air.

There was something pushing back: a spell pressing down on the planet's surface to keep Arven and his warriors from leaving. Arven used his mind's eye to test it. This was the hex that had killed Malachi, and whoever was behind it would pay for that crime. But what must he do to remove it without frying his, and his warriors', blood too? He could try to punch his way through the spell using another symbol – but there was no need. The spell was not really holding – *it was weakened.* As the planet imploded, the binding enchantment diminished. Arven pushed gently with his mind and then felt the hex that had killed his mage fall away.

His own symbol ignited before their eyes, lighting up the tent.

At that moment, the canvas tore and the final residue of Malachi's magic gave way. Arven pulled his concentration back to Jas's last location, keeping his mind on Kale. A circle of protection grew around the three of them like a golden sphere of light. Then it stretched to incorporate Malachi's body. Arven couldn't leave the mage to the elements. He must have the burial that he deserved.

One moment they could still hear the roar of the sandstorm against the sides of the ward, the next they were in Kale's tent, staring at a beautiful woman as she sat up in bed with the sheets pulled up to her neck.

Arven glanced around. He saw Malachi's body on the floor beside his feet. He let go of Prins' and Elee's hands. They had made it.

'You are belonging to Kale …?' Arven said in the English that Jas had taught him.

'I'm his wife,' she said.

'Juleeaa,' Kale said behind him. 'Her name is Juleeaa.'

Arven turned to see Kale standing in the tent doorway. The mage's eyes were wide with surprise.

'How did you …?' he asked in the Arrak tongue.

'That's a long story, my friend,' Arven said. 'Now, where is my wife?'

10

'What magic?' asked Jas.

'A spell has been cast that will make you all truly like us. The Earth women will no longer be inferior and the past can be put behind us all. We will all be Arrak Nah Tiamen,' said Prestin.

Jas tried to make sense of what Prestin was saying. She felt no different, so what did this mean?

'You mean *change* us?' Jas said.

'Enough,' said Marlin. 'We have a meeting with the council, Prestin. It is time to go.'

'Wait!' said Jas. 'Tell me what you mean.'

'It will all become clear,' said Marlin.

The mage and the councillor left. Jas waited for a split second and then made to follow. They had no right to keep her there. She would demand answers. If she had learnt one thing about the Jinx it was their unending loyalty to their leaders, and she was still the Empress. But as Jas reached for the door flap an invisible force pushed away her hand. She looked down at her fingers, wondering what had just happened. Then she tried again. This time her hand was slapped away with more strength.

Jas threw herself at the door in retaliation; she landed with a bump on the rug behind her. She wasn't hurt, but was shaken by the repulsion.

'A ward, then,' she said. 'I'm trapped.'

The baby kicked the side of her ribs in protest, then another kick or punch followed on the other side.

'Now you're a *contortionist*?' she said to her stomach before picking herself up off the floor. 'Okay. I'm listening. No more being thrown across the room. I don't suppose that's good for you, is it?'

She went to the nearest chair and sat down. She felt tired and anxious.

'Are you comfortable?' asked a voice.

Jas looked up to see a warrior standing in the doorway.

'I've been assigned to look after you.'

'What's your name?' she asked.

'Almani.'

'I'd be better if you'd let me out of here, Almani,' Jas said.

'I can't do that, Empress. Only the mage can allow it.'

Jas studied the warrior. He was young and had kind eyes that swirled with purple and green tones.

'What are they planning to do with me?' she asked.

'Protect you, Highness,' Almani said.

'Is that what they told you?'

Almani nodded, and Jas believed that he really thought this was the truth. There was no guile at all.

'You see, the thing is, Marlin is staging a ...' She searched for the Jinx word for 'coup' and couldn't think of one that truly fitted. 'A takeover,' was the closest she could come. 'Marlin wants to be the Emperor.'

Almani frowned. 'They said you would say things like this. I am not to listen. Can I get you anything, Empress?'

'Freedom,' said Jas.

Almani shook his head. The Jinx grew in different ways, reaching physical adulthood far sooner than mental maturity. By human standards he looked around 18. But really he was an adolescent – not of an age where a man would want to go to the marriage tent – and so Almani knew nothing about women. His mother had died of the pestilence some years back; Almani had had no contact with a female since. But Baulin had told him that their minds were ... wrong. That they made up untrue things. Especially these Earth women.

Almani remembered his mother as sweet and kind. The Empress, whom he had seen from afar, was an anomaly. A perplexing and confused soul. Or so he had been told. It appeared from her ravings that Baulin was right. After all, everyone knew that you could only *inherit* the throne. Marlin therefore would never be able to just 'take over'.

Jas watched these thoughts cross Almani's face. By his expression the boy was weighing up all of her words – and not believing any of them. What could she do to convince him of the truth?

'Fetch me some water,' she ordered, because she needed time to think.

Almani hurried away.

Left alone again, Jas studied the tent. All she needed was something sharp and she would cut her way out of there. She had done that before, and no magic was going to hold her captive.

Jas stood and walked over to the food-laden table. Fruit, cheese, meat and fish of every kind were spread out in a veritable feast. Jas wasn't hungry though, and this had more to do with her finding herself captive than her pregnancy. She looked for cutlery and found none. There was a small stack of plates however.

She heard Almani enter and asked him, 'How am I supposed to eat this?'

'I can give you a spoon,' Almani said. 'But no knife. You must use your fingers, Highness.'

He placed the carafe of water down on the table with a small clay cup.

'Leave me,' she said.

Almani lingered a moment and then turned and left. So far so good. At least the boy was taking orders from her.

She picked up the cup and smashed it down on the side of the table, but the pottery didn't break or even crack. She did the same with the carafe, but it remained intact no matter how hard she slammed it down.

Almani returned, and Jas guessed that he had never really been far away.

'Unbreakable, Highness,' he explained. 'No-one wishes you to hurt yourself.

Jas glared at him. 'I said *leave*.'

Almani bowed and Jas watched him exit the tent.

She scanned the furnishings, looking for anything that could conceivably be broken or used as a weapon, but Prestin had thought of everything: there was nothing breakable in this tent. Even the mirror on the dressing-table was made of polished metal. There were no jars of unguents, or crystal chalices to drink from. Even the chairs were solid. She tried to move one and found it rooted to the ground and therefore impossible to pick up and smash. It didn't take long for her to establish that there was nothing she could use to help her escape. Yet, the tent had every luxury she might need, including a bed cubicle and what looked like a pool room.

So I'm to be kept here for a while …

Jas sighed. She was tired and irritable and hated to have no control over her surroundings. But all was not lost. It was not a situation she found easy to accept or even cope with. Then she thought of Kale. She had to contact him. Maybe then he would be able to find and free her.

She sat down again and closed her eyes. She searched around for her connection with Kale, focused on the survivors as an anchor, but all she could feel was a huge wall around her. Her eyes opened and she scanned the canvas walls of the tent. She felt along them with the magic that fluttered around inside her. The tent might as well be made of brick. There was no way through; the whole place was cloaked: she was invisible to the world outside. Kale couldn't find her any more than she could find him.

'Damn it!'

How had this happened? How had Marlin been able to find and penetrate the barrier that Kale had so carefully constructed? Of course the major flaw was that Kale hadn't barred anyone from crossing into the camp. Just from finding it. But they had thought themselves invisible, and therefore it hadn't been a concern. How foolish they had been, and how clever Prestin and Marlin had proved to be. How conniving.

They've been planning this for some time, Jas thought, *and Arven didn't see it coming. Neither did I, or even Kale.* But then, Jas had been off planet and, according to Mallory, things had changed in Sharik since then. Jas couldn't help feeling responsible for this.

What made this whole coup so unsettling was that it was not a Jinx thing to do at all. Treachery was a human trait. The Arrak Nah Tiamen were notoriously loyal to their leaders. How could they have lost that devotion so easily?

She considered the curse that Prestin had mentioned. The thought was ridiculous. She wished she could discuss it with Kale, and experienced a spike of anger and frustration that she couldn't.

Jas stood up again and walked the perimeter of the tent, periodically touching the canvas. At some points her hand was gently pushed away, at others she could sense the strong force-field surrounding the tent and didn't try to touch the fabric.

By the time she reached the door again, Jas was feeling very irritated.

'Empress?' said Almani from beyond the door. 'Can I get you anything else?'

'No. *Leave me alone,*' she said again.

'Maybe you should rest. There is no way out of this place unless Prestin wills it.'

'I want to be let out, Almani,' she said. 'Do you understand me?'

'Yes, Empress.'

'Then let me out.'

'I can't. I would if I could,' Almani said, and Jas believed him.

'You're a loyal Arrak,' Jas said. 'And if the Emperor was here he would reward you for that. But listen, the men you are working for are not loyal. They have lied to you.'

Almani raised the flap of the door and looked in at Jas. The boy was frowning again, as though he was conflicted between what her enemies had told him and what Jas said now.

'They told me not to listen to you,' Almani said. 'But you are my Empress and I must.'

'Help me,' Jas said.

'I can do nothing,' said Almani sadly.

11

'I have sad news,' Marlin said.

They were in the council tent, which also doubled as a throne room, and the meeting had only just begun.

There were twelve councillors in all. Each represented one of the twelve districts into which the planet was divided. Within each of the council members' jurisdictions were more than 1000 towns. All of which had their own leaders, mages and council members who reported back to the council leaders.

The council leaders were all in attendance, and each had with him an assistant and a warrior, who stood behind his chair. Marlin had left his place and now loitered by the empty throne.

'Where is the Emperor?' asked Councillor Abeken.

'I'm afraid the Emperor is dead,' said Marlin. 'He left the planet on a fool's errand to the Eleventh Moon. He died there several hours ago.'

The council erupted with cries of horror. Some rejected Marlin's claim, demanding proof.

'The Emperor is not dead,' said Abeken. 'My mage would have told me if such a thing had occurred.'

Prestin came out from behind Marlin's chair.

'Unfortunately, Councillor Marlin speaks the truth. The Emperor learnt from Garuk that our race was suffering from the impact of a curse. An ancient hex invoked when our wives and daughters died. I believe that it was the Emperor who killed Al Kuzemen Garuk, so that he would not reveal this truth. Then he took it upon himself, using Plendura's mage, Malachi, to go to the Eleventh Moon to try to find a way to save us.'

'Preposterous!' said Councillor Abeken. 'The Emperor would never murder a mage! And if he did go to the Eleventh Moon he must have had good cause to believe he could fix this curse.'

'The Emperor was not himself,' Marlin said. 'He had lost his *Chio Mien*[1]

---

[1] Soul mate

and the separation was driving him insane. The Earth Empress had done something unprecedented when she left here with Al Kuzemen Kale … But this is old ground. Arven, in his insanity, believed he was doing the right thing for his people, I'm sure. But the fact of the matter is that Prestin felt the Emperor's death …'

'Is this true?' asked Abeken.

'Yes,' Prestin said. 'Ask your mages to search for the Eleventh Moon. The planet exists no more. And Arven and his warriors ceased with it.'

'And what of Malachi?' asked Abeken.

'Dead,' said Prestin. 'Led on this suicidal journey by the Emperor.'

'Which leads us to our immediate concern,' Marlin said. 'We have no ruler, no Empress … and no heir.'

Abeken and the other councillors grew silent as they took this information in. This was indeed an unparalleled situation. For generations there had always been an Emperor or Empress to take over from the previous.

'The throne is a birthright …' Abeken said finally.

'Unless there is none to take over,' Marlin said.

'This situation needs to be considered,' Abeken said.

'Indeed,' said Marlin. 'Prestin, as Sharik's mage, have you any suggestions on what must be done?'

Prestin smiled. 'Why we must choose another leader. And soon.'

Abeken was shocked. 'But who? Who would want to take on such a burden? For the throne is indeed the hardest role any Arrak Nah Tiamen could fill.'

Marlin smiled. This was going better than he had expected. Abeken was playing right into his hands …

'But of course,' said Abeken. 'Such a sacrifice would be for the greater good of the people.'

'Exactly!' said Marlin. 'Such a person would be unselfish … Thinking only of the good of the people.'

'Mmmm,' said Abeken. 'For this reason, I would offer myself for leadership.'

'What?' said Marlin. '*You*? I mean … you would?'

'Yes,' said Abeken. 'Or does someone else wish to take on this burden?'

Marlin was so shocked he did not know how to respond.

'I would propose … Councillor Marlin,' said Prestin. 'If I may. I know that would be a tremendous expectation, but the Councillor has been working in Sharik for several days now and …'

'No need,' said Abeken. 'I am happy to oblige. Now, if that is settled? Any other business?'

'A funeral for the Emperor must be arranged. Even with no body …' said Zeno, the councillor of Shandelin. 'We still must honour our dead.'

'Of course,' said Abeken. 'Followed by a coronation.'

Marlin returned to his seat and sat silent as the council members discussed the state funeral and coronation details.

'A vote, then?' said Abeken.

Marlin's attention returned to the room. 'Vote?'

'On when we announce the Emperor's death. A period of mourning must be observed ...'

'Yes. Soon. We should let the people know soon,' Marlin said.

'Tomorrow, then?' said Abeken.

Heads nodded in agreement, and Marlin went along with the flow. What else could he do? At the end of the meeting, when the councillors began to disperse, Marlin came face to face with Abeken. The man showed no guile. Perhaps his offer was as selfless as it appeared to be? But something in Abeken's expression told him otherwise. They had never liked each other, and Abeken was the most outspoken of the councillors.

'Councillor Marlin,' Abeken said. 'And Prestin. Please feel free to return to your town now. I will remain and begin to speak with the Emperor's advisors. We must make this transition as smooth as possible.'

'But ... you'll need a mage ...' said Prestin.

'I have one. But thank you for your service so far.'

'Who?' said Prestin and Marlin together.

'Taenan. He is already moving into the Al Kuzemen tent as we speak, and he has been telling me some very interesting things of late. A story of the Emperor trying to contact him and being *blocked* ... Though I'm sure the implosion of the planet could be blamed for that.'

Marlin saw the swirling stop in Abeken's pupils. There was a hard flint shell of blue beneath. Marlin shuddered as though he had been touched by ice. Then Abeken's pupils took up their usual rhythm and the moment passed.

'You should go now,' said Abeken.

12

'Highness,' Kale said, falling to his knees before Arven. 'I beg your forgiveness!'

'Stand up, old friend,' Arven said. 'You already have my pardon. We have to locate Jasmine.'

Kale remained on his knees until Arven took his arm and forced him to stand.

'We have no time for this,' he said. 'Jasmine is crucial. I need to find her, and quickly.'

'Crucial? To what, Emperor?'

'I will explain, but first we must find my wife ...'

Standing in the tent doorway, Kat was shocked to see the Jinx Emperor and two of his warriors suddenly appear. Stammering, she began to explain again what had happened to Jas.

'Thank you, I heard you tell Kale,' Arven said. 'We need to follow them.'

'They surely will have taken her back to Sharik,' Kale said.

'I doubt that,' said Arven. 'But let's make sure. Use your magic to search for her.'

Kale sat down cross-legged on the floor of the seating area with his staff lying horizontally over his thighs. He placed both of his hands on the wooden shaft and the gem lit up as he connected with his power. He cast out with his mind, searching for Jas. He did not tell Kale that he and Jas often communicated by telepathic means. As did he and Julia.

Julia, in the meantime, pulled the bed sheet around herself, got out of bed and went quietly into the pool room, emerging later dressed and clean. Kale had not moved during all of that time.

'I see *nothing*,' he said, coming out of his meditation. 'Though Taenan is in Sharik ... Should I ask his help, Highness?'

'Taenan?' Arven became thoughtful.

Taenan had been trusted by Malachi, yet the last contact his Al Kuzemen had with Taenan had resulted in Malachi's death. Arven wasn't sure if this meant that Taenan was working with his enemy. If so, the mage would pay dearly for his treachery. The death of Malachi had to be answered for – wherever that trail might lead.

'Do not reveal your presence yet, or mine,' said Arven. 'There is a traitor among the mages. He killed Malachi and. has taken Jasmine. He tried to prevent us from returning and would have killed me if he had been able to.'

The implication of Arven's words sank home. Kale climbed to his feet.

'And yet, after everything I did, you still trust *me*,' Kale said.

'More than you could possibly comprehend, unless I tell you what I learnt on the Eleventh Moon.'

'Then tell me Highness, so that I can fully understand.'

'But Jasmine …?' Arven said.

'Whoever took her is unlikely to harm her, and Jas is very resourceful. She's being hidden, but she'll try to find a way to get word to us,' Kale said. 'And when she does, we'll act.'

Arven nodded. 'Then I must be patient.'

Kale waited as Arven walked around the living area as though deep in thought.

'Very well,' he said finally. 'It is time I told you what I learnt. Prins, Elee, wait by the tent door. Ensure we are not disturbed.'

The warriors rushed to obey. Kat went outside with them. They closed the flap, making sure that the Emperor had complete privacy. But not before Kat said, 'What should I tell the others?'

'Nothing for now,' Kale said.

Julia in the meantime sat down at the dining table. Arven paid her no attention, because he realised she did not understand their language. He stopped pacing and turned back to Kale.

'The events of the past few years were foretold many thousands of years ago. Sit, my friend, for this is a long story, and in order to tell it well, I must start at the beginning.'

Both men took a seat on the cushion-covered chaises in the sitting area. Arven spoke slowly in the Arrak tongue as he told Kale about his powerful ancestor, Kil'n, and the crime he had committed against humanity.

'The two tribes!' Kale said. 'I always believed it a myth.'

'No myth,' Arven explained. 'At first there was one tribe of people led by Kil'n – an Emperor in possession of *all* magic.'

Arven had learnt that magic was a birthright, just as the throne was, and that it would pass from the ruler to his or her first born child, who would then take up the throne and the power when the Emperor or Empress died. Kil'n was the most powerful Emperor the tribe had ever had, and when Arven explained Kil'n's addiction to the magic, Kale nodded with understanding.

'Such power in one person's hands would indeed be problematic.'

'After the battle on Earth, Kil'n returned his people to the Eleventh

Moon. There his wife Shamila was plagued with visions. She said she saw the future of the second tribe – the Arrak Nah Tiamen – in the balance, and the only way they could save themselves at that time was for Kil'n to give up his magic.

'He did this for his people and to gain the forgiveness of his wife for the death of their son. He was sure his actions were the cause of all of their misery. You see, by ruthlessly attacking the other tribe, they had effectively committed genocide. The small number who got away had been swallowed up into other Earth tribes for the sake of their own survival. They had wed and bred with the other tribes, and their bloodline had been watered down, their heritage forgotten. All of the culture, faith and science that these people had, had been lost along with it. Kil'n's men might as well have killed everyone of the first tribe, from babes to warriors.'

'A crime for sure, Highness, but the punishment seems so harsh,' Kale said.

'I thought that too initially, but then I saw myself in Kil'n's place. He was obsessed with his magic. Hungry for power. Egotistical. But the magic was controlling him, not he it. He was even casting spells while he slept. I think I *know* him now. You see, I was inside his head. I was him, and I've come away believing that I am an old soul.'

'I don't know what you are saying,' Kale said. 'You are nothing like this Emperor. Your motives have always been for the good of our people.'

'I told myself that was the case, but were they? We too have destroyed almost half of a population. In a repetition of what my ancestor did, we laid waste to the planet that was once our home. Now it dies, and anyone left there will die with it. Its cultures. Its science. Its religions. All gone because I ordered it so.'

'But if it was foretold, how could you have prevented it?' said Kale.

'Therein lies my dilemma. And I have thought long and hard about this. Shamila's last vision revealed that if Kil'n gave up his magic, and the Guild of Mages was born, then disaster would be averted. But what she didn't disclose was that this would only turn aside the curse for a while. The curse would find its way back to the Arrak Nah Tiamen and exact its revenge regardless. Shamila manipulated Kil'n into accepting the terms, then she exacted her cruellest revenge. Look ...'

Arven placed his hand over Kale's and opened his mind to show the mage the story that had been revealed to him.

Until recent events their chamber had always been the place where Kil'n had been happiest: in Shamila's arms he experienced everything he desired. But no more. Despite their bond, Shamila would no longer be a part of Kil'n's life. Instead she mourned their child, refusing to leave the chamber, or to let Kil'n comfort her.

Kil'n had moved into another room to give Shamila time to recover, but every morning he came to see her. He wanted her to know he cared. It would have been so easy to let the distance between them grow, but he couldn't – being apart from her gave the Emperor such pain that he could barely function. This was partly due to the changes the Emperor had made to them both – the sex magic spell had made the bond even stronger.

He had done all that she said. He no longer had power; instead this had been passed on to the wisest among them to share in equal burden. This detail, however, still did not make Shamila forgive him. Neither did the fact that the loss of the magic was devastating to Kil'n.

Kil'n knew he had been wrong, but he also acknowledged that he had done the best he could for the future of his people. They were recovering – and he was learning to accept that he no longer had magic at the tip of his fingers. But his wife was not getting better. Losing a child was a distressing thing, but Kil'n believed that a new pregnancy would take Shamila's mind away from the problem.

Despite her rejection of him, he had to see her every day, and so that morning he entered the chamber, determined that she would begin to accept him once more as her husband.

Shamila was in their bed sleeping. Kil'n knew that the sex magic made it so that Shamila could not resist him. Her mind might reject him, but her body couldn't. They were **chio mien**, *and there was nothing she could do to stop herself loving him.*

But Kil'n was wrong.

Shamila had found a way to negate the bond.

When he pulled back the covers from the bed he found Shamila in a pool of her own blood. In one hand she held a scroll, in the other a warrior's blade. Kil'n fell to his knees before her corpse. He could not unsee … Shamila had cut her own throat on the razor-sharp blade and bled out onto the scroll and the bed.

Kil'n was plummeted into despair. He called for his new mage and advisor Sulemen.

'Oh, Highness!' the mage said when he saw the dead Empress. 'This is my fault! She told me she needed a spell scroll to help herself forget …'

Shamila had asked Sulemen to bespell the scroll so that the words she wrote on it would become so. Believing her motives to be genuine the mage had fulfilled her wish.

'Why would she kill herself?'

Sulemen opened the scroll and read the words that Shamila had written, which were now steeped in her life's blood.

'A curse, Lord,' Sulemen said. 'Everything she said was a lie. She has hexed you, and with you the tribe.'

'But how can this be so?'

'Her blood. Her death. It was powerful and dark magic. You see, your wife was an adept. Just as I was. The magic went to her as well as to your Al Kuzemen.'

Kil'n ordered the scroll burnt, along with any history to do with the curse. He believed that by doing this, he would negate its foretold future from ever happening.

'Sulemen, create me a spell that ensures that our two souls shall never meet again. This is the only way we can ever stop the curse from befalling our future generations.'

'Shamila used the magic scroll to reinforce *her* curse. There were no visions foretelling disaster – she lied in order to manipulate Kil'n. She could not forgive him for the death of Kisha,' Arven explained.

'But why bother making him give up the power?'

'Because she knew he loved magic more than anything else. It was the ultimate punishment. Also, when she cemented the spell by spilling her own blood over the scroll, she condemned her own soul as well as Kil'n's. Left as it was, Kil'n's magic could have easily negated the spell, but fragmented in the bodies of his wise men – who barely knew how to use it – the magic was almost useless to him. At the end of the scroll there was also a prophecy to the effect that when Kil'n's and Shamila's reborn souls finally met again, and bonded, the curse would be reactivated. The tribe of the Arrak Nah Tiamen would finally die out. Sulemen's spell was designed to ensure that the prophecy never happened. It worked for over 4000 years, and then there was this lifetime.'

'Then … you *are* Kil'n?' Kale said.

'Yes.'

'*Jasmine* is Shamila?' Kale asked.

'No. My first wife, Celin, was Shamila. When we met and bonded again, the curse was reactivated. It backfired on her, though, as all magic of dark persuasion does. She died again, taking our child and our wives and daughters with her. The Arrak Nah Tiamen were meant to die out after that. Just as Shamila wanted. But you, Kale, saved us.'

'I had a vision that led me to Earth,' Kale explained. 'I never knew where it came from.'

'Sulemen said he could not see all the way into the future. His magic was new, and as you know, the future depends on so many variables. And so he set another clause. He cast a spell using some of his own blood. It was designed to send a message at the right time to the right mage. It would point that mage at someone who could aid our future.'

Kale nodded. 'This one I know. The vision I had of Jas, before we found her and you bonded.'

'Yes. Jasmine is the key to our survival. She's also my *chio mien*. Kil'n did go on to find another wife, and she birthed him a child to take on the throne. After that, he had the Guild of Mages find them a new planet to live on. A new place to take the children away from the pestilence. As you know from our history, the tribe moved from planet to planet until they found Emin. Kil'n, however, remained on the Eleventh Moon. His lonely death left the residue of magic for me to find.'

'Since you are Kil'n reincarnated, only you could ignite that power once more.'

'That's right. But the magic in the pyramid revealed to me that souls can change. I *was* Kil'n, and that was enough for me to be able to use the magic. But now I am Arven. I am not the Emperor who was addicted to the magic his birthright gave him. That was never part of my early years. Kil'n's soul was reborn over and over, and lessons were learnt each time. It evolved. I am no more him than you are.'

'You have grown so much since we last spoke,' Kale said.

'I have changed. I think this is why some of Kil'n's power has remained with me. I don't know if this is forever, or just while I need it. Whatever happens, though, I need you to help me use it wisely.'

'I promise, Highness,' said Kale.

'And now the time to act comes to us. We must find Jasmine. She is the final piece in the puzzle to save our future. '

'Then you *know* how to end the curse?'

'Yes. We have to *save* the first tribe ...'

'Save them? I don't understand. I thought the tribe was all gone?'

'Not all. The first tribe lives on in Jasmine. It lives on in all remaining humans ...'

13

Baulin and his warriors waited as Marlin and Prestin climbed onto their el lien mecks. They were at the pens on the outskirts of Sharik, having been taken there by Abeken's warriors, who had duly left.

'What are your orders?' asked Baulin as the councillor's mount pulled alongside his.

'It's not over yet. You'll escort us to the oasis,' Marlin said. 'Then double back and take care of Abeken.'

'Let's be clear … you want me to *kill* Councillor Abeken?'

Marlin looked around, nervous that they might be overheard.

'Yes,' he said.

'And what of the mage Taenan?'

'The same. He knows too much for his own good. We need to rid ourselves of anyone who suspects our involvement in the death of the Emperor.'

'And when Abeken is gone?' Baulin said.

'I'll step in and take over the throne,' Marlin said. 'And you can go back to that camp and catch yourselves some females.'

Baulin gave a grimace that tried to be a smile. He was brutish in appearance – unlike Elidon, who had been handsome by Arrak standards – but so cold that it made him ugly. Baulin was in face what he was inside – and Marlin and Prestin knew it.

They rode away from Sharik now with Baulin in the lead, the councillor and mage between him and the men.

Marlin fell into his own thoughts. They were a two lecks' ride from the prison oasis and the Empress, but Marlin knew she was the hand he would play if all else failed.

'What if things don't go to plan?' Prestin asked. 'The Empress is tough, she won't be easy to control.'

'When Abeken is dead, Sharik will be thrown into a state of panic,' Marlin said. 'Baulin and his men will be there to handle the situation, but I expect a fight on his hands from Abeken's warriors. Bringing Jasmine back and announcing her pregnancy will ensure my place on the throne.'

'How so?'

'I'll declare a state of emergency and, under the guise of "Guardian Monarch" for the unborn child, I'll seize control of the capital and of Emin.'

'But … she won't go along with that,' Prestin pointed out.

'Obviously the Empress will have to look after her health prior to the birth, and being a weak human, will be unable to rule.'

Prestin realised that Marlin had it all worked out before they arrived at the oasis. Of course Jas's pregnancy would never make full term, and when the time came, they would announce the unfortunate death of the Empress and her child. By then it would no longer matter: Marlin would be fully in charge.

Prestin absorbed this information. He didn't like the idea of killing the woman or the innocent child, but he had thrown his lot in with Marlin and there was no going back. He was complicit in the death of one mage and directly responsible for the death of another. Now he also knew of Marlin's plans to murder Taenan: his soul was tarnished whatever he did, and so he did nothing.

At the oasis the warriors jumped down and took command of the animals while Marlin and Prestin returned to the prison tent.

'Build me a tent there,' ordered Marlin, pointing to the space beside Jas's prison.

Baulin and his warriors watered and fed the animals, and when they were sufficiently rested, mounted once more to go and complete the task that Marlin had set them.

Prestin went to obey his order, adding his own tent to the instruction. They were in for a long night while they waited for Baulin to return.

As the tents rose from the sand, Prestin experienced a peculiar sensation in the thread of his power – one of the tents collapsed back into sand. The other stopped building, half done and barely equipped. Marlin was heading into the prison tent when he heard the rumble of collapsing sand and turned back.

'What's happening?' he asked.

'I … don't know. My focus must be off …'

'Then get it back together,' Marlin said.

Prestin tried but nothing happened. 'The spell won't work,' he said.

'Your shortcomings never fail to amaze me,' Marlin said. 'I'll visit our prisoner while you correct this.'

Prestin sat down in the sand and examined his staff. The jewel on the top of it was dull and lifeless. It was as though the magic endowed to him for usage from the Guild had suddenly been revoked. But this wasn't possible. No mage had ever had their power taken back. Not even Kale after his treachery. Prestin tried to focus all of his energy into the staff, but nothing happened.

'You do realise that whatever you are planning will never work.' Jas said as Marlin entered.

'Be silent,' Marlin said.

'I won't help you, and when Arven's warriors get wind of this you'll find yourself in deep trouble.'

'For the good of your unborn child you will do as I say,' Marlin said. 'Now be quiet. Just a few more hours and things will be changed in Emin for my good.'

'You egotistical prick,' Jas said in English.

Marlin merely shrugged, because he had never made any attempt to learn any of the Earth tongues. He went to the food table and sat down, scooping handfuls of fruit, interspersed with cheese, into his mouth. Treachery had given him an appetite, but as he inserted a piece of meat and began to chew, Marlin found his mouth full of sand.

He coughed out the sand and reached for a carafe of wine. He took a long swig and then began to choke. The wine too had turned in the carafe. And as Marlin jumped to his feet, so did the rest of the food on the table.

Jas stood up from the chair she was sitting on just before it collapsed into a pool of sand at her feet.

'Prestin, you incompetent idiot,' Marlin said, hurrying to the door.

Jas hadn't expected her opportunity to come so soon. She watched as the sofa, tables, chairs and rugs all sank back into the ground, and understood that the spell Prestin had cast was somehow unravelling. She knew her chance to run could come any moment, but she didn't know where she was or how to get back to her friends. Hurrying to the side of the tent, away from the guarded doorway, Jas reached out and touched the fabric. There was a flutter against her hand as the spell to prevent her leaving tried to activate, and then, it was gone. Her hand connected with the canvas, which fell into decay, crumbling to dust. Jas glanced over her shoulder, then threw herself forward at the fabric, expecting to be thrown back.

She passed through a waterfall of sand and found herself outside of the prison. Luck was on her side!

Prestin was sat on the ground outside. He was holding his staff, eyes closed as if in prayer, while he concentrated, trying to regain his power.

'What is happening, you fool?' Marlin shouted, and Jas took a step back, hiding in the shadows of the half-fallen tent.

'It won't work. It's gone!' wailed Prestin, burying his head in his hands. 'I cannot feel even a thread of magic.'

'Give me that thing!' Marlin said, snatching the staff from Prestin's hands.

'It's no good. It will work only for a mage,' said Prestin.

Marlin became aware of the disintegration of the prison tent. He dropped the staff and turned back. Jas hesitated for a moment, recalling how Kale's staff had reacted to her in the past. Could she use Prestin's staff in the same way? She stepped out from the shadows and reached for the mage's power source.

I hope this works! she thought.

Jas had learnt enough from Kale to know how to channel the modicum of power she had, and she focused all of her energy on igniting the staff.

Kale. I'm here! Come and get me! She closed her eyes and concentrated on her tent in the survivors' camp.

The gem began to glow.

Prestin lifted his head from his hands. His mouth fell open as he saw the beam illuminating Jas: covering her in a blast of radiance. And then, Prestin blinked and the Empress and his staff disappeared.

14

She was in a bubble of warm light, floating in the space between dimensions. From where she was, Jas could feel nothing. It was like the time when she had dream-walked and found herself on Emin long before she knew the planet existed. She was in a place where only Kale had been able to see her. She had been drawn to him, or his magic, as though it were a homing beam.

Within the bubble Jas still held Prestin's staff. She glanced at it now; saw her hand – though her skin glowed luminous and corporeal.

Not Prestin's staff, she thought. *Mine.*

Jas's fingers tightened possessively on the staff. The wood grew warm and the gem glowed brighter as though the channel was accepting her now as its new mistress.

She turned her mind outwards. She was away from Prestin and Marlin – that was important. But how could she get back to the survivors' camp where she belonged?

Jas cast her mind out and gasped. She was not on Emin. Wherever she was, she was 'off planet'. Then she took a breath to steady her fear.

I'm fine. I'm safe. I'm in control.

She tapped the staff down inside the bubble, as she had seen Kale and the other mages do. There was a surge of energy through the staff that made her fingers tingle. It told her that she was being given a certain amount of magic to use. She hadn't known that the taps represented a request for a certain amount of energy from a shared pot. But she could feel that energy now. It was limitless, but was doled out fairly to all mages as they needed it.

'Take me back,' she said. 'Back home.'

The bubble she was in began to spin and turn; first it pointed one way, then the other, as though the magic did not understand where Jas's home was.

The gem glowed and she saw a flash of Earth and the Trafford Centre; then the power showed her Emin's capital Sharik; but it did not take her to either place.

'Emin,' she said. There was no point in going back to Earth, and not without Kale and the others anyway.

The magic found its focus. Jas felt the bubble move. She was drawn to another form, a being so powerful that she was almost blinded by the light coming from inside him. This creature had lived, died and been reborn countless times. His lives were infinity. A soul as old as time. She saw those lives flashing before her eyes as though they were her own life, and then …

A *female* figure. Far away from this first bright light and born from another tribe … *She* was on Earth, as the male soul travelled through the stars. Destined to be born and born again. Her life would always feel unfulfilled, and each time it ended … alone.

'What is this?' she asked the power now.

You, came the reply.

She saw then a history, a pyramid – or was it a Mayan temple? Despite the hieroglyphic language this was not ancient Egypt. This tribe came from somewhere else over 4000 years ago. Jas had no knowledge of geography and yet she understood, as though the magic drip fed her the information, that this was South Eastern Mexico. This place was swollen with magic, and it gave birth to many kings and queens who held the bloodline and controlled the power. It was all inside them, bubbling like a volcano ready to burst. And the architecture was part of it, infused with it: glorious in its artistic beauty. The temples were built to last because they had been created from the soil by *Kil'n's* magic. But who was Kil'n?

Jas recognised one soul in particular. *Hers.* Or at least a spark of it – the beginning of a long journey through many lifetimes.

But the images jumped. One minute from childhood, the next to a bonding ceremony. In this montage she learnt that her sister Shamila had bonded with the Emperor. How fortunate Shamila had been!

Neferia – that was Jas's name then – had also been paraded before the Emperor in the hope that they would bond. But Kil'n had eyes only for Shamila. Even though her face was veiled, Shamila's alabaster skin was attractive and unique. She wore a silk chemise and her arms glowed in the torchlight. Although he pretended to look at five other women before, Kil'n tested only Shamila. The bonding magic sparked, and Neferia knew that the Emperor had subconsciously made it happen.

She said nothing at the time, for she had never revealed the secret of her own magic. Neferia could see into a man's soul. And when she looked at Kil'n, she saw the first stages of a man drowning in his own obsessions.

He was not a bad soul though, and Neferia thought he would make her sister Shamila happy. It didn't matter that the bond was not true … many a marriage was made by suitability rather than real love. And who wouldn't love Kil'n? He was the Emperor and he was beautiful and strong, pleasing to any female eye.

Neferia saw all of this with no romance: it was just a fact of their way of life.

In time Neferia was bonded to one of the senators – Aris. She knew that this bond was not true love either, but more that she pleased Aris as Shamila had pleased Kil'n. But the marriage was reasonably happy. They lived a simple life until the uprising, when Aris, along with Hren and many others, betrayed the Emperor.

Then there was the parting, and one tribe became two …

When the Emperor left Earth with his bride and followers, the world Neferia knew changed. Magic was frowned upon. Neferia hid her true self even more. Had she married one of Kil'n's followers she would have been able to leave with the Emperor, but unfortunately as Aris's wife she couldn't. She had been made to stay home as the coup occurred; learning only when it was too late what her husband had been involved with. She was angry and disappointed by his treachery, but as a woman she had no right to voice such an opinion.

Afterwards they entered a world of science. Aris had a fascination for architecture. He and Hren were friends, and so Aris supported all of his wild ideas and schemes. No-one pointed out that in the old days, Kil'n could have created the structures Hren designed from sand in a matter of moments instead of through the laborious construction work that took years to complete. Neferia missed the wonders the Emperor could produce, and she watched as her husband grew closer to those who had ousted Kil'n. Without meaning to, she withdrew from their company as much as possible. Hren disgusted her, as did Aris more and more. She believed that what they had done was a serious mistake.

The first year after Kil'n's departure, there was a famine. For all of Hren's boasting that his science had saved the crops, Neferia knew this to be untrue. Hren lied often, and there was a black shadow around his heart that only she could see. Unfortunately Aris believed in him, and anyway, they had little choice since Kil'n was gone now. They had to make their agriculture work without the Emperor's help, because he would never return.

Hren took up leadership – Neferia knew this had always been his aim. The farmers employed his methods and the crops began to grow once more. He was hailed as a saviour. Neferia wondered when his luck would finally run out and the Mayan people would learn the truth about him: he was more corrupted by his science than Kil'n had ever been by magic.

Neferia gave birth to a daughter, but no more children sprang from her womb. And few births came from others too. This was seen as a blessing at first, but with infant mortality on the rise, Neferia could not help but wonder if this was another form of punishment for their betrayal of their Emperor. She tried to broach the subject with Aris, but he didn't wish to discuss the past. Already magic was mentioned only in tales to scare children, and never recalled as something that had been real or alive in their society.

Neferia kept it alive in her heart though. Her dreams were coloured with visions of magical occurrences, including tables laden with food created by nothing more than sand. In her fantasies she saw the Emperor living in his golden pyramid, her sister's belly swollen with child, and then …

Terror struck as night beasts plagued Neferia's dreams. She saw them attacking the second tribe. People died of a poisonous sickness. Kil'n was afraid. She could feel it across the universes.

She tried to warn Aris.

'They will return,' Neferia said. 'They have to – they are dying.'

'It's just a dream,' he said.

But the dreams got worse.

The world beyond the stars was more real to Neferia than the one she shared with Aris during the day. She became dazed and confused when awake, as though this were the dream and the other her reality. She tried again to tell him what she was seeing, failing now to hide that spark of magic she had retained even after Kil'n left.

'That evil man, Hren,' she would say. 'He caused this ...'

'He's our leader. You should be careful what you say!' Aris told her.

Aris thought her ravings were the onslaught of insanity. He had her confined to her quarters and gave her little contact with the outside world – none with their daughter. She was fed, bathed and cared for only by trusted servants.

Aris took a mistress: any womb, even one that you hadn't bonded with, could bring forth more offspring. No-one would blame him under the circumstances, and deep down, the bond had always been second best for Neferia – she knew it in her heart. Just as she knew when he stopped visiting her that there was someone else.

Sometime during those strange early years Hren had noticed that the people needed faith and religion as much as science. He had appointed spiritual advisers who soon became priests. They controlled the citadel and the people, keeping them in a state of fear, and offered up innocent souls for sacrifice to obscure deities – a thing that Kil'n and the second tribe would never have permitted, for all life was precious and it was not for man to take it.

All of this Neferia saw as the years passed and she spent them more and more alone.

The second tribe through all this had one thing that the first tribe had lost: they retained their authentic spirituality. It was real, because the magic that the universe granted Kil'n was used always for their greater good. Neferia had never believed the lie that Hren had spouted about the consequences of using magic. The power was pure, not dark as their human science could be.

Ten years went by. She spent many hours alone, often drifting in and out of sleep, barely talking or eating. When she slept, she followed the lives of the second tribe. She understood that these were not dreams, but real events that she could somehow see because she was still connected to the magic. She saw their struggles and triumphs, the highs and lows, and finally the day when the children there were struck blind. When this vision came, Neferia knew that there could be only one outcome.

This time Neferia did not call for Aris and beg him to listen. Instead she got out of her bed for the first time in months. She washed and dressed herself, putting on her finest clothing. The servants were too shocked to stop her as she left her quarters. They had become complacent because she never tried to leave, and so they were uncertain what they must do if she did. One – a servant girl that Aris had recently taken to his bed – had the presence of mind to go and find him. But, by the time he arrived at Neferia's rooms, his wife was nowhere to be found.

A search was made and it was discovered that Neferia had taken Allsa, their daughter. Fearing for the child's safety, Aris ordered a hunt for mother and daughter, but no-one found them.

Meanwhile, Neferia and Allsa left their town. The vision had shown her the outcome and she had to get her daughter as far away from the capital as she could.

The Arrak Nah Tiamen arrived that day, and Aris's servants and warriors abandoned their search in order to fight for their homes.

The Mayan empire had grown but it hadn't been preparing for an attack for the last ten years. The Arraks had, and they were strong, unstoppable, superhuman.

Hren and Aris died at the hands of Kil'n.

Neferia saw the town burning in the distance. She took Allsa's hand and they continued their journey away from the land of their birth forever.

The montage continued, and Jas saw the mixing of the first tribe's blood as Allsa married and bred with the prince of another land, as did others who had escaped the slaughter. She knew then that the blood was diluted, but still inside her ancestors. She was born and reborn through her own kin, always as a prophet bearing bad news that no-one wanted to believe in.

In Troy her name had been Cassandra …

Jas tapped the staff and sent the images away.

'No more. I can't take any more.' It was too horrible. And she had been so alone in every lifetime. No wonder she was always ready to fight for those she loved in this lifetime. The past explained a lot about Jas's personality and behaviour. What it also revealed was that she had been trying to fight her destiny all this time, even though it was, probably, all predetermined. Knowing this, Jas forgave herself for all of her mistakes. She had been foolish to leave Arven, but she could understand now why she had been so resolute about returning to Earth.

The light of the first being shone before her again: Jasmine knew who he was now, and that it was with him, not in any particular place, that she truly belonged.

'Take me to Arven,' she said.

She tapped the staff down twice and the bubble of light burst.

15

She was outside the tent.

'You almost gave me a heart attack!' Kat said.

'Highness!' Prins and Elee bowed before her.

'How did you escape?' asked Kat.

Jas was spaced out, plummeted as she was back into the survivors' camp and facing two Arrak warriors. It was as if the world had altered in the few hours since she had been taken by Prestin and Baulin.

'I was supposed to find Arven …' she said, bemused.

Kat pointed at the tent.

'He's *here*?'

Kat nodded. 'Talking with Kale.'

'Thank god!'

Jas blinked, shaking away the replay of the other lives she had lived. None of them was important anymore. She knew that this was all about *now*.

She opened the tent flap and stepped inside.

'Jasmine!' said Arven.

He leapt to his feet and came to her, but halted a foot away. For a few moments there was an awkward tension between them, but then Jas stepped into the breach and took Arven's hand. Arven pulled her into his arms and held her as though he was afraid to ever let her out of his sight again. The hug was awkward because Jas did not wish to let go of the staff also. Eventually Arven stepped back and looked into her face as though he still could not believe her appearance.

'I'm a mage,' she said, holding the staff aloft.

'That belonged to Prestin,' Kale said.

'Not any more. He's lost his magic, which is just as well, because he and Marlin wanted to take over the world.'

'How did he lose his magic?' asked Kale.

'I'm not sure,' said Jas.

'Treachery is a serious crime,' Arven said.

Exhaustion overwhelmed Jas then. The baby kicked inside her as though furious.

'Ooh!' Jas said, placing her hand on her stomach. 'It kicks a lot these days.'

Arven looked at Jas's stomach, and then he did a very human thing. He placed his hand on her and stroked.

Julia had been silent while Arven and Kale had chatted in their own tongue, and although she didn't understand what was being said, she saw Jas's exhaustion and came to her aid.

'Sit,' she ordered.

For once Jas obeyed.

'We have much to do,' Jas said in English. 'Arven, we need your help. You have to protect these people. I won't allow your warriors to murder the men …'

'Of course,' Arven said. 'We must guard them.'

Jas sat back, surprised that her request was agreed to so easily.

'There is treachery in Sharik,' Arven said. 'I have to bring my people back in line …'

'I feel … weird …' Jas said, and then the staff slipped from her hands and she slumped.

Arven scooped her up in his arms and carried her over to her bed. Her face was deathly pale and perspiration beaded on her forehead.

Kale placed a hand on Jas's head.

'There's a fever burning through her. She has never become sick before,' he said.

'The baby?' asked Julia

Kale ran his hands above Jas's stomach. 'All is well with the child … but …'

Arven met Kale's eyes and confirmed what he already knew, 'There are two.'

'Twins?' Julia asked. 'How wonderful!'

Arven glanced at Julia, 'What are *twins*?'

'Wait. You have never had twins before?' Julia asked. The two Arrak men looked blank. 'Two babies born from the same womb? No? Sometimes they are from the same egg and are identical, other times they are from two eggs that were fertilised.'

'This has never been known in our world,' Kale explained.

'Well, you weren't with Earth women before, so I suppose this is another difference we have. But anyway, I don't understand why twins would give Jas a fever. That has to be something else. She's caught a virus or something – which isn't surprising, as she's been burning the candle at both ends since we got here.'

'I need to examine her properly,' Kale said. 'Her back …'

Jas was in a feverish haze and unable to respond to their request that she sit up.

Julia helped Kale roll her on her side, and they pulled the robe away from her shoulder. Kale gasped.

'What is it?' Julia said.

'No. It's not possible. The Earth women are *immune*.'

'What?' Julia asked again. 'Tell me!'

'The same symptoms of the virus that killed our women. It started with fever and rash. Nothing worked to cure it,' Kale said.

'But how can this be?' asked Arven.

'Changed us …' Jas murmured. 'Prestin cast … spell. Said he would make us like you …'

'That fool!' Kale said. 'But such magic was banned. How did he know the spell?'

Arven shook his head. He saw in his mind's eye the symbol that Kil'n had drawn to give his people the sex magic that had changed them all into Arrak Nah Tiamen and taken away their human weaknesses. But how could Prestin have known this spell? Especially when their order had banned the use of magic that changed their physical form, ever since the dawn of their civilisation …

Kale brought his staff to the side of the bed and tapped it lightly on the ground. He held his other hand over Jas's forehead. The fever diminished and she slowly came round.

'You've cured her,' Julia said.

'No. It's temporary. Despite everything we've done to negate it, this is still the force of the curse working.'

'Curse?' Jas and Julia asked together.

Jas sat up and was able to take some water that Julia brought to her in a crystal chalice. Then she lay back down, because she still felt an overwhelming weakness in her limbs. Her joints ached as her immune system attempted to fight the sickness.

'It's time we told you about the two tribes,' Arven said.

When Arven finished his story, Jas filled them in on the history she knew of the first tribe and the part of Neferia.

'She was connected to Kil'n,' Jas said to Arven. 'I think perhaps he made a mistake choosing Shamila. His *chio mien* was always Neferia. But humans are flawed that way, Arven. We fight against real love. Maybe it frightens us. And at the time, Kil'n was still human, despite his obvious magical ability.'

'What does this all mean?' asked Julia. 'Are we all going to die? After everything we've done, how hard we've fought to survive, it's all going tits up anyway?'

'There's a chance we can undo the damage,' Kale said. 'Reverse the change spell. It hasn't fully taken hold yet anyway; Jasmine has not grown in height and her skin does not have the golden hue we have.'

Jas glanced at her arms. 'All true. And Prestin has lost his power. Maybe it will reverse itself like the prison tent and the oasis did.'

'We need to learn what he did and make sure,' Kale said. 'Are you strong enough to show me where they are?'

'Yes. I'm feeling much stronger by the second. Whatever you did, I'm myself again.'

Jas stood and reached once more for the staff. The minute she touched it the power ignited for her.

'This is mine now,' she said, as much to herself as to the others.

Arven went outside and brought Prins and Elee in.

'Where's Kat gone?' Jas asked.

'A man came and she took him away to explain I think, Highness' said Prins.

'Was his name *Taylor*?'

'I think that was what she called him,' Elee said.

'Julia. Will you go and find Taylor? Fill him in on the details, inasmuch as Arven is back and he is willing to help. Don't tell him anything about my sickness. It shouldn't affect anyone in this camp, though it might be working on the women in the Arrak towns. We have to find out, and I don't want anyone here to panic.'

Julia nodded. 'All right. What are you guys going to do?'

'We're going to go to Marlin's hide-out and get hold of Prestin.'

'Be careful,' Julia said. Then she hugged Kale.

Arven watched this with no judgement. It made his heart ache with sympathy for them both. He liked to see the mage so relaxed and comfortable with the woman. Why shouldn't the mage also find love? Didn't everyone deserve happiness?

Arven, Kale, Jas, Prins and Elee stood in a circle outside the tent.

'A vortex?' asked Kale.

'No. A bubble,' said Jas. 'Like this.'

She tapped her staff down once and the group found themselves surrounded by the golden orb of light that Jas had conjured earlier to exact her escape. This time they were not thrown off planet: Jas was a quick learner. Arven recognised it as the same spell he had used to get them off the Eleventh Moon.

'She's channelling your power,' Kale said, his eyes wide with wonder. 'She's your royal consort and carrying your child. That is powerful magic brought over from Kil'n's heritage.'

Jas tapped the staff down once more. The bubble burst and they stood now before the remnants of the prison tent. It was mostly disintegrated but not completely destroyed.

'A bit less messy than a vortex for a short hop, don't you think?' Jas said.

Jas turned around, looking for Marlin and Prestin, but neither the councillor nor the former mage was anywhere to be seen.

'Search for them,' said Arven. 'They can't have gone far.'

Prins and Elee drew their swords and ran to search the remnants of the camp. They came back with Almani. On seeing the Emperor, Almani fell to his knees and begged forgiveness.

'You have done nothing to need it,' Arven told the boy.

'Look!' Jas said. She was squinting out into the desert. 'Warriors. Probably Marlin's men returning.'

There were only a few men riding toward them on el lien mecks, and as they drew closer Jas recognised the warrior that had captured her, Baulin. The band looked tired and wounded now though, as though they had fought a battle and, after losing, had fled to save their own lives. When he saw the collapsed oasis and Jas among the others, Almani still kneeling at their feet, he charged toward them, failing to recognise Kale or Arven

'Get the Empress!' cried Baulin.

Arven drew his own sword on reflex, and as Baulin galloped toward him, the Emperor ran out and leapt into the air with impossible agility. He swung his sword: it bit through flesh and bone easily and Baulin's head rolled across the sand.

The el lien meck he had been riding galloped onwards with its headless rider until the body of Baulin flopped and crumpled to the sand a few feet from the camp.

The three other warriors pulled up their mounts and stared at Arven as though they had just seen the devil.

'They said you were dead!' one of them gabbled.

'I'm very much alive,' Arven said. He held his sword in a battle-ready stance.

Elee and Prins flanked Arven's sides, swords drawn as they expected the remaining warriors to attack. But faced with the Emperor, the misguided warriors leapt from their el lien mecks and grovelled in the sand at his feet.

'Where are Marlin and Prestin?' Arven asked.

'We thought they were here. Marlin gave orders to attack Abeken and kill him and Taenan.'

'You attacked a councillor and a mage?' Arven said, appalled.

'They still live,' pleaded the warriors. 'The councillor was ready for us. We were outnumbered and barely escaped with our lives. We didn't know, Highness! Marlin told us stories that made no sense, but we had to believe were true. At first he said the orders were coming from you. Then that you were dead and had left instructions we must follow. He said that Abeken and Taenan had killed you.'

Arven didn't believe the warriors, but knew he would deal with them later.

'Kale, rebuild the prison tent, please,' he said.

Kale did so with just one tap of his staff, and the three warriors were sent inside. The ward was set, banning them from leaving.

'Without magic, Marlin and Prestin would have to have left on foot or el lien mecks, but where would they go?' Jas said.

She turned around in a circle, then tapped the staff down twice. A spark from the gem sent a beam of light up into the air and around and behind her. She turned and squinted once more into the desert. There she saw movement in the distance.

'I'll deal with this,' Arven said.

Then he did something he had never thought possible before his trip to the Eleventh Moon: he raised his hand and drew a symbol of power in the air.

Jas felt a thrill of excitement as Kil'n's magic once more coursed through the Emperor's veins. The symbol ignited. Hair stood up on her arms and the back of her neck as she felt the magic ripple in the air. Arven's energy was strong.

One minute Marlin and Prestin were riding away from them, the next they were riding back. When the two traitors saw Arven, Jas, Kale and their warriors, they halted their mounts and turned them around, but no matter how hard they tried, they always found themselves approaching, not retreating from, the oasis.

Finally exhausted, the el lien mecks came to a halt in front of the prison tent. Elee and Prins pulled the men off the animals and dragged them across the sand, throwing them at Arven's and Jas's feet.

'You have betrayed me,' Arven said.

'There has been some misunderstanding,' said Marlin, summoning up all the guile he could. 'Everything we have done has been to protect the Empress. Abeken has staged a …'

Marlin paused.

'On Earth we call it a "mutiny",' said Jas. 'And you were the instigator of this treachery. Not Abeken.'

'No. No, Highness. My men have tried to take Sharik back from the traitors.'

'Prestin,' said Arven, 'you are a disgrace to your order. The punishment of losing your magic has already been dealt for your crime. You will be forced to live as a low-rank Arrak, a station that is fitting for such a misguided and unwise man. But first you'll tell me of the magic you used to change the Earth women.'

Prestin bowed low before Arven, relieved that his life at least would be spared. He did not consider the torment that life without magic would be. Arven knew only too well what that was like, and fully understood the punishment he had given.

'A spell, Highness. I found it in your mage's tent among the ancient scrolls that Kale once took care of.'

Kale and Arven glanced at each other.

'Where is this scroll now?' asked Kale.

Prestin pulled it from inside his robe. 'Some men struggle with the differences between our races. I wanted only to bridge that gap.'

'You're a fool, Prestin. Did it never occur to you that by changing the Earth women into Arrak females you would be opening them up to the pestilence that killed our women in the first place? The only reason the Earth women have survived here is because as humans they are immune to it. By breeding with them we are protecting future generations from the disease. They must *never* become us!'

Prestin was shocked by this revelation: it hadn't occurred to him at all, but this did not excuse his treachery. Arven took the scroll from the former mage's trembling hand.

'Take them into the prison tent,' Arven ordered.

When Prins and Elee pulled the traitors away, he unrolled the scroll and read.

'A curse, not a spell,' he said. 'Written in the hand of my wife, Celin.'

'But that would mean … Celin *knew* who she was …' Jas said.

'In which case she deliberately took the life of all of the females, including our daughter,' Arven said. 'What evil her magic wrought so long ago. How could it have existed still inside a soul that was born and reborn over and over? Did she learn nothing in those lifetimes?'

'She cursed herself to see this hex through, Highness,' Kale said. 'She could not evolve as you did.'

'May she rot in hell,' said Jas. '*Bitch.*'

Then all the energy went from her body again and she sank to her knees.

'The plague!' Kale said. 'It grows stronger inside her!'

Jas's skin was glowing: a golden tone, contrary to her usual paler skin colour.

'The change is still happening. But it seems impossible when Prestin's recent magicks have all been reversed,' Arven said.

'Not this spell, though, Highness. It was not Prestin's magic behind it, but tainted with the death of our entire female population. Billions of Arrak women died to give this the potency it has,' explained Kale. 'Not just one mere woman taking her own life.'

Arven read the words of the spell over and over. Then he looked into his soul, at that residue of connection he still had with Kil'n. A symbol came to his mind, but he doubted its validity. Kil'n's magic could not always be trusted.

'I see something, but it isn't right. It is a symbol to create the change, but I need one to reverse it.'

Arven thought through the enchantment. In his mind's eye he looked at the pattern of the sex magic symbol. After discovering that each symbol had rudiments that represented what the spell needed to achieve, he analysed each curve and swirl. This sign was oval: it had the Arrak symbols for male and female drawn within it. Other elements represented change, power, strength, and all were brought together with a binding mark.

Arven was unused to analysing spells, and even though the magic had once been his birthright, he did not know how to interpret and reverse what he saw.

'I don't know what to do,' he said to Kale.

'Show me what is in your mind.'

Kale took Arven's hand this time, and he searched inside the Emperor's mind to find the symbol of sex magic in the forefront.

'This should be removed,' he said, indicating the binding sign. 'The male element too, as we are reversing only the spell worked on the Earth women. Combined with the binder used in Celin's spell.'

Then Kale added an image that Arven hadn't thought of. A small grey circle with a ring around it, representing the Earth and its orbiting moon. 'The Earth women have altered since contact with us. We cannot eradicate the change Prestin started without damaging the good transformations that have occurred,' Kale said. 'And so I would add this ... It will stop further change.'

The image that came to Arven's mind was instantly recognisable as an improved version of Earth women. They would be strong, healthy, have the longevity that the Arrak men had. That couldn't be a bad thing, could it?

'How?' asked Arven.

'This image is a code for the first tribe's bloodline.' Kale said, indicating the Earth symbol. 'They all carry a trace of it inside themselves. This symbol will enhance that connection, effectively making them *more* like their ancestors. They will change a little, in some ways they will be further human. But by not reversing what has happened so far, they will retain the elements we need them to.'

Arven nodded. He pulled together the rudiments Kale suggested, adding Celin's binding symbol back at the end, and then raised his hand in the air. His lilac and blue swirling pupils froze as he drew this powerful sign, and then the air ignited.

The symbol hung like a ring of fire in the air, and then the magic flashed outward and into Jas. She threw out her arms, taking the power into her chest. She felt it coursing through her veins and out again. It used her as a conduit as it sent waves of energy across the planet.

'I feel them!' said Arven. 'Every one of the women. They were growing sicker as the change crept upon them.'

'The magic is cleansing the change,' said Kale. 'Yes, there will be modifications, but for the better.'

The magic pulsed for a few more moments and then the symbol extinguished and vanished from sight.

'Jasmine?' Arven said.

'I'm all right,' she said, using the staff to help her stand. 'And so are the others. Now we need to do the same for the Earth men who have joined us too.'

Arven and Kale studied her face. She looked the same as she had earlier, only now her aura glowed bright and visible, and a cloak of white light surrounded her head like a halo. Then the light slipped into Jas's normally black hair. It turned pure white and waved over her shoulders. The transformation gave Jas an ethereal quality.

'How do I look?' she asked.

'Like a goddess,' said Arven.

16

Al Kuzemen Taenan and Councillor Abeken were waiting in the Emperor's tent when Arven arrived back at Sharik with Jas and Kale. Prins and Elee had remained at the oasis to keep an eye on the prisoners until Arven sent reinforcements to bring them back.

'Highness!' Abeken said falling to one knee. 'We've been awaiting your return.'

'When I realised Prestin's treachery and felt Malachi's death,' said Taenan, 'I enlisted Councillor Abeken's help. The league of mages sent you the foresight and strength to use Malachi's staff. But we couldn't reach you, even so …'

Arven knew instantly that the mage and councillor were telling him the truth; he felt it in the core of his new found power.

'Now I see why the thought to try it came into my mind. You did reach out to me, Taenan!'

'Taenan saw into Prestin's mind as his guard was down, trying to prevent Malachi from bringing you all back home. He saw how Elidon had murdered Garuk, and we knew that he and Marlin were planning a takeover. Forewarned, I was ready to thwart them.'

'You had a trap waiting for Baulin's warriors?'

'Yes, Highness. The attack was … predictable,' said Taenan.

'We have Prestin and Marlin and the three warriors held in an oasis four lecks away,' said Kale, and he gave the location to Abeken, who left the tent to give the order to bring the men back.

'I need your help still more,' Arven said when Abeken returned.

'Name it, Highness. We are always your servants,' Taenan said.

'We need to call a council meeting as soon as possible. I have learnt some interesting things on my expedition to the Eleventh Moon, all of which I can share with you. But it's going to need trust and faith from all of us to make this work. You support will be crucial to our success.'

'You have it unconditionally,' Abeken said.

Arven explained what he had learnt.

'We need to learn to live side by side with the people of Earth,' Arven began. 'You see, we committed a serious crime when we attacked them. The curse of Shamila was ours to bear. Had we known of it before we attacked, then I would not have given the order. This curse is destined to repeat itself unless we find a way to negate it permanently. We have to make the two tribes one again.'

'How do we do this?' asked Taenan.

'There are 500 Earth survivors in a camp ten lecks south,' Kale said. 'Among them, human males. None of them must be harmed.'

'Where did they come from?' asked Taenan.

'I brought them with Kale,' said Jas. 'We think they are all that's left of humankind, because the Earth was poisoned. They are few in number, but they must be brought into the fold and given equal rights.'

'I'm not sure how we would put this to the Arrak who have no wives ...' Abeken said.

'Things have changed. The Earth women here and in the camp have also altered. We haven't finished with this magic yet, as we need to enhance the human males too, if they are to survive,' Jas said.

'I see the transformation in you, Highness,' Taenan said. 'It is indeed miraculous.'

'We already have one human male here. Prestin kept him locked up in a warded tent,' Abeken said. 'I didn't know what we should do with him.'

On Arven's order they brought Gerald to the imperial tent.

'Tell us what you told Prestin,' Arven ordered.

Gerald drooled on the rug, saying nothing but gibberish.

'What's wrong with him?' asked Arven.

Kale placed a hand on Gerald's forehead. 'His mind is a mess. Prestin raided his memory. *This* is how he knew the location of the survivors' camp.'

'What else did he reveal to Prestin?' asked Jas.

'I cannot get anything from him. Prestin has destroyed him beyond redemption.'

'I can't say it's not a fitting end,' Jas shrugged.

Prins and Elee arrived and requested an audience with Arven.

'Come in, friends,' said Arven. 'Are the prisoners now in Sharik?'

'Yes, Highness,' said Prins.

'Bring Prestin to me.'

Prins hurried to obey, and Prestin was brought before him. Prins pushed the former mage down to his knees before the Emperor and Empress as Abeken, Kale and Taenan bore witness.

'What information did you get from this man?' Arven asked.

Prestin was shocked as he looked at Gerald. He had thought the human long since executed.

'He … is the vilest of humans,' said Prestin finally. 'He deserves only death …'

'We didn't ask that,' said Jas. 'Now speak unless you want Kale to do to you what you did to him …'

The thought of having his mind invaded horrified Prestin. As a mage he could have protected himself, but now his magic was gone he knew he could do nothing. He observed the Empress, noting her change. This was not the work of the spell he had cast but of something else. He noticed his staff in Jas's hand and reached for it.

'Mine …' he said.

'The Guild revoked your magic after I reported your crime to them, Prestin,' said Taenan.

Jas tapped the staff on the ground. The gem on the top sparked and illuminated the room in indigo light.

'It's mine now,' said Jas.

'The Empress is an adept …' Taenan said, surprised.

'No,' said Kale. 'She's a fully-fledged mage.'

Faced with this anomaly, Prestin told them all he knew.

'And so,' Arven told the 11 remaining councillors, 'there must be some changes if we are to avert the curse. First I want to introduce you to two new council members. This is Sylvia and Kat. They are human and they will be representing the humans on Emin in future.'

Sylvia and Kat entered. Both of them bore the mark of the change. Kat's hair was now a glowing mass of vibrant red, streaked with silver white, and Sylvia's previously white hair was now a golden blonde. They were both enhanced and youthful in appearance, even though Sylvia had been in her seventies prior to the magic.

They had been briefed by Kale on what to anticipate, but no-one had expected the total silence of the councillors as the two human women took the seats that had been allocated to them.

The councillors had listened carefully to Arven's recounting of Kil'n's and Shamila's story, followed by Jas's revelation of her history in the first tribe. It was a tale that could be thought of as legend or myths, but none of them refuted it. The evidence of this ancient curse, so recently invoked, could not be denied.

'We welcome you into our community,' Abeken said, bowing his head to the two Earth women.

'If I may?' Taenan said, leaving his place beside Abeken. 'Kat, is it?'

'Yes,' Kat replied.

'You have something else that few others do. Something that will be beneficial to our joint communities.'

Kat smiled and looked at Jas, 'What is he saying?'

'I wish to invite you to the Guild of Mages,' he said. 'We know you to be an adept of great ability. The Guild can feel it. You will be the first woman ever to be a member, and we will teach you to use your gift for the good of your people and ours.'

'I don't know what to say …' Kat said.

Taenan held out a staff. It was the perfect height for Kat and the gem on the top looked like a ruby: her favourite jewel.

'Take it, Kat,' said Jas.

Kat took the staff, and immediately the gem flared in recognition.

'It knows it belongs to you,' Jas said.

The councillors cheered in astonishment. It was a confusing and surprising turn of events, but one that they all were ready to embrace. It was time for change, and no-one could object. Even their Emperor could wield magic, an anomaly they could never have expected.

'And now to our final business,' said Abeken. 'You know what must be done. Do we have a yes?'

The vote to return to Earth to put right the wrong was unanimous.

17

Prestatyn, Earth

They were only eight days free of the base when they heard the helicopter flying overhead.

The fifth columnists had settled into their new protected home after Harrington and some of the other men had moved the trucks and cars into the garages of the abandoned local houses. Any vehicles too big to be hidden had been driven further away. The majority were near enough to get to if needed, but out of obvious sight if Handley's men came looking.

The lives of the columnists had become somewhat Bohemian. They were glad to be able to relax and not have their superiors breathing down their necks. It was particularly freeing for the women, who felt no pressure to cook and clean. But it soon became clear that someone had to do the basic tasks or the living conditions in the hotel would become unbearable. After all, it was not really safe for any of them to go outside: the air had thickened into a dense smog that hung around the hotel as though it knew there was clean air inside and wanted to taint it.

To give them all focus, a rota of work was set up, suggested by Donovan.

'We had to do this at the Trafford Centre,' he explained. 'It was the only fair thing to do.'

Donovan had recovered well from the beating he had received at the hands of Handley's thugs. And after the men had told him that all of the Trafford Centre survivors had escaped the military's clutches, he had to accept that he might never see Caroline and his children ever again. He tried to believe that they were safe somewhere. He trusted Jas and Taylor and knew they would have at least tried to make sure everyone was okay. Jas was by nature a leader; even, some might say, a heroine. Donovan had always seen that in her.

'The girls are recovering well,' Kerry said to Tremaine as they met in the bar. 'The drugs are out of their system and they don't appear to remember anything of the last few years. I think that's a blessing, and I'm hoping they never recall what happened.'

'According to the file, they were administered a variant of flunitrazepam,' Tremaine explained. 'A form of rohypnol that didn't send them to sleep but had a powerful hypnotic quality that made them easy to manipulate. The side effect was that it also caused amnesia. They might remember something eventually – but it will feel like a dream rather than reality.'

'What about the second injection you were given?' Harrington asked.

'An adrenaline-based drug that could have beneficial properties as long as the recipient hadn't been exposed to the smog outside. So my source hadn't lied. The girls won't need it now, though, and I wouldn't risk it, just in case. Especially after what happened to Alan Kenney.'

The women were no longer behaving like asylum patients and had begun to communicate, first with Kerry as she took it upon herself to look after them, and later with each other. As they improved, Kerry assigned them all tasks to do, thinking that having some focus would be easier on them all.

'What's that?' Kerry said. 'That sound …'

The chatter of the occupants relaxing in the bar area ceased. They all heard the whirring as air beat against powerful rotors, like the wings of a giant bird fighting to stay in the air.

'Shit!' said Harrington. 'It's a helicopter.'

'Don't panic, it could be just flying over, searching,' said Tremaine.

'I'll go and check,' said Kerry.

Kerry hurried to the dining room where the former P Class women often congregated. The women were calm, failing to notice anything peculiar outside. All of the hotel windows had shutters that were firmly closed and airtight to keep the poison outside from leaking in. There was a camera monitor set up in the dining room of the front of the hotel, though, and Kerry glanced at it now.

She saw a stream of military vehicles pulling up outside. Masked and armed soldiers got out of the backs of the trucks and moved toward the hotel.

Kerry ran back into the bar and told the others what was happening. By then, Harrington was already manning the door and airlock.

'Masks on, everyone,' he said. 'Take the exit route out of the back. Kerry, get the girls masked and their coats on. You all know the escape drill.'

They had been over what to do if James's or Handley's men showed up. Now the families were in a state of panic. Kerry left the doorway and went into the dining-room with a box of masks and instructed all of the women to put one on and find a coat. Outdoor clothing and masks were always kept handy in case of such an emergency.

'They're ready,' Kerry said. 'I'll get them downstairs. Come with us

Harrington!'

'I have to make sure the airlock isn't breached,' he said. 'But the damn metal blast shutter on this side won't activate. It seems to have rusted in place. Fuck! If I can get it down it won't keep them out but will slow them down. That should give us at least some chance of escaping.'

'Leave it. We can't stay now they know we're here …' Kerry said.

'I know but … we'll lose everything. The provisions we've spent years saving …'

'Harrington,' said Tremaine. '*Love*. Come on. This place is fucked.'

Harrington put on a mask, pulled on his coat. He gave the metal blast sheet one last try. Then he was thrown back as an explosion blasted through the grille and the first airlock door.

Tremaine pulled him to his feet and they both ran for the stairs, down into the former spa area and out through the door that the survivors had prepared for such an eventuality.

'How the fuck did they find us?' Tremaine cried into his mask.

As the air outside hit his face, his mask steamed up. He could barely see, but he held onto Harrington's arm as they ran toward the promenade.

'Where to?' asked Harrington.

'Head for the dunes, hide where you can,' said Tremaine. 'Then we'll make our way to where we hid the other trucks.'

The smog worked in their favour. As the people poured out of the building, the helicopter above couldn't see them. It circled around, stirring the poisonous air with its rotors. Another explosion came from the hotel and Harrington knew that the inner airlock door had now been breached. The hotel was lost to them, and everything in it. But they couldn't think about survival beyond escaping capture. There was no going back, even if they all died today.

Donovan was leading the P Class women with Kerry, and some of the wives and their children followed behind. They ran as hard and as fast as possible toward the former arcade just off the promenade. Beyond that, perhaps a mile along the beach, were the sand dunes and a possible hiding place.

Then, the ground churned up beneath their feet. Collectively the women and men stumbled. Gina, one of the P Class women, fell on the concrete of the promenade. Blood seeped through into the knee of her jeans and she nursed her knee, staring in fascination at the blood.

'Come on Gina,' said Kerry, grabbing her arm. She hoisted the petite woman up onto her feet, and that was when the spinning vortex opened up in front of her.

Kerry screamed. She clung to Gina, unable to run as her legs froze.

'Come on!' said a very human voice in front of them. The smog cleared as Jinx magic repelled the poison from around the vortex, and fresh air from

Emin poured through onto Earth.

Kerry looked up and saw a beautiful woman with white hair holding a bejewelled staff. She was wearing a long kaftan, and Kerry couldn't help thinking how she looked like one of the fey in the *Lord of the Rings* movies she had seen years ago as a kid. She had to be one of the Sidhe, or maybe she was an angel.

'Get inside,' the woman called. 'We've come to save you!'

Tears streamed down Kerry's face as she ran forward, still holding Gina, and the other women followed her as though she were their saviour.

They ran into the centre of vortex, as armour-clad Jinx hurried out at the sides and headed towards the hotel.

'Oh god! It's the Jinx!' one of the soldiers' wives said.

'I'm human,' said Jas, 'and we're here to help. Trust me for the sake of your children. Get inside!'

The soldiers and their families were terrified, but something about Jas's voice and appearance gave them confidence. They entered the spinning tunnel of sand and air and turned as one to look out at the hotel as members of Handley's and James's militia swarmed around the building toward them.

They were greeted by the Jinx warriors.

Jas raised her staff and tapped it down on the stable platform inside the vortex. Outside, the soldier's weapons backfired, and the fifth columnists and their kin watched as their enemies were mercilessly cut down by the Jinx.

Jas swallowed. This brought back so many memories of the first attacks on Earth by the Jinx. The death and the horror and the slaughter. Though she understood now why that had happened, and recognised the predicament that the Jinx had found themselves in, she still couldn't erase those images of men and woman being cut down and slaughtered by the giant Jinx warriors emerging from a terrifying spinning vortex in the sky. Was what she was doing with the Jinx now, any better?

'Good riddance to bad rubbish,' said Gina.

Kerry met the woman's eyes and saw a small tear slip down her gaunt cheek.

'You'll be all right now,' said Jas, placing a hand on Gina's arm.

'Jas?' said a voice behind her.

'Donovan! Oh my God. I never thought we'd see you again,' Jas said. She hugged him. Tears welled up in her eyes. The whole experience of being here, rescuing these poor people and bringing the might of the Jinx down on the enemy, was almost overwhelming. Then – finding Donovan alive among the group. She had a conflict of emotion – both happy and sad all at the same time.

'You look *different* … Is Caroline okay?' he asked.

'She'll be better than okay once she knows you're alive,' Jas said, wiping her eyes.

Having despatched most of the soldiers, the Jinx warriors returned to the vortex. There Jas tapped the staff down once more and the wormhole closed, shutting out the poisonous atmosphere.

Then two of the warriors, shorter than the average Jinx, removed their helmets, and Donovan found himself face to face with his captain, Taylor Arch, and Sergeant Harvey.

They barely had time to speak before the vortex reopened on the outskirts of Sharik.

The survivors huddled together in terror as they looked out onto the vast plains of Emin, with the city of Sharik in the middle-distance, and twin suns shining in an alien sky.

Jas could appreciate what they were going through, and remembered her first sight of the alien city and landscape.

'Explanations soon!' Jas said. 'Let's get these families settled in their new home.'

18

'Every day when I wake I have to pinch myself. I can't believe we are working with the Jinx,' Harrington said. 'And they are helping us. *Saving* us.'

'Things have changed in both their world and ours,' Tremaine said. 'I for one will be relieved to see those women finally freed.'

Kale was leading this attack; and after briefing the fifth columnists on their agenda, Jas, Arven and Kale had their full support. The intelligence they had been able to gain from one captured soldier revealed the location of most of the bases on Earth, and there had been several simultaneous attacks that had successfully rescued the P Class and breeder women from the clutches of James's men.

This one, Tremaine wanted to be present for. He wanted to see the breeders of MD59 finally freed. And hopefully also to salvage the children who had been born into this awful place over the last five years. He felt responsible for them and it was the only way he could ever live with himself for letting Handley control them for so long.

They had been living with the Jinx for several months before hitting MD59. On Earth no time had passed at all. They arrived at MD59 at exactly the same time as Jas was saving them and the other fifth columnists over in Prestatyn. Tremaine tried not to think about this, because it made his head hurt as he worried about the paradox.

'There's no such thing,' Jas laughed. 'And we have to do these raids this way. All effectively happening at the same moment in order to ensure that none of them has the chance to raise the alarm. We want to get those bastards. No matter how long it takes us.'

Of course they couldn't physically attack the bases one after another. Warriors needed rest and recuperation between battles. The soldiers didn't give up their cowardly new world easily. They fought for the right to keep their bigoted lifestyle. But they all went down in the end. Those who didn't fight were given amnesty and brought back to Emin with the rescued females and children. Some of them proved to be fifth columnists from other bases. There had been a shocking number of the men willing to renounce James's and Handley's corrupt lifestyle.

'A big day for us,' said Harrington. He was wearing Jinx armour, and a visor down over his face protected him from the poisonous Earth atmosphere. Tremaine was wearing combats and one of the gas masks they had retained from their own escape.

Taylor and his men, as well as many Arrak warriors, marched into Kale's vortex, which had been opened beside them.

'I need to make contact with you,' Kale said to Tremaine. 'To see the base … we are going to try to materialise inside.'

'Okay,' said Tremaine. He offered his hand awkwardly to Kale.

The vortex closed and Tremaine felt a momentary surge of claustrophobia as the walls swirled around them, then the portal opened up.

There was screaming and chaos as they arrived. Handley's soldiers were depleted, out as they were currently attacking the Beaches Hotel.

The portal's appearance inside the base was so disruptive it undermined the structure. As Taylor's men and the Jinx warriors swarmed out, huge lumps of concrete dislodged from the ceiling, tumbling down beside the vortex. Kale tapped his staff down inside and the vortex span, snake-like, to a safer location where the men were not at risk as they exited.

No matter what happened, the warriors would not be stopped. They emerged in an endless stream, swords swinging. The first soldiers who opposed them fell.

After that the rest were cowed. Jas and Arven wanted to spare as many lives as possible. Some would be given a chance to earn their redemption.

'Which way to the medical centre?' asked Taylor.

Tremaine led the way. Taylor gave a guttural order in the Arrak tongue. He had picked up the language well in the last few months and was respected by the warriors, who acknowledged his brave leadership.

'Andy, go with the doc!' Taylor said, and Jas's former pupil, now a grown man, hurried to follow his captain's order.

A platoon of Jinx warriors followed Tremaine, Harrington and Andy, while the others split into several groups that swept through the bases, finding and rescuing any females and children. There were many, and a few men among the soldiers who surrendered willingly when they recognised Taylor. He was ready to give them all the benefit of the doubt. After all, not every man on the bases was evil: many had been caught up in this against their wishes. Their only crime was that of not saying 'no' to the situation for fear. After all, like warring countries of old, if you didn't stand with your enemy then you were against them, and liable then to become part of the fodder.

'This way,' said Tremaine as they reached the medical centre. He keyed in his passcode and found it still worked. He had hoped that security would remain tardy. Handley had not run a tight ship – he had been too concerned about his baser instincts and too secure in his position.

Now Tremaine led the warriors through the centre and to the breeders' wards.

'Where are they all?' Tremaine said as he opened the door to the first ward. The beds were empty and none of the women that had been there was around.

In the next ward he found five women, heavily pregnant.

Startled by the sight of the Jinx warriors, the women screamed and cowered.

'It's all right!' said Tremaine. 'We're here to rescue you.'

'Dr Tremaine,' a woman called Cilla cried. 'We thought you were dead.'

'Where are the others?' he asked.

'A few hours ago Handley and James came in with some soldiers. They took anyone who wasn't pregnant,' Cilla said. 'We think to the P Sector.'

'Those bastards!

'Go with Andy,' he said to the women.

'But the Jinx …'

'They won't hurt you,' Tremaine explained.

Andy and six of the warriors led the women back to the vortex.

'Come with me,' Tremaine said. 'This way.'

The warriors passed through a set of corridors and came out of a door at the back of the medical centre. There Tremaine led them through a short cut to the P Sector.

'That's the nursery,' he explained to one of Taylor's men. 'We'll go on the way back and take any of the babies left there. But first we need to get those women out of here.'

As they approached the P Sector, Tremaine saw the guard-house and, trying not to remember the last time he had been here picking up Alan Kenney's body, he hurried forward.

'There's no-one manning it,' Harrington said. Reaching inside, he opened up the drawer in the guard desk. He took out the emergency key card and they went to the airlock, swiping the card down the scanner.

The door opened and Harrington and Tremaine took some of the warriors inside.

'It'll take too long to get everyone through,' Harrington said as the door opened up on the other side.

Tremaine turned to the platoon leader and, with a spattering of Arrak words and gestures, managed to explain the dilemma.

The Jinx warrior studied the glass airlock door that had closed behind them. Then he raised his sword and smashed it down. It was reinforced glass, but it shattered as though it were cheap crystal, spitting fragments out into the sentry area.

The remaining warriors and soldiers passed through, kicking the glass clear as they did. The P Sector was now truly compromised.

Harrington hurried ahead, looking in the windows of the rooms used for individual conditioning. All were empty. They reached the end and Harrington swiped the card down. The door opened.

What greeted them shocked and sickened Tremaine to the core. The women were all on the beds, hooked up to IVs that pumped the hypnosis drug into their systems. Each was naked, with a soldier between her legs, fucking her. In the corner Handley's fat bulk crushed a petite girl beneath it, and James was pressing his cock into the mouth of the same girl – it didn't matter that she was too drugged up to do what he wanted her to do and suck him off.

'You bastard!' said Tremaine. One of the soldiers fell away from one of the women. She wasn't fully under and had been sobbing as the man had been brutally raping her.

Tremaine looked at the Jinx platoon warrior and said. 'Kill all the men.'

There would be no mercy for these men. Not after this.

Handley and James were pulled away from the woman and hauled before Harrington and Tremaine. The two men were forced down. They were half dressed, cocks going rapidly flaccid as they realised that they were in a bad situation. But still Handley had to try to take back control.

'Tremaine, you treacherous bastard ...' said Handley. 'I'll have you executed for this.'

'No you won't.'

The other soldiers were yanked away from the women and Jinx swords sliced through them until a pile of bodies was in the centre of the room.

Harrington went to the aid of the women, removing the IVs and pulling blankets around them.

The Jinx platoon leader came to Tremaine's side. He seemed to understand that the two men kneeling before the doctor were somehow important.

'Kill?' he said.

Tremaine held out his hand. The platoon leader nodded, then he gave Tremaine his sword.

'You're never going to do this to another woman,' Tremaine said.

At that moment, James pulled a small pistol from his boot. He grabbed Handley's arm and yanked him to his feet as the warriors, and Tremaine and Harrington, looked on.

Tremaine was amused by the two pathetic leaders' attempt to escape. A quick death was too good for them both. Tremaine raised the sword and swung it above his head, as he did so, James squeezed the trigger. A bullet flew from the barrel and headed towards Tremaine. Harrington dived in front of him. The bullet burst into Harrington's arm, shattering bone as it passed through, but he did what he had set out to do: he saved the man he loved.

'Jesus!' Tremaine said. Handley and James used the distraction to exit through a door that led to the back corridor.

'Get them!' said Tremaine, as he dropped the warrior's sword and, tearing up the shirt of one of the fallen soldiers, created a tourniquet to wrap around Harrington's arm.

Three of the warriors followed Handley and James through the door. There were further gunshots, and some guttural cries from the warriors as the bullets grazed their armour.

Once Harrington was taken care of, Tremaine retrieved the sword and followed the warriors to learn what had happened to Handley and James. He found the two men cornered in one of the labs. Handley had a large syringe in his hand; James still pointed the gun, but had apparently run out of bullets.

On seeing Tremaine, Handley began to plead for his life.

'Help me. I defended you, even when you betrayed us ...'

'You cowardly bastard,' James said to Handley. Then he hurled his gun at Tremaine.

One of the warriors caught the weapon, then tossed it down on the floor behind them. The warriors were amused by the efforts of the two men – whatever they said, however they begged, in their eyes the two men were already dead.

Tremaine stepped forward now, holding the sword toward them both. In a last attempt to flee, James threw himself forward. Tremaine raised the sword between them. James ran at him like a madman. The sword cut through his chest like the proverbial knife through butter. Tremaine felt no resistance, even from the ribcage, which cracked open effortlessly.

Handley gasped as he saw James fall. Tremaine could see that in this moment Handley realised his last hour had come.

Even so, he dived at the nearest warrior. The syringe now held above his head in attack. The warrior reacted with all the skill of the Arrak Nah Tiamen, and he caught hold of Handley's arm, even as it swung downwards, and twisted it, back and toward the Major. The syringe pierced Handley's stomach. The warrior's weight fell onto Handley as he buckled, and the plunger was slammed in, pushing all of the contents of the syringe into the man's body.

Handley fell to his knees, even as the warrior regained his equilibrium and stepped back.

Handley looked down at his stomach, then pulled the syringe out of his blubbery flesh. He looked up at Tremaine. His eyes went bloodshot. A dark madness filled his gaze, and the major began to cackle like a coke-drunk crone.

'That shit was …' Handley managed. 'I'm gonna be a drone. I'll be unstoppable …'

'No,' said Tremaine. 'You'll just be insane.'

Handley tried to stagger to his feet, but it was as if his limbs had all turned to jelly. He couldn't get up, and he fell down on the floor. Like a large salmon pulled from a lake, he jerked and flopped as though drowning on land.

White foam burst from his lips. 'Help … me!'

'You think you deserve less?' Tremaine said.

'Kill?' the platoon leader said again, standing over Handley's now unconscious body.

'Too good for him,' Tremaine said, shaking his head. 'He'll die eventually. 'Alone and insane. It seems like a fitting end to me. Let's get the women out of here.'

The warrior nodded and turned without argument.

They returned to the holding room, and one by one the warriors lifted the women and carried them out of the P Sector – most were still too drugged to be afraid and lay complacent in the Jinx warriors' arms. Tremaine went to help the girl that Handley and James had been abusing, while Harrington supported a woman who sat in the corner sobbing. But as they both reached the door, Handley staggered into the room behind them.

The front of his uniform was soaked with drool and rabid foam and his eyes were rage-filled – insanity had set in quickly as Tremaine had predicted. Handley still had enough of his own memories though to recall that he hated Tremaine. Fingers curled into hooks, he dived at the doctor, catching him off-guard from behind.

Tremaine released the woman he was helping as he was thrown to the floor. Handley jumped on his back, clawing at his head and scalp and then suddenly, Handley fell away and Tremaine was free.

He staggered to his feet to find Handley unconscious on the floor and the girl he'd been helping – Tremaine remembered her name suddenly – Alma – holding a chair. She had hit Handley full in the face, knocking him clear of the doctor.

Harrington had almost been out into the corridor when the fight had erupted behind him. He came back into the room and saw what had happened.

'What do we do about Handley?' Harrington said.

'Help me pull him onto one of the beds,' Tremaine said.

With both Alma's and Harrington's help, they strapped Handley down onto one of the tables. There, Tremaine hooked him up to one of the mind control IVs.

Then Tremaine bent down and slapped Handley full in the face. The sting of the blow brought him from his stupor.

'I haven't finished with you yet,' said Tremaine. 'Not until you know this. Right now every one of the bases is under attack. The Jinx are killing your soldiers and leaders and they are rescuing the women you've so badly abused. Then, we're all leaving this planet to the fucked up mess you created. And you know what? You're gonna *die* Handley, and there will be no-one left to help you.'

Handley spat at Tremaine and struggled and tugged at his restraints to no avail.

'It's going to be a slow death. The drugs will keep pumping into you until you're nothing but a vegetable,' Tremaine continued. 'But that could be days away, and you'll be wishing I'd finished you off and shown mercy. But people like you don't deserve that.'

Then Tremaine switched the IV on. The liquid dripped into Handley's arm, despite the major's attempts to pull himself free.

Hissing and spitting like an enraged cat, Handley twisted and turned and tugged – and that was how Tremaine, Harrington and Alma left him.

Back at the vortex, the last of the Jinx warriors had entered by the time Tremaine and Harrington reached it. As he entered, Tremaine smiled. There were the children, there were the women, and so too some of the men who had thrown themselves down and asked for clemency.

The vortex closed and they travelled back. Tremaine's heart was thudding in his chest. This was it. It was over, and the promise he had made to himself to help these women had finally been kept.

Epilogue

The months passed in relative harmony. Kat and Sylvia were the council representatives for Maya – the name the survivors had chosen for their city based on their Mayan ancestry – and they resided with the former Trafford City council in the place the humans now called home.

Not all human females had remained in the camp. Some had chosen to seek a union with Arrak males as goodwill to their saviours and now friends.

Mallory was one of those who had put herself forward, and hearing of her journey to the marriage tent, Prins had also proposed himself. The Arrak warrior hadn't understood his feelings for her until then.

They bonded immediately.

They chose to live in Maya, where Mallory still took care of the orphan children until the newly formed families began to offer them a place in their homes and hearts. Life on Emin became the utopia they had all dreamed of.

'Jas is in labour,' said Kat. 'I can feel her pain. I must go to her.'

She was sat drinking a herbal tea with Mallory. The two women had become friends and often sought each other's company.

'I'll come with you,' Mallory said.

'I hoped you would,' said Kat.

Now they went out into the desert and Kat summoned a small sphere – or 'bubble' as Jas had named it – to take them to Sharik.

The town was already celebrating when they arrived. The Empress was about to give birth, not to one but to two babies, and there was much excitement.

Mallory and Kat were welcomed inside the imperial tent, and they went quickly to the royal sleeping quarters, where they found Jas with Julia, Kale and Arven.

It was not known for an Emperor to remain while his wife gave birth, but, as had been the case ever since her return, Arven rarely let Jas out of his sight. She didn't mind this, though, because she always wanted to be around him.

Now he held her hand like any human male might have done back on Earth when it had become the norm for the father to be there too.

Things have certainly changed, Mallory thought as she looked on.

'Can we help?' said Kat.

'Yes,' Kale said. 'You can disperse the pain, making the birth easier. Hold her hand.'

Kat was not quite a full mage yet, but she was almost there. She had studied hard, and had progressed so much faster than the Al Kuzemen generally did. But Kale knew that she and the other women that had entered the Guild were unique.

She went to the other side of the bed and took Jas's hand. There she smiled down at her friend and, using empathy, took the pain into herself and sent it out into the sand beneath her feet. Jas felt immediate relief, and a few moments later the first baby was born.

'A girl!' said Julia, wrapping the child into a blanket. It wasn't long before the next child, a boy this time, also came into the world.

Arven took his daughter and looked down into her very human eyes. For a minute his Arrak pupils stopped their buoyant swirling.

'What shall you name her?' Kale asked.

'Allsa,' said Jas immediately. 'And our son is Kisha.'

'You would name them after such tragedy?' he said.

'This is who they are.'

Arven handed Allsa to Jas and then took his son from Julia's arms. He looked down into the child's swirling pupils, so like his own, and knew that, yes, this was the son Kil'n had once loved and lost. They were rewarded by the return of these precious souls to the world of the Arrak and humans – two tribes that had become one. They were whole again, and the curse, this time, was fully broken.

'Now that you're a mother, I must get back to my little girls,' said Julia.

'How are they settling down?' Mallory asked, for she had been instrumental, with Tremaine's help, in bringing the five little girls, aged between one and five, back to their natural mother.

'Our daughters are wonderful,' Kale said.

Julia hugged Jas, and she left with Kale to return next door to the royal Al Kuzemen tent and their new family.

'I'm so happy for them,' said Jas. She held Allsa and kissed the baby on the top her head. She noted then that the little girl had white blonde hair, just like her own. 'I now know how it feels to love your own child.'

Mallory nodded. 'And I will too soon. I'm pregnant.'

'That's wonderful news!' said Kat.

'Congratulations to you both,' said Arven.

Mallory did not add that she was surprised it was even possible. She shouldn't be; everything was different on Emin, even her ability to conceive.

'We'll leave you to rest,' said Kat as she noticed Mallory's sudden fall into reflection.

The two friends left the tent.

'I should visit *him*,' Mallory said.

'Why do that to yourself?' Kat asked. 'He did you so much evil.'

'I know.'

But Kat turned and accompanied Mallory away from the imperial tent to the destination she now sought: a small tent alone, outside the capital.

The desert night was warm as they approached the hermitage, outside which an Arrak warrior stood guard alone, though his presence was unnecessary.

'How is he?' Mallory asked.

'Insane,' said the warrior.

'He always was …'

The warrior lifted the tent flap and Mallory glanced in to see Gerald sitting in the centre of the floor. The place smelt of piss and shit, but she knew that the Arrak mages kept Gerald as clean as they could.

'Someone should put him out of his misery,' said Kat. 'But that's not the way our new world deals with things, is it?'

'We have pity,' Mallory answered. 'Or maybe he just deserves to be left suffering.'

Dementia was after all the only way a broken mind could continue to exist. And Kat knew, though she didn't share this with Mallory, that Gerald was broken and suffering. It was a fitting end for one such as him.

'Goodbye, Gerald,' Mallory said. 'I won't return. I have my own life now, and I'm having a baby. Maybe it is Jinx magic that has healed me, or maybe the fault was always yours. Perhaps you used this as another weapon to hurt me. You were evil and it took the Jinx entering our world in order for me to learn the truth. But I'm happy, Gerald, and I don't care if you're not. You see, we women are survivors, and it is only the weak who have to hurt others.'

She turned away before the warrior dropped down the tent flap, shutting Gerald inside.

The twins lay side by side in a crib. Allsa looked up at her mother with alarming focus, and Kisha slept as though his journey into the world had been truly exhausting.

'I feel as good as new,' Jas told Arven. 'Should I be concerned?'

'Kale said there were changes. You have all of the good that Kil'n's original spell had. None of the bad.'

'Thank you again,' she said.

'What for, Jasmine?'

'For saving my people. For bringing the two tribes back together. For your patience … For loving me.'

'I had no choice in that last part,' Arven laughed.

Over the last few months he had learnt to relax more around her. Developing and using a sense of humour that Jas could never have imagined would be housed in a Jinx male body. He was a wonderful companion in every way.

'Come. You need to rest,' he said, taking her hand and leading her to the bed. 'But promise me one thing.'

'What?'

'If you want to save humanity again, come and talk to me first!'

Jas laughed. 'My running days are over. Don't you realise I'm forever Jinx bound?'

They lay back on the bed together and Arven kissed her soft lips, then he pulled her into his arms and held her in that protective way that he had sometimes. As though he still thought she would run. As if he never took for granted what they had.

Jas closed her eyes and pushed back the memory of her previous lonely lifetimes. Sometimes they came back to haunt her, but always Arven's presence sent the fear of another failed life scurrying away. She still found it difficult to believe that they had finally joined, and more importantly that Shamila's curse could no longer find a way to hurt them.

About The Author

Award winning author Sam Stone began her professional writing career in 2007 when her first novel won the Silver Award for Best Novel with *ForeWord Magazine* Book of the Year Awards. Since then she has gone on to write several novels, three novellas and many short stories. She was the first woman in 31 years to win the British Fantasy Society Award for Best Novel. She also won the award for Best Short Fiction in the same year (2011).

Stone loves all types of fiction and enjoys mixing horror (her first passion) with a variety of different genres including science fiction, fantasy and Steampunk.

Her works can be found in paperback, audio, screen and eBook. www.sam-stone.com

More Telos Titles
By Sam Stone

KAT LIGHTFOOT SERIES
Steampunk, horror, adventure series
1: ZOMBIES AT TIFFANY'S
2: KAT ON A HOT TIN AIRSHIP
3: WHAT'S DEAD PUSSYKAT
4: KAT OF GREEN TENTACLES
5: KAT AND THE PENDULUM
6: TEN LITTLE DEMONS

JINX CHRONICLES
Hi-tech science fiction fantasy trilogy
1: JINX TOWN
2: JINX MAGIC

THE VAMPIRE GENE SERIES
Horror, fantasy time-travel thrillers
1: KILLING KISS
2: FUTILE FLAME
3: DEMON DANCE
4: HATEFUL HEART
5: SILENT SAND
6: JADED JEWEL

THE DARKNESS WITHIN: FINAL CUT
Science fiction horror short novel

ZOMBIES IN NEW YORK
AND OTHER BLOODY JOTTINGS
Thirteen stories of horror and passion and six mythological and erotic
poems from the pen of the new Queen of Vampire fiction.

CTHULHU AND OTHER MONSTERS
20 Tales of Horror and Cosmic Horror

OTHER TITLES BY SAM STONE

POSING FOR PICASSO

Other Telos Steampunk and Horror Titles

<u>TANITH LEE</u>
BLOOD 20
20 Vampire Stories through the ages

TANITH LEE A-Z
An A-Z collection of Short Fiction by renowned writer Tanith Lee

<u>GRAHAM MASTERTON</u>
THE HELL CANDIDATE
THE DJINN
THE WELLS OF HELL
RULES OF DUEL (With William S Burroughs)

<u>PAUL FINCH</u>
CAPE WRATH AND THE HELLION (Horror Novella)
TERROR TALES OF CORNWALL (Ed. Paul Finch)
TERROR TALES OF THE NORTH WEST OF ENGLAND (Ed. Paul Finch)
Forthcoming

<u>RAVEN DANE</u>
THE MISADVENTURES OF CYRUS DARIAN
Steampunk Adventure Series
1: CYRUS DARIAN AND THE TECHNOMICRON
2: CYRUS DARIAN AND THE GHASTLY HORDE
3: CYRUS DARIAN AND THE DEMON (forthcoming)

DEATH'S DARK WINGS
Alternative History Novel

ABSINTHE AND ARSENIC
Horror and Fantasy Short Story Collection

<u>SIMON CLARK</u>
HUMPTY'S BONES
THE FALL

www.ingramcontent.com/pod-product-compliance
Lightning Source LLC
Chambersburg PA
CBHW070937190726
48292CB00004B/1212